FINAL PARADOX

the second in the
OSGOODE TRILOGY

FINAL PARADOX

The Second in the OSGOODE TRILOGY

A Novel

Mary E. Martin
author of Conduct in Question,
the first in the Osgoode Trilogy

iUniverse, Inc.
New York Lincoln Shanghai

FINAL PARADOX
The Second in the OSGOODE TRILOGY

iUniverse books may be ordered through booksellers or by contacting:

iUniverse
2021 Pine Lake Road, Suite 100
Lincoln, NE 68512
www.iuniverse.com
1-800-Authors (1-800-288-4677)

Cover design by Memacom

ISBN-13: 978-0-595-40760-6 (pbk)
ISBN-13: 978-0-595-85125-6 (ebk)
ISBN-10: 0-595-40760-9 (pbk)
ISBN-10: 0-595-85125-8 (ebk)

Printed in the United States of America

To my family, David, Stephen, Timothy and Susan and to my muse.

CHAPTER 1

▼

On Harry's last visit, Norma Dinnick wore a flaming red wig and served sherry in crystal glasses. Despite her advanced age of eighty-seven, she chatted brightly about the stock market and the roses in her garden. Hearing loss seemed to be her only trouble.

Arriving at her apartment house, he prepared himself for another loud, but lively hour of banter. He rapped sharply and waited.

"Go away! My mind is filled with holes," she cried out from behind the door.

He frowned. "It's me, Harry Jenkins, your lawyer. You asked me to come."

Straining to listen, he heard the awkward shuffle of slippers on the bare floor. Her tiny whimpers made him think of a frightened, caged animal. The door handle rattled, and metal scraped on metal until the door creaked open. Just above the knob, suspicious eyes peered out.

"Who are *you*?" she demanded.

"For heaven's sake, Norma, it's me, Harry."

"Where's your beard then?"

"What? I've never had a beard!" Without thinking, Harry rubbed his chin and pushed back the strands of his thinning hair from his forehead.

"Are you the plumber? Show me your card."

Sighing, Harry took his business card from his suit pocket. "It's me, Harry Jenkins, your lawyer."

"We have an appointment about your will," he reminded her.

Suspicious and confused, she stood before him in a faded green house-dress stitched up at the shoulder with a black thread.

"Well come in, then." She backed away from the door, giving him just enough room to enter.

Harry stood speechless as he surveyed the apartment. A naked bulb swayed gently from a broken fixture and cast shifting shadows across the once elegant living room. He saw the outlines of her furniture, now draped with dingy bedsheets. Oddly, all the lamps had lost their shades and, in the dining room, the mahogany buffet sat buried under piles of old newspapers.

Once seated, Norma seemed to forget him.

"Norma, what on earth's happened?" he asked.

She occupied herself with picking fussily at the arm of the settee, as if to remove creatures visible only to her.

Sitting beside her, he asked gently, "Are you all right?"

She tilted her tiny face upward to the light and gazed out the window. "I think it's safe to talk now," she whispered.

"Safe? Is someone listening?"

Pointing at the ceiling, she said crossly, "You should have come in the back way. Now they've seen you, they'll be quiet."

As far as he knew, Norma had only one remaining tenant: a shy and silent man named Grieves. Last year her investments did so well that she decided to close the other five suites, not needing the income or the worry.

"And they've not paid one cent of rent!"

Harry dutifully made a note. "You mean Mr. Grieves?" he asked.

Norma shook her head. "No. The ones directly above me."

"But that apartment is empty."

"And furthermore, they listen in on my phone."

Sadly, Harry shook his head. Only months ago, Norma's blue eyes had sparkled with lively intelligence and her knowing laugh accompanied a razor-like wit. Now she rocked back and forth beside him, glassy-eyed.

"How do they listen in?" he asked. Although the paranoid delusions of the elderly held little humor, Harry struggled to suppress a smile at the absurdity of imaginary tenants. He knew a lucid mind could inexplicably drift without warning into madness.

She seemed lost, focusing on the flickering shadows at the window.

"How many tenants are in the building?" he asked, although he held out little hope that his client's problem could be solved by a Landlord and Tenant court application.

She shook her head fiercely. "Just the ones above me!"

"Have you seen them?"

"No! But I hear them every night, carousing like drunken sailors." Again, her fingers chased the invisible creatures running amok on the arm of the settee. When she glanced up at him, he saw a glimmer of the old intelligence in her eyes.

"Do you think Archie's causing all the trouble?" she asked. "I think he's trying to drive me mad so I can't change my will."

Harry, who did not want to worry her, spoke reluctantly, "Actually, Archie called to tell me not to come today. He claimed you didn't want a new will and that you didn't have the capacity to make one."

Her eyes flashed in anger. "Of course! That greedy lout will suck me dry. He even wants the shares my Arthur left me."

"What shares, Norma?" He couldn't recall any share certificates in Arthur's estate.

"George Pappas-that dangerous animal-is after them too!"

"Who is he?" Although the name was unfamiliar, he dutifully jotted it down.

"Vicious," she shivered, drawing inward like a shrinking flower.

Harry took her hand.

When she resurfaced, she asked, "Will you come upstairs to see where the trouble is, Harry?"

"Are the tenants in?"

"I don't think so."

Fussing with a jumble of keys, Norma teetered to the top of the narrow stairs. At the door, Harry knocked sharply. He could hear the accusations in court. *Unauthorized entry by landlord, with her solicitor in tow.* With exasperated sighs, Norma worked one key after another until the door swung open into the silent room.

Light flooded through the extraordinarily large bay window. Harry set his briefcase down and drew in the cool, musty air. He looked through the living room, dining room and on into the kitchen. His view of the apartment was entirely unobstructed by rugs, drapes or furniture. Dust motes floated in the light and the silence was broken only by laughter of children playing in the street below. Norma stood off to one side, dwarfed by the cold and empty fireplace.

"Please, Harry, you must get them out. They're driving me mad."

"But Norma," he said quietly, "I don't see anyone." He edged closer to her.

Her face puckered with annoyance. He thought she might stamp her foot. "Of course not! They're only here at night."

"But I don't see any furniture, either." Harry knew that his client was at least partially delusional. Fortunately, the law recognized that you could still make a will even if you saw the occasional apparition.

Norma's lower lip trembled as she muttered "Those cursed shares! Must I pay for them forever?"

Gently, he touched her shoulder and felt her whole body shaking. "What shares do you mean, Norma?"

"Please. You must get the tenants out. I can't stand it any longer."

"All right, Norma." He put his arm around her. "I'll try my best," he concluded doubtfully, wondering how to give legal notice to a phantom.

"Thank you, Harry."

Downstairs, over tea, she seemed more her old self. He probed gently, asking if she still wanted to discuss her will.

She nodded vigorously. "Archie's to get only a quarter—not half—the estate, and Bronwyn Saunderson the rest."

Clear enough in regard to beneficiaries, he thought. "Is Bronwyn related to you?"

"She's my goddaughter. I knew her mother well when we were just starting out. Young and foolish, we were!"

Harry made a note. Desire to benefit a goddaughter was sufficient reason to cut down Archie's share. After all, the man was only Arthur's business associate and her executor. Although she was clearly delusional about her tenants, when it came to will-making; the law only required she be aware of the approximate size of her estate and the *natural objects of her bounty*, that is, her next of kin. With no children of her own, or nieces or nephews who might inherit, Bronwyn would be her logical choice the courts would honor.

"If you're concerned about Archie, do you still want him as your executor?"

Norma reached for his hand. "No, I want you, Harry. I know you'll look after me."

"About these shares…"

Confusion spread across her face. "Goodness! Sometimes I get muddled up. I must have been thinking of something else."

"Who's this George Pappas?"

"That dangerous man!" she declared. "Arthur had such strange business associates." She lapsed into silence.

Harry stared at his client before closing his briefcase. She was perfectly clear in her intent to benefit her goddaughter, and Brinks had no moral or legal claim to anything at all. "I'll be back in a few days with the new will. I'll bring my secretary, Miss Giveny, as a witness."

She clasped his hands. "Good. But you *will* do something about the tenants?"

Harry frowned as he stood at the door. "First, I'll have to find them, Norma."

Once outside in the foyer, he heard the scrape and screech of wires being wound around latches. *A deadly security precaution, especially in the event of fire,* he thought.

Harry paused on his way down the front steps. Coming in, he had not noticed the vines and bushes choking off the light from the apartments or the wild grasses growing through the cracks in the steps. Arthur would be dismayed at the dilapidation of his once impressive apartment building. As he drove off, he wondered what to do about the nonexistent tenants.

Taking the long route downtown, he was plagued with visions of Norma creeping upstairs to the completely empty apartment. Stuck in a line of cars, he sighed. Dundas Street was a jumble of cars and delivery trucks, overhead wires and tracks for streetcars. But, surrounded by the chaos of life in downtown Toronto, he felt safe and contained.

His mind wandered back to Norma's husband, Arthur, who was a professor when Harry was at law school. A tall and somber man, he had been an inspiration to all first-year students crammed into lecture halls with rows of scarred wooden desks.

Dinnick would begin with a courtly bow in the direction of the two female students. "Ladies, and gentlemen," He gave a perfunctory nod to the rest of the class.

"Civil Procedure is not a dry and colorless book of rules. It is a code of honorable conduct for the litigant, as well as an invaluable source of strategy."

Looking about the class, the professor then intoned, "Without the restraint of law, our darker natures, like storm clouds, will prevail—making civilized society an impossible dream. You see, ladies and gentlemen, rules are essential in the real world."

Harry thought the law was more like a blunt and clumsy tool, but Arthur Dinnick pushed and prodded legions of first-year law students to a fleeting perception of the law's higher purpose. Now his widow saw invisible tenants.

Archie Brinks, Norma's soon to be dismissed executor, had brought a whiff of scandal to Arthur's otherwise exemplary teaching career. Rumors of suspicious stock trading swirled around the two men, and while Archie bellowed and bluffed, Arthur grew pale and silent and finally retired. On vacation in Florence, he died of a heart attack. Archie, obviously, was still very much on the scene.

Before visiting Norma this morning, Harry had received a call from Archie.

"I'm calling about Mrs. Dinnick. I'm her executor," boomed Brinks.

"You know I'm not at liberty to discuss her affairs."

"I don't want you to. I'm *telling* you, Mr. Jenkins, Norma does *not* want a new will. Besides, she's incompetent to make one."

"How interesting. I suppose you've had her assessed?"

"What?"

"Then you're a psychologist?" Harry had dealt with bullies before.

"Listen. Don't be smart with me. She doesn't know what day it is."

Harry sighed. The man was tiresome. "I thank you for your views, sir. I've made a note of our conversation and will discuss it with my client as soon as possible."

Brinks was apoplectic. Harry smiled and hung up.

Still lost in recollection, he turned his car northward into a long-forgotten neighborhood of narrow houses jammed together. He pulled up in front of 147 Cecil Street. The subconscious destination of his seemingly aimless drive was now painfully obvious to him. The house still listed to one side under the weight of fussy Victorian detail. Only one thing was missing. When he lived there as a student, a sign in red and black lettering announced *Madame Odella—the future foretold.* Only thoughts of Norma and Arthur could have brought him here.

CHAPTER 2

▼

Shortly after Harry left, Norma heard the banging upstairs. Clutching her cane, she hobbled up the flight of stairs. With the deep, gravely voice of George Pappas rolling about in her mind, she quivered to think he was waiting for her.

When she opened the door, she saw, not the empty apartment, but Arthur's study in their old house on Barclay Street. A brass lamp glowed on the desk underneath the bay window, illuminating stacks of her his important papers. She ran her hand over the purple velvet couch, fingering the white piping along the edges of the cushions. Her George, of years ago, leaned against the fireplace looking every inch the handsome gentleman. For just an instant, she wanted to touch his golden locks of hair, curling about his collar. But his icy eyes riveted her. He did not smile.

Hoping to gain the upper hand at the outset, Norma used her sternest tone. "George, don't wear your hat in the house. It brings bad luck."

Anger flashed in George's eyes, but he removed his homburg. "Where the hell are the shares, Norma?"

"I don't know. Arthur never told me. Besides," she continued bravely, "he always said they were rightfully ours." Her face darkened in disgust. "Anyway, you deserve nothing. You were all show and promise, but in the end you were a complete disappointment."

A flush grew from his collar. "Goddamn it! A woman like you..." He broke off and stared at his shoes.

"You're a fraud, George Pappas."

He stared at her in disbelief. "You stupid woman! Obviously Arthur told you where he hid the shares."

When he grasped her hand, she cried out.

He growled, "I can easily snap your fingers off, one by one," He yanked her arm up so that she dangled from his fist like a faded rag doll.

Norma's eyes rolled back in her head, and she thought she would faint. George flung her to the sofa and stood over her.

"Don't toy with me, Norma. You know the consortium raised the money for medical research. Arthur squirreled it away, and *I* am going to find it."

Norma began to breathe normally. She played with the piping on the cushions and struggled to clear her mind. She wanted to dismiss George with a wave of the hand, but it was never that easy. She thought back to 1963, to the snowy December evening at the King Edward Hotel. She and Arthur had rushed from the black limousine through the freezing sleet and into the hotel foyer, lit by the tallest Christmas tree Norma had ever seen.

That night had been George's show.

Under the immense crystal chandeliers of the ballroom, Pappas courted five hundred of Toronto's moneyed elite at a one hundred dollar a plate black tie dinner to raise capital for Elixicorp Enterprises. Eager talk swirled about Norma and Arthur.

"Has Pappas really patented the elixir?" asked a portly man, tugging on the vest of his tuxedo.

"A wonder drug to prevent memory loss?" breathed another as he chewed his cigar.

When a waiter thrust a tray of hors d'oeurves in front of her, Norma frowned at the array of toast covered with glistening black beads.

"Caviar, Madame?" inquired the waiter.

Helping herself, she scanned the room for George. There he was, surrounded by women. He tossed his massive head of curls back to laugh in deep, rolling cadences. Norma held her breath. When she caught his icy blue eyes, she hurriedly turned away.

A woman in a pink sequined gown crushed against Norma to get a look at him. "My God! Isn't he gorgeous? He can tuck his shoes under my bed anytime." The woman winked at Norma and sipped her champagne.

Dinner in the ballroom was a luxurious affair. Silver candelabras and tiny, embossed menus were set out on snowy white tablecloths. Norma turned over her dinner plate to check the name. Her hand flew to her lips as she read, *Spode.* The twenty-piece orchestra began to play.

Waiters delivered salads, clam chowder and then Beef Wellington. Norma gaped at the labels on the innumerable bottles of French red and white wines. After coffee, Archie, sweat dripping from his brow, introduced George to the guests. *Too many drinks*, thought Norma. Next to Arthur, he was a buffoon and a pale imitation of George.

The chandeliers were dimmed and a spotlight swept across the ballroom to the stage. Pappas rose before them like a magician weaving his spell. The audience was ready for seduction.

"My dearest friends! In life, we cherish our memories. We remember Mom as she tucked us in and kissed us goodnight and Dad when he taught us how to ride a bike. What could be sweeter? But what if mother or dad lost all memory of you, or their darling grandkids?" His voice rose with a preacher's zeal. "Wouldn't that be one of the most heart-wrenching experiences anyone could have?"

With microphone in hand, George stepped into the audience. Touching one woman's shoulder, he gazed into her eyes. "Wouldn't you do just anything to bring them back to you?" Wide-eyed, the woman nodded dumbly.

"Well, friends, Elixicorp Enterprises *can* bring them back to you." George, followed by the spotlight, strolled further into the audience. Pointing to one and then another, he crooned, "Soon as we've raised the capital and cut through all that red tape, we will have the one pill—the *only* pill—that reverses the effects of aging and reverses memory loss."

George sauntered back to the podium and loosened his tie. "Now I know what some of you are thinking: 'that George Pappas must be some kinda snake oil salesman. Nobody's got a pill for that!'"

The audience held its breath. Another woman, next to Norma, nudged her. "I hear he's absolutely fantastic between the sheets." Waving her champagne glass in front of Norma, she laughed. "A real tiger!"

Norma glanced at Arthur, pale in the shadows.

Swirling his jacket like a sorcerer's cape, Pappas patted his red satin cummerbund and laughed. "But we do have that pill!" His voice dropped to a hoarse whisper. "Stretch yourself, my friends! Buy as many shares as you can tonight. Why? Because in three months time, those shares will be worth three times as much."

The eagerness of the crowd surprised even George. Men, waving check books, rushed to the back of the room to subscribe. George slapped Arthur on the back, saying "Artie, that's the lovely rush of money."

Then Norma was back in Arthur's study, and George was still towering over her. "Please, George! Don't hurt me. I've got holes in my mind today. I'll try to remember, and when I do, I'll call you right away."

George shook his head angrily. "You stupid old bitch. You think you can fool me with that? That money was raised for legitimate medical research, and we need it now."

In fury, Norma twisted away from him. "You're just a bully with no brains and no style. You bilked everyone in Toronto, but you got greedy. And then you got sloppy."

George gripped her arm so hard she screamed out.

"I'll be back, Norma. You can't hide it from me forever." He walked to the door. Turning, he growled, "I will tear you apart if I have to. And you'll be begging me to take those shares."

He slammed the door. Norma waited in the cold apartment until she was sure he was gone. Then she hobbled downstairs and made a cup of tea.

Harry strolled slowly along Cecil Street, wondering what had become of Madame Odella. Most likely dead, he concluded. But where was her beautiful daughter, Katrina? With no real explanation, Katrina had grown cool and disappeared from his life. A pang of longing touched him. It seemed that the past was always just an instant away.

During law school, Harry had shared the second floor flat with a class-mate, Peter Saunderson. His lumbering presence in the tiny rooms always made Harry feel cramped. And then, one night, Peter ran his hand over Harry's chest as he squeezed past him in the hall. Harry jumped back, banging his head against the wall. Peter pretended innocence, but Harry caught the lonely, hungry look in his eye. The thought disgusted him, but he refused to consider moving that year. After all, the lovely Katrina lived downstairs. They reached an uneasy truce, but Harry spent many hours with Madame Odella and her daughter in their front parlor. From what he could tell, Peter lived a solitary—rather furtive—life, and that suited Harry just fine.

Unless a reading were in progress, Madame Odella kept the red velvet curtains drawn back to keep an eye on her tenants. She sat at a card table with a purple robe draped over her mountainous body. White wisps of smoke curled up from the cigarette in her ashtray, turning the room blue with haze.

"I will read your cards tonight, Harry. Come. Sit."

Harry laughed and shifted the immense tabby cat from the chair. "And pray tell, what will Madame Odella see tonight?" The cat's green eyes glimmered up at him.

Harry watched her place the cards in a mysterious pattern known only to her. The first card she turned up was The Fool. With good humor, he examined the brightly colored card, which depicted an idiotic looking young man, in a green peasant suit, stepping off a cliff. He smiled and thought the game ridiculous.

Madame Odella drew solemnly on her cigarette. "You are a young man, Harry, with many challenges ahead of you." Her yellowed finger tapped the card. "See how The Fool steps confidently into the unknown?"

"He looks pretty stupid to me," he laughed. The tabby cat hissed and slunk under a chair in the corner.

"The Fool represents the blithe spirit in you. You must cherish him, Harry. He is the force that teaches you to let life happen in order to find happiness. To learn, you must take risks."

Solemnly, she made a fist in the air, then relaxed and opened her hand. "You must not cramp life out of fear and misunderstanding. If you do, you will never conquer the emptiness within." Across the red and white checked cloth, she reached out and grasped his wrist. "If you fail in this, you will drive love from your life."

Impatient, Harry frowned and shook his head. "Where do you get all this? I mean just from this one card?"

"You must listen carefully, Harry. It comes from the forces within and outside you." Her eyelids flickered. "But The Fool also represents naïveté. You must guard against this in your nature. You are very trusting, but your chosen profession may change that."

She turned over the next card and sighed, "It is as I thought."

"What?" Harry heard the trepidation in his voice. But, of course, it was only a game. He stared at the card with the pale moon looming over a dark and barren landscape. A sense of unease crept over him.

"The Moon card warns of someone in your life who hides behind curtains like a cowardly puppeteer." She stared deep into his eyes. "He is an enemy, Harry, who will prey upon your naïveté. He is an instrument of your destiny."

"Who *is* he?" Harry demanded.

Madame Odella shrugged. "The cards do not say, but he is close by now." She bowed her head in study. Shadows flickered on her broad face. "He is the trickster who erases all your carefully constructed boundaries to make way for the new. You are paired with him, and he will follow you along your life path."

Glancing about the room, Harry wished he could open a window. The old woman was talking nonsense. Where were the usual, happy predictions like *your true love will last a lifetime?*

"You will have three women in your life, Harry," she said. She turned over the Priestess card, which showed a bejeweled, ethereal being with eyes cast upon some distant world. "But your true spirit guide, the third woman, will come only later in life when you need her most. She is beautiful beyond all your imaginings, and you will be in her thrall."

Harry grinned and shoved back his chair. Without warning, the huge tabby cat sprang to his lap from a bookcase.

"Sit," she commanded. "You must accept this woman just as she is. She is the *good* in you."

"Terrific, Madame Odella. I'll think about all that." Harry caught a glimpse of Katrina in the kitchen. He stood, almost knocking over the table. Katrina smiled over her mother's shoulder and pointed upward to his bedroom above. Harry hurried up the stairs.

Still gaping up at the Cecil Street house, Harry suddenly realized how odd he must look, a middle-aged man lost in reverie on a street corner. So much time had slid by. His thoughts darkened as images of Katrina swept over him.

He remembered her as young and lovely, lying on his narrow bed tucked up under the eaves of his bedroom. As she set down her philosophy text, she tossed back her long blonde hair. Her eyes came alive with challenge and readiness to argue. Laughing when she scored a point, she would beckon him to the bed. Sliding in beside her, in awe, he touched her lips and traced the line of her neck with his fingertip.

He never understood what went so terribly wrong. Suddenly, she was slipping out of his life. She no longer came to his room. They no longer met downstairs, at school or at their favorite spot, the bridge. Climbing the stairs one day, he found her in the upstairs hallway with her books and notes clutched to her breast. The winter light from the tiny dormer window cast a sickly glow upon her face. Edging past him, she rushed down the stairs.

Whenever he tried to talk to her, she drifted further away. He would see her walking across the campus or in the library stacks. When he did catch up with her, she was always polite, but cool and distant. Better if they had argued or she had simply left him for another guy. Nothing. No explanation. He shook his head and turned back to the car. Any fragment of the past was always waiting to surface.

What could he have known at twenty-one? Back then, he saw only a well-lit path leading ever upward. No dark twists or cavernous pits in sight. Like most of his eager classmates, he had seen admission to law school as a ticket to the land of riches and comfort. How like the blithe fool! But his world had darkened when Katrina left without a word, and he thought the emptiness of spirit would always be with him.

Turning the car's ignition, he wondered if his father had plunged into the same void when his sister, Anna, died. He never saw his father shed a tear, but his pain was written in the twisted lines on his graying face.

As he edged the car back to Dundas Street, Harry continued with his recollections—but this time with a smile. Madame Odella had predicted the appearance of his spirit guide later in life. She could only be Natasha, who had come into his life last year like a soft breeze when he needed her most.

CHAPTER 3

▼

Back from Norma's, Harry hurried through the atrium of his office building. As always, the plush, blue carpeting and the marble, with its gold fittings, enlivened his step. He entered the glass elevator and rose through a profusion of greenery and flickering light and shadow. It was a huge change from the dark, dank offices he had inhabited less than a year ago, where the sight of chipped windowsills and rusted fire escapes depressed him. The wash of sunlight from the skylight banished for a moment his dark thoughts of Norma and Katrina.

Sarah, the receptionist, welcomed him. Her warm voice and smile further raised his flagging spirits. But the grim staccato of Miss Giveny's typewriter, blasting from her office, set him on edge. Clearing his throat, he stood at her door. She scarcely took time to nod in his direction.

"You know, this Dinnick business is very strange," he began. "She's hallucinating that there are tenants above her." He sighed. "God save us from the vagaries of old age."

The typewriter ribbon broke. Miss Giveny, hunched over the machine, muttered under her breath.

"Why don't you use the computer?" Harry asked. "Then you wouldn't have to mess with ribbons."

She glared at him over the tops of her glasses, which had slid to the tip of her nose. "This is a form. I can't do it on a computer. Besides, is my work not satisfactory?"

He shrugged. Although her stubborn resistance to technology annoyed him, he backed off. "Do as you please." Still compelled to talk about Norma, he added, "She says she hears them only at night and that they listen on her phone."

"How do you know they're not?" Miss Giveny asked crossly.

With strained patience, he said, "Because I went up to look and there wasn't a stick of furniture in the place."

"Maybe someone is playing tricks on her. I can think of one person who wants to see her gone." She tapped out an impatient rhythm on her typewriter. "Maybe you should take her complaints more seriously. That Archie Brinks is up to no good."

"That much is obvious!" He began shuffling through the mail.

She stopped her typing. "Mr. Jenkins, why would Jeremy want a copy of Mrs. Dinnick's will?"

Harry paused. His junior, Jeremy Freemantle, appeared highly competent, yet something about the boy him nagged at him. "No idea. Did you ask him?"

"Yes. I found him rummaging through your filing cabinets. He said he needed it for a precedent."

That's probably the reason." Harry turned to go.

Miss Giveny said, "Did you check his references when you hired him?"

"Yes, of course."

She glanced at him balefully as she adjusted her glasses. "Well, I wouldn't trust him to look after a goldfish."

Harry shrugged. "I'll ask him about the will myself." He started down the hallway.

Miss Giveny called after him. "But about Archie Brinks. Mr. Crawford always said he was trouble. Mr. Crawford would have…"

Harry did not wait. He could fill in the blanks. *Mr. Crawford was an excellent judge of character. He would put a stop to such nonsense.*

Richard Crawford was Harry's deceased law partner, who lived on in Miss Giveny's mind as the paragon of virtue, intelligence, and wit. Undoubtedly she thought the firm was sliding into a yawning void without Mr. Crawford at the helm. Of course, she overlooked the fact that he was an unrepentant womanizer and had dropped dead at Harry's feet, overcome with lust for his client, Marjorie Deighton. It seemed no female was entirely safe alone with him. Muttering, Harry marched into his office and firmly closed the door.

Sinking into his chair, he surveyed his desk. After the morning, he welcomed the few hours of tedium ahead. Dismissing Norma as delusional made him feel momentarily guilty, but the problem still remained; how to remove non-existent tenants? When he glanced out the window, he saw huge, soft snowflakes wafting down.

A knock came at the door. Jeremy, his junior, entered.

"Got a minute, Harry?"

Harry nodded and motioned him to take a seat.

"This won't take long." Jeremy sat on the edge of the chair.

Uneasily, Harry thought the boy's keen glance and tilt of the jaw gave him a calculating appearance. In the initial interview, his humility had charmed him. His references checked out, except for one who could not be tracked down. But lately, Jeremy's boyish modesty seemed barely to conceal an unsettling arrogance.

"Something about the Parrish estate?" Harry prompted.

"No. Not that sort of thing." The boy flashed a smile.

"Then?"

Jeremy sighed and bent his head. "It's about my uncle, Peter."

Harry knew the folly of acting for relatives. "What's the problem?"

"Seems he's in some trouble professionally at his law firm, Blackburn and Swanson."

"You mean, Peter Saunderson, Bencher at the Law Society?" How strange, thought Harry. He had heard little from his roommate over the past twenty years, and now, after his musings, his name was cropping up. He watched as the boy gnawed a thumbnail. Odd behavior for someone usually so composed. "Go ahead."

Jeremy's gaze was level and appraising. Shoving a lock of his dark hair to one side, he asked, "This is confidential, isn't it, Harry?"

"Not precisely. It depends on what you tell me."

His junior squirmed in his seat and said, "He's gay."

Harry shrugged. "So? That's no crime these days."

Jeremy shook his head impatiently. "That's not the problem. I think he's being blackmailed."

Harry considered the tilt of the jaw and the cool, appraising eyes. "By whom?" he asked.

Jeremy threw up his hands in futility. "Who knows? I think he's also got some pretty unsavory connections. Ever heard of George Pappas?"

Harry sat up straighter. Norma had mentioned the name Pappas this morning. "I don't think I know…"

"Sometimes he's in the papers. But nothing ever sticks to the guy."

"Listen, Jeremy. First you tell me he's gay—which is, of course, an entirely private matter. Then you say he's being blackmailed. And as if that's not enough, you're suggesting he has underworld connections."

"Yes," said the junior stubbornly. "But here's the worst. I think he's dipping into trust funds to pay them off."

The tale was growing more outrageous by the minute. Next Jeremy would be accusing his uncle of murder. "Pay off whom? His alleged gangster friends?"

Jeremy stared at the floor. "I was afraid you wouldn't believe me."

"How do you know all this?" Harry asked quietly.

"From his wife, Bronwyn. She says he's experiencing weird mood swings…"

Jesus! Yet another connection! Now Norma's goddaughter was involved in this mess, thought Harry. It was also another reason for Jeremy to look at Norma's will. He said, "Allegations about trust funds and underworld connections are extremely serious, Jeremy. A solicitor is required to report them to the Law Society."

"You won't, will you, Harry? His eyes were pleading. "I wouldn't have said a thing, if I'd thought…"

"All you have is hearsay? Nothing concrete? Or have you?"

Jeremy rose swiftly from his chair. "No. Nothing. Bronwyn's probably worried about nothing."

"Then I suggest you be extremely careful. You can't make wild accusations. If you have substantial proof, then you must report it to the Law Society."

At the door, Jeremy nodded vigorously. "That's good advice, Harry. I'll say nothing more."

Harry nodded and said, "Miss Giveny says you wanted to make a copy of Norma Dinnick's will. Did you?"

"Yes. It's a good precedent for the McWilliams will I'm drafting."

"Then you know your aunt Bronwyn is mentioned in it. You understand that information is privileged and must not be divulged to *anyone* under *any* circumstances."

Jeremy appeared shocked. "Of course, Harry. Absolutely. I'd never do that."

"Good. Just be certain you don't"

Jeremy flashed a smile and backed out the door.

Harry stared up Bay Street at the old City Hall clock. After such an odd conversation with Jeremy, he felt all the more wary of the kid. Why had he not given his uncle as a personal reference?

Although he never cared much for Peter Saunderson, he could not help but pity him. One night, years back, Harry had been rushing to get ready for a date with Katrina and had banged on the bathroom door.

"Peter! When the hell will you be out of there?"

"Go away." Peter groaned.

"Just tell me. How long?"

"Fuck off, Jenkins!"

Harry leaned hard into the door. "I want to brush my teeth and shave." He banged again. "Let me get my stuff, and I'll use the kitchen."

"Open the fucking door yourself, asshole!"

Harry turned the knob, and the door swung open.

Peter, shirtless, was bent over the sink. Straightening up, he lowered the towel from his face and turned to Harry.

"Jesus, Peter," Harry whispered. "What happened?"

Peter's face was black and bruised. Blood flowed from a slash on his cheek. His chest was covered with nasty welts. He sat heavily on the toilet seat.

"What d'you think? I was beaten up."

"Let me take you to the hospital." Harry moved toward him.

"Stay the fuck away!"

"Who did this to you?"

A sob broke Peter's voice. "The whole goddamned fucking world did this." He held out the blood-soaked towel. His face was swollen into a Halloween mask.

Harry wet another towel and began to dab Peter's forehead. "What are you talking about?"

"Couple of guys in the park jumped me. One held my arms back, and the other beat the shit out of me."

"But why? What were you doing?"

"What the fuck do you think? I was doing absolutely nothing. I cut across Queen's Park to get to class. They called me a pervert, a queer." Peter stifled another sob.

"Did you tell the cops?" Harry began to work around the bridge of Peter's nose.

"That's really funny. The cops would probably give them a medal."

"I think you need stitches."

Peter shoved his hand away. "Don't try to play the Good Samaritan, Harry. Most of the time, you treat me like I'm some piece of shit, that'd pollute your pristine self."

"But I don't mean…"

Peter's laugh was ugly. "You know, I don't get it," he began quietly as he dabbed his lip. "Guy like you sees a girl, and right away you get a hard-on. The whole fucking world says, *Great guy! Go get laid.* I can't help it. Same thing happens when I see some guy. Then everybody yells *sicko! Pervert!* Then they beat the shit out of me."

Peter turned to Harry. Tears ran down his bruised and swollen face. "And it's not the first time, either. Is that fair?"

Harry had no words. He just shook his head.

Giving Harry the finger, he said, "So, Jenkins, get your stuff out of here and leave me alone."

Torn from his recollection, Harry stretched back in his desk chair. Being gay certainly had made Peter's life hell, at least in the early years. Maybe it was the pain, all bottled up, which had made him so vicious and cunning. He just *knew* Peter had a lot to do with Katrina's leaving—the end of his first serious love affair. He shook his head, wondering if life had become any easier for him since then.

Scanning his list of calls, he brightened. Natasha had called this morning. He had not heard from her for three or four days. Picking up the phone, he thought of Madame Odella's prediction.

"Natasha?"

"Harry, I'd love to see you. Are you free tonight?"

"Of course. Should I come over?"

"Yes, please. Be sure to come hungry. Say around seven? Ring up from the desk." Her laugh was warm and inviting. "And I will let you in."

With a grin on his face, Harry hung up. Only with great effort could he immerse himself in the stack of files on his desk.

Ten minutes later, Miss Giveny interrupted him. "A Mr. Claus Oldenburg is on line one. He says it's urgent."

Harry frowned and snatched up the receiver. "Jenkins here."

"Is Stanley Jenkins your father?"

"Yes, he is." Harry held his breath.

"I'm his neighbor. I was wanting to borrow his snow shovel, and I found him unconscious at the bottom of the cellar steps."

"You called an ambulance?"

"Of course. They're taking him to the Toronto General."

"Thanks very much for calling. Was he all right when they left?"

"He was still unconscious. They bandaged up his head."

There was a silence on the line. Then Oldenburg spoke. "I didn't know your father owned a gun, Mr. Jenkins."

"What?"

"He had it in his hand when he was lying on the floor. I gave it to the paramedics."

"Thank you, Mr. Oldenburg, I'm very grateful."

Harry's anger mounted as he raced up University Avenue in a taxi. His father had fought his way out four retirement homes in the last three years. For the past few months they had tried his living at home, but Harry could never stop worrying.

Nobody's going to push me around, his father would say to the nurses. Dad was like a troublesome kid getting kicked out of schools. Nothing seemed to work, but the thought of the gun frightened Harry. He couldn't spend all his time worrying about him. No more nonsense! They'd have to make something work.

Harry was told to sit in the emergency waiting room. Impatiently, he flipped through magazines. Sitting off to his far left, a man dressed in a suit and tie was pressing a bloody towel to a gash on his forehead. Harry picked up an old issue of *Car and Driver*. A loud bark made him jump. *What the hell? They're letting dogs in?* He lowered his magazine but saw no animal. When he returned to his magazine, a long, pained howl arose, filling the waiting room. The man with the towel bared his teeth and growled. Spittle flew everywhere.

A nurse and an attendant rushed out from behind double doors. "Mr. Franklin," the nurse said, "the doctor will see you now." With a few yips, the man consented to be led away. Harry suppressed a smile. *Surely not a clever ploy to jump the queue?*

Finally, he was ushered into cubicle four. Expecting to find his father awake and looking rather sheepish, he was shocked. Harry entered the cramped, darkened room to see his father lying motionless in a snakelike tangle of wires and tubes. A green line bleeped across the heart monitor with little enthusiasm. Underneath the flimsy hospital sheet, his father lay shrunken and shriveled, like a broken bird. When a low growl came from the next cubicle, Harry winced. *Must be Mr. Franklin in his lair.*

"Dad? It's me, Harry. Can you hear me?" He waited for a flicker of the eyes. Nothing. Next door, Mr. Franklin began to howl. In a welter of that man's pain and his own, Harry felt his annoyance mount. *Next he'll be looking for a lamppost! Why in hell don't they give him a sedative?*

"Please, Dad, talk to me," Harry whispered urgently. He suddenly felt clammy. *Good God! Maybe this time, he's really done it.*

He reached for his father's hand. "Dad? Say something." This obstinate man, reflected Harry, accused his son of trying to run his life, when he was only trying to keep him safe. Always having to worry about him. Harry touched his own cheek and was surprised to find it damp. Next door, Mr. Franklin had settled down to a low but persistent whimper.

The curtain was torn back. The doctor stood silhouetted in the hall light. Harry introduced himself.

"I'm Dr. Patterson." They shook hands.

"Your father lives alone?"

"Yes. He's very stubborn. He's been in and out of retirement homes. Nothing seems to work."

The doctor nodded sympathetically. "He's suffered a blow to his head, apparently from a fall down the basement steps. All his signs are normal, but I've ordered a CAT scan."

"Can you do anything to waken him?" Harry asked.

"Simple things sometimes work. Talk to him. Touch him. Sometimes a familiar voice helps a lot. I'll call you when we have the test results." The doctor turned back. "Mr. Jenkins, did you know your father had a gun?"

Harry's chest constricted. "Not until today. The neighbor said so."

"Do you see your father often?"

"At least once a week. Sometimes more."

"Has he seemed depressed lately?"

Harry shook his head. "No, not particularly. No more than usual." His father had been so depressed since Harry's older sister Anna died that he hardly ever spoke.

The doctor rattled off his list. "Any complaints of sleeplessness, fatigue, change in appetite, or unusual behavior?"

"No. No more than usual."

"Do you have a close relationship with your father?"

Irritation flared in Harry. "As close as he would allow."

The doctor gazed at him for a moment and made a note. "I'll let you know when we have all the results." Then he was gone.

Flooded with shame at his own anger, Harry sank into the chair beside the bed. Little snorts and wheezes came from underneath the sheet.. For moments, he willed his father to open his eyes, but to no avail.

"Dad! Please talk to me." *Ironic*, Harry thought. They could never talk even at the best of times and now he expected words from a comatose man. He tried to hum a few tunes from childhood, songs he remembered his mother singing. Exhausted, he rested his cheek against the cool metal bed rail and closed his eyes.

When Harry's sister had died of polio at thirteen, his father had slipped into a dark silence. Now, fifty years later, they had found him at the foot of the cellar steps with a gun in his hand. Jesus! Was he intending to end it all?

Except for a few low growls, all was quiet in Mr. Franklin's cubicle. If only his own father would make a sound, give some evidence of life! At last, Harry checked his watch. Almost six o'clock. Leaving his cell number at the desk, he headed out.

At seven, he was at Natasha's door. She commanded his sweetest fantasies, but nothing compared to the real thing. Marveling at her shining black hair, he reached out to touch it. Her pleasure at his presence widened her deep brown eyes, and when she brushed against him with a light kiss to his lips, her soft voice was filled with promise.

"Harry! Come in." With a smile, she took his coat. He felt his shoulders lighten and his breathing slow. Her kiss was long and searching.

Holding him at arm's length, she asked, "What's wrong, Harry? You're troubled."

Following her into the kitchen, he slid his arm around her waist. "Not anymore," he said simply. Even after almost a year, she had a tremendous hold on him. *In her thrall,* he thought with a smile.

Reaching for the wine bottle, she moved away from him. "Would you pour the wine? Dinner is almost ready."

He handed her a glass of wine and sat at the counter. "I spent the afternoon at the hospital with my father."

"What happened?" She set down the salad bowl and turned to listen.

"The neighbor found him unconscious at the foot of the cellar steps."

"Do you know how it happened?"

"No. Nothing." Harry shook his head. "I'm running out of places for him. He's been kicked out of four homes in three years."

"He cannot live alone?"

"Not really."

"Why?"

"He forgets stuff."

"Like what?"

"Like turning off the stove and opening the mail…oh, and not getting groceries or cooking proper meals."

"Is it possible to get someone in to help?"

"He won't allow it."

"But…"

"Natasha, when they found him, he had a gun in his hand."

"Oh, Harry." She set down the soup ladle and came to him. "You think he was trying to…"

Harry shrugged. "What else?"

She laid her hand on his arm. "How is he now?"

He looked at her sadly. "Still unconscious."

"Do you want to go back to the hospital? We can eat now, and you can go back."

"No. I've got my cell phone. They said they'd call if he woke up."

At the table, Harry poked at his veal and pasta. He sipped his wine. "For some reason, sitting around in hospitals sure takes it out of you."

Natasha set down her fork and looked at him carefully. "You sound resentful."

"I do?"

"Yes. Do you need to straighten anything out with him?"

Harry sighed. "The doctor asked if I had a good relationship with my father." He shrugged. "I guess it shows."

"A bit. But there is a real touch of sadness."

Abruptly, Harry rose from the table to gaze out the living room window. Except for a few pinpricks of light out at the Island Airport, all he saw was darkness and himself reflected back into the room.

He spoke rapidly, almost to himself. "He says I don't really give a damn about him. That I'm trying to run his life, just so he can't cause me trouble. Then he says just to forget about him. Get the hell out of his life because he doesn't want me meddling in his and ordering him around." He rubbed his neck and squinched his shoulders in pain.

Moving behind him, she said, "I know it hurts when someone you love seems unreachable."

"Hmmm…" He did not turn to her.

Then she whispered in his ear, "You're all knotted up, Harry," She held him close, and he felt the warmth of her breasts as they grazed against him. "Would you like a massage? I mean a real one."

Her low, intimate tone always inflamed him. His eyes widening with pleasure, he drew her close to him and whispered, "That would be fabulous."

She took his hand and led him to the bedroom. She was gone only a moment and when she returned, she said, "Lie on the bed, Harry."

"Your wish is my…" he smiled.

"Quiet!" she teased, her tone severe. She turned her ankle for him to see her shiny, leather boot.

Grinning, he reached for her and asked, "What else has my mistress planned for me?"

She shrugged. "You shall see what lies in store!"

Momentarily, a strange guilt crept over him. How could he celebrate such wild passion when his father lay comatose? Too much thinking! Life surged in him. His excitement rose swiftly as he stripped off his shirt and trousers and stretched out on silk sheets. Someday he would lie where his father now lay, but not yet. Not for a long time. When she straddled him, he was conscious only of the intense pleasure from the pressure of her thighs and the smooth coolness of her leather boots on his legs. Gently, she smoothed oils on his skin. With deft fingers, she coaxed the tightness from his shoulders. As she slowly worked far down his back, he thought he would swoon with pleasure.

He twisted around to see her smiling above him. She was naked and in the light and shadow, so desirable, she took his breath away. Life throbbed within him.

With his teeth, he pulled down the zippers of her polished boots and slid them slowly off one by one, caressing her legs as he went. He pushed back her hair and felt her quiver as she pressed against him. He kissed her neck just beneath her earlobe and, slowly sliding his tongue along her shoulder and down her breast, he memorized, all over again, each taste and texture of her skin.

When she ran her fingers across his chest, he marveled at the energy her touch created within him as if their bodies were one. Why did this woman, his spirit guide, draw him so forcefully that he scarcely knew where he ended and she began?

And then he laughed at himself as he slid beneath the covers. No sane man would question such free and voluptuous pleasure, as if it could only be valued through thought. Only an idiot or a *fool* would try to analyze love and passion.

She sighed deeply, and when she was ready, she turned for him to enter her. Every time they made love, he experienced a dark and mysterious world he had never found anywhere else. At last they fell together on the bed, laughing and panting, and marveled at the utter satisfaction flowing through them. Then she rose and wound her robe about her. He dressed and shuffled into his shoes. In the kitchen, she made coffee.

For Harry, Natasha was always part fantasy. He did not know what was missing, what made her seem to drift beyond his reach. One moment, she was so close and warm that he thought they might melt together in bliss. Next, she was drifting into her maddeningly remote world beyond his reach. He longed to secure her in his world, but did not know how to do so.

Sipping his coffee, he said, "Natasha, you know how much I love you."

She only smiled.

"Now that I'm downtown, do you think we could try living together?"

She set down her mug carefully. "Perhaps, Harry, sometime."

"But it's silly to have all these expenses, when I'm here so much. My place is big enough for the two of us." They had discussed the question before. He knew expenses were not the *real* issue, but he could not bear rejection over any serious ones.

She smiled and touched his cheek. "We can think about it." He heard coolness creep into her tone, and he hesitated to push further.

His cell phone rang. "Jesus!" He snatched it up. "Yes."

"Mr. Jenkins? I'm calling from the hospital."

"About my father?"

"Yes. Just to let you know, he's been moved to Room 509 in the Eaton Wing."

Harry sank with relief. "Is he awake yet?"

"No, but he's muttering a few words we can't make out."

He hung up and turned to Natasha. "He's okay. At least he's making some sounds."

"Good. Can you stay with me tonight?"

He drew her close. "Indeed I can."

CHAPTER 4

▼

George Pappas paced his living room, a cigar clenched between his teeth. With red, rat-like eyes, he scanned the ravine beneath the bay window. Age had turned his rich, gravely voice into a hoarse whisper and had wizened his body. Images of the pudgy and complacent Peter Saunderson flashed in his brain.

"Victor! Get me my hunting rifle."

Aghast, Victor struggled to keep the disapproval from his voice. "But sir, shooting wildlife in the city is illegal."

The old man glared at him and then cackled, "That's really funny, boy. You, of all people, can't harm a squirrel."

Victor took the rifle from its cabinet and handed it to his boss. Together, they stood on the terrace jutting out over the treetops. Pappas scanned the floor of the ravine through the sights.

"Perfect target!" The old man licked his lips and followed a fox darting through the underbrush. Gently, he squeezed the trigger. The snap of the unloaded gun echoed in the ravine. Grinning, he returned the rifle to his assistant.

Inside, Pappas asked, "Tell me Victor, what should I do with Mr. Saunderson."

"I'd see what he has to say, first, sir." Victor locked up the rifle.

"It'll just be more excuses from the useless son of a bitch." In the library, he settled into his leather chair and began slurping his tea. "I think," said Pappas, relighting his cigar, "he's gotten fat and complacent. It's time to shake the little queer up. I'd entrust that job only to you."

Peter rose upward in the private elevator to Mr. Pappas' suite. Victor, looking grim in his three-piece suit, let him in.

"Mr. Pappas has been waiting for you in the library, sir."

Peter smoothed his jacket and tie as he gazed through the expanse of foyer and living room to the huge bay window at the far end. Beyond the barren ravine, pine trees on the far hill were bent in the wind. In silence, he followed Victor to the darkened library.

To Peter, the old man looked swallowed up by the huge leather armchair. When he held out his hand, Pappas did not move.

"Well, Saunderson, I've been waiting for your report."

Peter sat down on the edge of the chesterfield. "Certainly, Mr. Pappas." He fumbled with his case and realized there was no place to set his papers down. He looked up into the red-rimmed eyes of the old man.

"Sir? We're making all efforts to be certain that the shares are not in the David Parrish estate."

"Fuck! You were doing that two months ago."

"Yes, sir, but as an added precaution, I've assigned a man to follow up any possible leads."

"Bullshit! Tell me something new, Saunderson."

"Now we're taking steps to look into Archie Brinks affairs. He was, after all, one of the original members of the consortium."

"Christ, man! Don't tell me what I already know. I was there. Brinks doesn't have the shares. If he did, do you think he'd be wasting his time looking after Norma?"

Peter tried to contain the sickness welling up in him. Pappas dug his fingers into the arms of the leather chair. His eyes flashed in anger. "Peter, you have failed me miserably."

Peter stared at the old man. He was mesmerized by the flecks of spittle on his chin. Strands of yellow-gray hair touched his collar. Inanely, Peter wished he had been able to keep his hair for as long as Pappas.

"But sir. I've looked everywhere for the shares." Peter threw up his hands in dismay. "I've been to Germany, France, and Italy. Nothing's turned up." His stomach was churning. Suddenly, he was aware that Victor was standing nearby, his arms folded across his chest.

"Then look harder, Saunderson. I'm telling you Norma Dinnick has them. That damned woman is crazy like a fox."

"Yes, sir." Peter bit his lip. "That's why we're concentrating our efforts on Archie. I think Norma has left her estate to him and her goddaughter."

"And who is the goddaughter?" Pappas asked.

Peter kicked himself. He had not planned to drag his wife, Bronwyn, into the mess. But, hell, if it bought him more time, it was worth it.

"What's her name?" the old man persisted.

"Bronwyn Saunderson," Peter said quietly. "She's my wife."

A thin smile broke across Pappas' face. "Now we're getting somewhere. If Archie is out of the way, then everything goes to your wife?"

"I think so, sir. But I don't really know." Peter stifled a cough.

"I'm sure you could find out." Pappas said puffing leisurely on his cigar.

Victor spoke. "And your wife's estate would go to you?"

The old man grinned. "Now Victor, that's very clever. Peter, you wouldn't be planning anything as foolish as hiding them from me, would you?"

Peter turned pale. "Oh, no sir! Please. I would never think of such a thing. I've been completely loyal to you, Mr. Pappas, for over twenty years."

The old man slapped his knee. "And I believe you, Saunderson. You may not be too bright, but I'm sure you are an honorable man." He paused. "If you betray me, I will personally see you suffer a horrible death."

"Yes…I mean no, sir. I would never do that, sir," Peter stuttered as he rose to go.

"Sit down."

Peter sat gingerly on the couch. "Yes, sir?"

"You have disappointed me, Peter, far too many times." Pappas struggled forward in the massive chair, waggling a bony finger. "You've got one more chance to get those shares. Do you understand?"

Peter nodded. Clouds swiftly covered the sun and darkened the library. Pappas said quietly. "Victor, show Mr. Saunderson out, please."

Thank God the meeting was over, thought Peter as he climbed into his car and headed downtown for his office. He thought he might throw up. He breathed slowly and deeply to ease the pain constricting his chest. His cell phone rang.

"Yes?"

"Peter?"

"Yes, Roger." Peter's voice was flat.

"What's wrong? You sound like you've been strangled."

"Nothing. Just business."

"I want to see you, Peter." Roger's voice was filled with promise.

"I've got a million things to straighten out. When?"

"Tonight."

Peter fussed. "I'll try to get away around eight." He had promised Bronwyn he'd be home for dinner.

"Marvelous!" Roger exclaimed in a burst of enthusiasm. "Roxanna will be waiting for you."

As fantasy took over, Peter breathed heavily into the phone. Images of Roger, in drag, floated before him.

"Or would you prefer Delilah, tonight?" Roger teased.

"No, Roxanna." Peter pumped the brake. He had almost gone through a red light.

"See you at eight, lover boy."

Everything was closing in on Peter. His attraction to Roger was very expensive, with huge sums of money going out to prop up his faltering antique business. But the thrill was the payback. With Roger, he could sink into a world of fantasy and desire where no one, not even Pappas, could reach him. What Roger left over, Pappas would chew up in an instant. And then there was Bronwyn. What man could succeed in a major law firm without the obligatory wife and hostess at his side? A lawyer had to be part of the straight world, at least on the outside—or so it was back then. But what did it matter now? Most of those "happy" marriages had gone down the toilet years ago. Even though acceptance was preached, pretence really *did* still matter.

Peter could see the Bloor viaduct arching high above the valley road. A favorite place for ending it all. He imagined standing at the top in the cold, unremitting wind. After one last look at a world, where he had always been the outsider, he would close his eyes and jump. Probably, his heart would stop before he hit the road.

He had met Roger through Bronwyn. In the days when he sought to please and placate her, he had agreed to stop in at Roger's shop, Paramour Antiques, to pick up a print for her. When the front door swung open, Peter's mouth went dry. Before him towered the tallest man he had ever seen, dressed in tight white jeans and a blue silk shirt. His hair, gray at the temples, was pulled back into a ponytail.

"Yes?" the man said.

"My wife asked me to pick up a print she ordered." Peter thrust out the crumpled receipt.

"Step in," was all Roger Blenheim said.

Peter followed him through a dark and narrow passageway into a large room at the back. Dazzled by light and overwhelmed by detail, Peter slowly set down his briefcase. Each wall was crowded with small oil portraits framed in gilt. Men in long, tight frock coats gazed sternly at him. The women were pale in their pearls, surrounded by ugly children with unnaturally rosy cheeks. Peter was lost in a dark and richly colored world.

Roger's voice was deep, sonorous, and mocking. "I don't sell prints, Mr. Saunderson. The lowest one could sink here would be a pretty little lithograph." He was intrigued with the soft, slouching man before him. Not his usual type at all.

"My wife bought a lithograph?" Peter croaked. "How much did she pay for it?"

He tried to smooth out the receipt. "Jesus Christ! Eight thousand five hundred dollars!"

"Wives can be such a nuisance, can't they, Peter?" Roger smiled benignly, thinking the man would certainly be an interesting challenge.

"Cheer up," he said happily. "It's a mere bauble compared to what I usually sell."

"Well, you'd better get me the picture." Peter checked his watch. "I'm already late."

"Let me show you around first, Peter." His glance silenced any objections. Touching his elbow lightly, Roger guided him to a staircase.

Mesmerized by Roger's sinuous motions as he mounted the stairs, Peter followed at his heels.

"I established this little business fifteen years ago. The Rosedale matrons—they're fabulously wealthy and have far too much time on their hands—are my very best customers." At the top of the stairs, Roger brushed against him saying, "They go for the chinaware, sterling silver, and paintings. But my special collections of really interesting works are in the bedroom. I have a fantastic collection of North American Indian masks you simply must see." He motioned Peter into a bedroom. "They're in the cabinet behind the door."

Peter entered the room and stopped. Roger closed the door. An immense four-poster bed covered with a gold and burgundy spread lay before them. Mountains of cushions were stacked before a triptych of mirrors. The air between them throbbed.

From the cabinet, Roger took down a mask and held it out to him. Instantly, Peter was drawn. Running his fingers lightly over the shimmering surface of the honey-colored wood, he quivered inside. A semi-circle of tiny figures curved upward from the chin around the cheekbones.

Roger's breath was warm in his ear. "The figures close down by the chin are contorted in torment. They represent our earthly existence, trapped in a world of pain and sorrow. But see?" Roger reached across Peter to trace the progression of the figures. "Higher up, they become willowy and floating, signifying the transformation of the soul from its wretched state in this world to its pure and free form in the next."

Peter handed the mask back.

"Try it on." Roger was driven to provoke him.

Hastily, Peter shook his head and backed away.

"Go ahead. It's an amazing experience."

Peter did not understand why he consented to Roger's lowering the mask over his head. His throat constricted, and he struggled to lift the heavy, wooden piece from his shoulders. Roger adjusted the mask. Moments later, Peter felt a lightness lifting him up and breezing throughout him. His breathing slowed and deepened. His hands dangled at his sides.

Roger led him to the mirrors. His voice was languorous and soothing. "See yourself transformed by the power of the mask. It awakens your true spirit. With masks, we find the 'other' within ourselves."

Energy flowed through Peter. From unknown depths, his anger spurted upward into his consciousness. Always the yes-man for Pappas and all his law partners. Forever trapped under Bronwyn's thumb. Hiding his shameful desires—Peter was sick of the pretence of happiness. Trapped in his own carefully constructed world, he was now suddenly gasping for air. Quickly, Roger lifted the mask from his shoulders.

"Enough of that," he said briskly. "I can tell you need to be led more gently to your freedom. I'm afraid you'll have a heart attack casting off your shackles."

Peter was caught. He wanted desperately to feel once more the smoothness, the power, and the release of the mask. But he had been stricken with fear, and so he had not reached out until the moment had passed.

By then, Roger had set the mask back in the cabinet, saying, "I have no idea how you lawyers don your straight jackets every morning to slay the dragons, or whatever it is you do."

Shaken, Peter sought to call back the moment, but he was left stranded in frustration and longing, with only a taste of the real power of being himself.

"One more thing to show you! My pistol collection." Roger unlocked another cabinet near the bed. "See? My Gautier flintlock dueling pistols. They really are my most prized possessions." He held out a box that contained two beautifully scrolled silver pistols. "I keep them well oiled and locked up. After all, it *is* hard to find a dueling partner these days."

Peter glanced briefly at the pistols and handed them back. He said stiffly, "Could you get me the lithograph now?"

Blenheim nodded. He sensed that the strange little man's true spirit was buried under an unholy pile of garbage. Maybe that was part of the attraction he felt. But Roger sensed that he *did* show promise. Within five minutes, Peter was stowing the artwork in the trunk of his car. Weariness flooded through every inch of him as he backed from the driveway

Since their first meeting, Peter had frequently visited Roger at his shop, but he still remained trapped in his life. He could get away from the office in the afternoon for a few hours more easily than he could escape from Bronwyn in the evenings. The secretiveness had acquired a thrill of its own. But it was becoming outrageously expensive. He was single-handedly bankrolling Roger's failing business. Tonight, he decided, they would talk finances first.

That afternoon, Bronwyn was shopping at Holt's with Meredith Harcourt. Past the cosmetics counters, aglow with the promise of youth, they rode the escalators to the suit and dress department. There it was. The little black dress. Bronwyn stroked the filmy silk and checked the tag. Size six. Twenty-five hundred dollars. Perfect. But for what? It scarcely mattered since Peter had never found her attractive. How could he? Upon marriage, she had willfully blinded herself to his true nature. Now she was weary with self-deception. Glancing in a mirror, she thought she and Meredith looked sallow and dried out in the mirrors, despite their rigorous diet and exercise regimes.

In the dressing room, she tried on the dress. Its folds fell over her bust and hips with flawless grace. "What do you think, Meredith?"

"Perfect. It looks positively elegant on you, sweetie!"

"You're absolutely sure?" she asked turning once more before the triptych of mirrors.

"Trust me. It *is* you. Besides, you can wear it to one of Peter's cocktail parties. The gentlemen will find you ravishing." Meredith smiled broadly.

Bronwyn handed over the credit card to the saleslady at the door.

After ten minutes, she complained, "Why is she taking so long?"

"Service is deteriorating everywhere, Bronwyn." Meredith flipped through a magazine, and Bronwyn undid the back zipper of the dress.

The saleslady was at the door. "I'm so sorry, but the credit department has declined your card, madam. Perhaps you have another one?"

Bronwyn was incredulous. "There must be a mistake!"

"I'm afraid not, madam. I tried twice and even called upstairs."

Bronwyn's face froze like an alabaster statue. Letting the dress waft to the floor, she stepped out of it and began to dress. In one deft motion, the saleslady retrieved it. Meredith busied herself with her purse.

When Bronwyn's head emerged from her collar, her face an ugly knot of fury. "This is a shoddy way to treat a customer of twenty-five years!" she cried.

"But Mrs. Saunderson, your husband's account was put on hold for arrears," the woman blurted out.

Bronwyn swept from the room. Meredith followed at a safe distance. When she did catch up with her at the curb, they made kisses in the air and Bronwyn hailed a cab, smiling so hard she thought her face might crack.

"Wonderful to see you, darling, but I must run. Give my love to George."

Meredith smiled back—*what a delicious story for the club!*

At home, Bronwyn seethed over the statements she found in Peter's desk. Gift upon gift danced before her on the page. A silver cigarette case, an eight hundred dollar silk robe, a leather bound volume of Shakespearean love sonnets. And finally, items from the lingerie department, set out in embarrassing detail. One black lace corset. Two garter belts. On and on. Bronwyn found the thank you note further back in the drawer.

Peter, you naughty boy. The gifts are totally divine. Friday night, Roxanna will begin the fashion show. Till then, Roger.

Bronwyn poured herself another glass of wine. She would straighten her bastard husband out tonight. Right now, she had other problems.

That morning, before the Holt's scene, Peter's nephew Jeremy, had shown her Norma's draft will. His brilliant blue eyes had borne in to her.

"Here's your chance, Bronwyn. The old lady has to kick off soon. Half her estate is already yours, and soon you'll be entitled to three quarters.

Once she dies, you can dump Peter." He winked and patted her bottom. "Then it'll be just the two of us," he said as he rose from the bed.

After saying good-bye, Bronwyn thought, *Shit. I don't want Brinks in the will at all. What right does he have to anything? I'm going to need all that money if I'm going to keep Jeremy and get the hell out of here.*

Shortly afterwards, the mailman arrived with a registered letter from Norma containing an early birthday present, a check for five thousand dollars. Standing in the foyer, another thought struck her. *If Archie dies first, I'll inherit everything. Jeremy said so.*

She caught her reflection in the hall mirror. In the harsh light, her eyes looked like hollows in her worn and gray face. *Almost forty*, she thought, *but looking fifty—so much for all those spa treatments.* She closed her eyes and pressed her face to the cool mirror. The anti-depressants weren't working. She felt slowly sucked into a dark well where she would be lost for days on end. Opening her eyes, she smiled slowly. *There must be people who could arrange something accidental for Archie. Peter would know. Peter knows everyone.*

Her mind drifted back to Jeremy. Such a good-looking kid, and only fifteen years younger! Thank God he wasn't gay. She'd almost given up hope of being actually loved instead of tolerated as a needed accessory. Jeremy might not actually love her, but at least he was good at the pretence. But Bronwyn, being no fool, knew she needed Norma's money and everything she could get out of Peter.

She carried the half empty wine bottle into the solarium overlooking the garden and poured another glass. The lawn and flowerbeds fell away to the cliff, which overlooked the downtown. As she watched the sun's downward path brilliantly reflected in the columns of glass office buildings, she tried to control her anger enough to devise her plan. An hour later, when the garden was in darkness, she held the bottle up and tried to estimate how much she had drunk.

When Peter entered the house, he immediately knew something was wrong. Bronwyn's venom was like an all-pervasive odor.

She swayed in the foyer.

He tried to assess the damage. How drunk was she?

"You bastard!" she croaked, reaching for the hall table to steady herself. "Do you know what you've done?"

Peter stood completely still.

Ugly red splotches covered her hardened features. Her voice slid from a hoarse whisper to a shrill blast. "Answer me! Do you?"

Made reckless by the wine, she screeched, "I know you've been buying your lover boy gifts!"

She raised her arm. He grabbed her wrist.

"For God's sake, Bronwyn, you're drunk. Exert some self-control. The staff will hear you."

She broke away from him. "Beautiful gifts…silk robes and garter belts!" Her heels made a sharp staccato on the tiles.

"Jesus! Keep your voice down."

"That's right! Always worried about what people will think. Never giving a shit about me!"

Peter saw her tears. The mascara had begun to blotch in ugly black clumps under her eyes. Turning away, he forced into his mind's eye, the tiny willowy figures of Roger's mask, which he longed to caress like a totem for its power. In response to her harsh breathing, he consciously slowed his own. Suddenly, he didn't care about her histrionics. He scarcely cared about anything, anymore.

"Don't go on with this. It won't change a thing. This marriage has been dead for years. You don't give a damn about me. You're only waiting for Norma's inheritance so you can leave."

Bronwyn spun on her heel and marched across the black-and-white tiled foyer.

"Besides, I won't give him up, regardless of what you do or how many scenes you make." Suddenly weary, Peter sank to the hall chair.

Turning back to him, she hissed, "You think I care about your infatuation with your boys? We don't sleep together anymore and never will again, so it's nothing to me."

"Good! Then it's settled. We stay out of each other's lives." Peter rose and turned to straighten his tie in the mirror. He saw Bronwyn's contorted features looming behind him. Her brightly painted lips made an ugly slash across her face. *Just like the faces from hell on the mask,* he thought with interest.

"I'm not talking about your lovers!" she screeched. "If you want to make a fool of yourself, go right ahead. I'm talking about the scene in Holt's today. They refused your credit card. Meredith heard everything, so you can be sure the story will be all over the club."

Bronwyn halted her tirade. Her wine glass dangled from her hand. The last few drops of wine splattered across the black-and-white tile floor. "Pay the fucking bills around here before you buy baubles for your lover!"

Peter was sick to death of money. Bronwyn and Roger were the millstones around his neck. She used credit cards to castrate him. At least Roger gave something in return. Disgusted with the smell of alcohol and the pretence, he sank to the chair and buried his head in his hands. Maybe he should get rid of both of them. Start over.

A sharp crack sounded above his shoulder. Looking up, he heard the splintering, cascading sound of shattering glass. A warm trickle came from under his left eye. Aghast, he shouted, "For God's sake, Bronwyn! What have you done?"

She was gone. She had flung her wine glass at the mirror, sending shards of glass flying everywhere. Millions of tiny pieces were strewn across the checkerboard floor. In panic, he swung around to examine his cheek in the mirror. An inch-long gash ran from the outer corner of his left eye toward his nose. He dabbed the wound with his handkerchief.

Cold fury seized him. He took the circular stairs two at a time to the bedrooms above. Chest heaving, he beat on her door.

"You bitch!" He shoved the door open. The room was pristine in its neatness. *What else?* he thought, *Bronwyn would never vent her rage on precious things. She went for human flesh.* He threw open the bathroom door.

In the mirror, she glanced briefly at him. With casual strokes, she continued brushing her hair.

"Look what you've done!" He thrust the bloodied towel at her.

She shrugged and said calmly. "I only want two things from you, Peter. And I'm going to get them."

"What?"

"A divorce. I take half the assets, and you pay me monthly maintenance."

Peter looked beyond her into the mirror. Clutching the towel to his wound, he drew back from her hard, thin face. *Venomous*, he thought.

Methodically, she slapped the hairbrush in the palm of her hand. "Peter, sit on the bed. You and I are going to get some things straight."

He sank onto the bed. She stood over him.

"You've failed miserably at hiding your secret life from me." Her smile was cruel. "You're a weak and gutless fool. And you make yourself a ridiculous target. If you don't do exactly as I say, your dirty little secrets will be all over the office and the club."

"For God's sake, Bronwyn. You're blackmailing me?"

Her smile was pitying.

Peter felt ice forming in his stomach. Where was the flow of energy from the mask?

"What a sniveler you are. It's not just the boys. You've really thrown caution to the winds, all for your darling Roger."

"How do you know his name?"

"You've given him all sorts of money. Just imagine the whispers at the club and the office. Senior corporate counsel of Blackburn and Swanson, esteemed Bencher of the Law Society, has not only loaned his boy very large sums of unsecured personal and client funds, but he has also diddled with trust funds to cover up the sorry mess."

Peter turned a ghastly green. *At least she hasn't mentioned George Pappas*, he thought inanely.

"But, if you do one little thing for me, you can keep your lovely Roger, and your secrets will be safe with me."

Peter saw only her bright red lips parted in a mocking smile. Rising up, he struck her hard across the face. She dropped to the bed. Instantly, he was on top of her, jamming his knee between her legs. He clutched her neck and saw her face turning purple. Little gurgling noises came from her throat.

Flailing frantically, Bronwyn grasped the bedside clock and smashed it on the side of his skull. He crumpled on the bed.

"You fucking bitch! You almost killed me."

"Jesus! You were strangling me."

Panting, Peter sat up on the bed. "We better get out of this unholy marriage before we kill each other." Blood trickled down his cheek. "It's not as if you didn't know me, before we got married. I'm just an endless river of money to you."

She held out a towel to him. "Hold this on your cut. It's still bleeding."

He pushed her away. "What in God's name do you want from me."

"I want you to give me a name. A contact."

"For what?"

Suddenly, she became nervous. "Someone who can arrange an accident." She picked up a nail file.

"What? You mean a hit man? I don't know any one like that."

"I suppose that's what you call them."

"Are you out of your mind?" Peter shouted. "You're asking me to find someone to kill me? How sick are you, Bronwyn?"

"Don't be ridiculous! I'm not that stupid. It's for someone else.'

"You hate someone else more than me? Who is it?"

"You don't need to know."

"I goddamned well *do* need to know! Who is it?"

"Archie Brinks."

"Good God! What has poor Archie done to incur your wrath?"

"Nothing." She paused to file a nail. "He's a beneficiary under Norma's will."

Peter began to laugh. "How very slow of me, my dear. He stands in your way to Norma's millions." He shook his head. "Poor bugger!"

"All I need is a phone number."

Jingling the change in his pocket, Peter considered the matter. Undoubtedly, Bronwyn was right on the edge. One little push and she'd be a basket case. He smiled and said, "All right. I'll make a few calls." For Peter, it was an opportunity not to be missed. Didn't matter who got screwed. The whole fucking world was to blame for his shitty life.

"Good. I knew you'd see it in the proper perspective." She returned to filing her nails.

Downstairs, Peter entered his study and called Roger. "I can't come tonight."

"But sweetie, Roxanna is all gotten up and waiting for you."

Peter sighed. Images of Roxanna and her lace corset swirled in his head. He said, "I'm sorry, but business has come up. I can't get away."

"Wifey won't let you out?"

"Something like that."

"All right, then. But Roxanna can't wait forever."

"I know," Peter said softly. "I'll call soon." Peter hung up.

CHAPTER 5

▼

Archie Brinks breathed deeply and snapped his red and blue suspenders. He took Norma Dinnick's will from his office vault. Settling into his desk chair, he swung his feet up onto the desk. On the stiff blue backing sheet was typed *Original Last Will and Testament of Norma Dinnick, prepared by Harold Jenkins, Crane, Crawford, and Jenkins, solicitors.* He examined the first page.

I, NORMA AUDREY DINNICK, NOMINATE CONSTITUTE, AND APPOINT my dear friend, ARCHIBALD R. BRINKS, as my Executor and Trustee. IN THE EVENT THAT he predeceases me, I NOMINATE, CONSTITUTE, AND APPOINT my solicitor, HAROLD JENKINS, in his place and stead.

Archie irritably scanned several pages of boilerplate clauses and stopped at Clause Four which read,

I BEQUEATH the entire residue of my estate as follows: One half to my god-daughter, BRONWYN SAUNDERSON, and one half to my friend, ARCHIBALD R. BRINKS. If either of them fails to survive me, then his or her share shall be paid to the survivor of them.

After polishing his glasses, Archie gazed out his window onto the city twenty-five stories below. He had a clear view of the lake and the condominiums posted like sentries around it.

Norma was at least twenty years his senior. Fine looking woman in her day, but now she was a dried out husk. Completely batty, too. He knew she had the shares, all the money raised by the consortium, which Arthur had hidden. Crafty bitch.

That smart-ass Jenkins could cause no end of trouble with a new will. As executor of her estate, he could control the inventory. If he ever found the shares, he needn't tell anyone. Half of what? Not the shares. His watch read four o'clock. Time to visit Norma again.

Lying still on her bed, Norma Dinnick could see the crisp red and yellow leaves on the trees outside her window. In annoyed tones, Arthur called out to her. "What are you waiting for? Hurry! Get the shares."

The black figures surrounding her bed had come from upstairs to steal her silverware. When she finally dared to move, the figures disappeared.

Nearly crippled with arthritis, she gasped at the poker-hot pain grinding in her knuckles and up her arms. She hunted for the pills Archie brought. Although they did ease the pain, they cradled her in such darkness that she did not know who or where she was. When she tried to open the bottle, the capsules shot out and onto the floor. In the humps and hollows of the bedspread, she found one pill and popped it under her tongue.

An hour later, she awoke to banging at the front door. "I'm coming!" she cried out. At the door, she struggled with the latches and wires and peered out.

"Who is it?"

"Let me in. It's me, Archie." Pushing past her, he threw his coat on the sofa. "Did you take them?" he demanded.

"Take what, dear? Would you like a cup of tea?"

Archie hesitated. If he pushed too hard, she'd go off into her crazy world. "All right, Norma, I'll have a cup."

In the kitchen, she said, smiling brightly, "I took two pills last night, dear, just as you said."

"That's a good girl, Norma." He lounged comfortably against the counter as she got down the teapot. "If you want to get better, the doctor says you have to take the pills regularly."

"Which doctor is that?" She looked trustingly at him.

"You remember, dear. Dr. Greenberg. You saw him last week down-town. The medicine is for your arthritis."

"I don't like the downtown, Archie. It frightens me. So many strange people in such a hurry."

He smiled indulgently and helped her with the tray.

"I was so hungry that I ate all the doughnuts you brought last time. Will you shop for me today?"

"Of course. I'll get more for you. You like the chocolate ones?"

"I'd like a little bit of chicken, Archie." She fumbled in her pocket. "I think I have enough money."

"For heaven's sake! Of course you have enough money. I showed you the bank statement, didn't I?"

"Oh! I guess I forgot." She set down her teacup and sighed. "Archie, I don't like those pills. They make holes in my mind. And those tenants upstairs are driving me mad."

"Listen!" He held up his hand. "If you keep talking about holes in your mind and tenants who aren't there, people *will* think you're crazy!" Archie waggled his finger at her. "And if you don't take the pills, you won't be able to live here. Dr. Greenberg will commit you to an asylum."

Norma was aghast. "He could do that?"

"Yes," said Archie with grave authority. "I'm only trying to look after you like Arthur wanted." Alarmed at the distant expression on her face, he said, "Are you listening to me, Norma?" Awkwardly, he grasped her wrist. "Where are the pills? You're due for one now."

Norma could make no sense of his words. Shaking her head in frustration, she set down her cup. Archie thought she was refusing him.

Rising abruptly, he cursed. "Jesus Christ, woman! Just take the damn stuff." Alarmed at his anger, he clenched one hand in the other. So easy to do it. The top of her head was covered with wispy strands of white hair. Stunned by his murderous instincts, he turned away.

"Norma?" he began more gently. "Where are the pills?" He saw her eyes glaze over. It was only to get her attention that he grabbed her shoulder.

She shrieked, "Don't hurt me, please!" She heard the banging upstairs. Clutching both his hands, she begged, "Oh, Archie, please get them out! They're upstairs right now."

"What? Who?" Archie shook his head. "If you're hearing ghosts, you're nuts. I can't hear a thing." He studied her carefully. The crafty bitch was probably trying to keep him from finding the pills.

Norma struggled to stand up and drifted down the hallway, humming a tune.

"Where are you going?" he shouted.

"The bathroom. I'm going to be sick," she said faintly.

He listened intently to hear the toilet flushing. Then he heard a thud, like a heavy bag of laundry landing on the floor. Archie banged on the door. "Are you all right?" Hearing only silence, he shoved open the door.

She had fallen awkwardly and was now heaped on the floor like a bird with a broken wing. Her head lolled backward, and her arm curled over the side of the tub. She did not move.

How convenient; a fall in the bathroom! Kneeling beside her, he felt for her pulse. No sign, not even a flutter. No chance to change her will. He stood up.

One eye flew open. "Help me Archie. I want to get up." Breathing hard, she raised herself up on one elbow.

Archie was quick. "Of course. You've had a nasty fall." His tone was solicitous. "Let me help you."

Archie grunted and heaved. *Goddamned heavy for a little old lady!* He hadn't budged her. With his arms hanging helplessly at his sides, he asked, "Nothing broken, I hope, dear?"

She shook her head uncertainly.

"Because I am going to have to pull you out of here." Tossing off his jacket, he grabbed her under the arms and dragged her, shrieking, from the bathroom down the hall to her bedroom. By the time he had hoisted her onto her bed, his shirt was soaked, and he was red faced and panting.

"Archie, you've hurt me horribly. My arthritis…" she groaned.

"You have to take the medication, Norma." He shoved her to the center of the bed. "I'll get you a glass of water."

When he returned, she was breathing heavily with little snorts and sniffles. The empty pill bottle sat on the night table. "What happened to them all?" he asked.

Her eyes opened, and she seemed to brighten. "They spilled on the floor."

Archie dropped to his knees and searched through the carpet. At last, he had collected most of them. Puffing, he sat on the bed.

Norma sighed. "I'll take the pills if you insist. But you must tell that doctor they make me sick."

He patted her hand. "I'll call him tomorrow." He held out the glass of water and one red pill.

She took the capsule and popped it under her tongue. After sipping some water, she fell back, her eyes riveted on him. "I suppose you think I have the Elixicorp share certificates. Well, I don't. Arthur never even showed them to me. Now let me sleep." She closed her eyes and began to snore.

Stubborn old hag, he cursed under his breath. *Don't go to sleep. The pills don't work that fast.*

With her eyes shut, she smiled wearily, "You've been talking to my lawyer, Harry Jenkins."

"What?" Archie froze.

She spoke dreamily. "You don't want me to change my will."

"Why would you?" he demanded. "I've spent years looking after you. Just as Arthur wanted."

Now she really was drifting off. Collecting the pills, he put a dozen in his pocket and the rest in the bottle. Just in case she decided to throw them out, he would still have some left over. Silently, he rose from the bed and left the apartment. When Norma heard the door close, she waited only a moment. She found a Kleenex and spat the pill out.

CHAPTER 6

▼

Arriving at his office next morning, Harry was met by two men at the reception desk. His client Brian Frost, a tall and somber man, rose to introduce his short and rotund companion, Ross Brackley. Although the pair reminded Harry of Laurel and Hardy, he found little humor in their demeanor.

"Gentlemen. What can I do for you?"

Frost spoke. "We need to see you on the Parrish estate. You remember; I'm the executor." Brackley scowled in the background.

As Harry ushered them into the boardroom, he mentally reviewed the file. Except for a few clerical details, the estate was wound up and distributed to several charities. It had taken years to finish it off due to some lengthy and complicated trusts. Harry took a chair across from the two men.

Frost began stiffly, "Mr. Jenkins, Mr. Brackley is a forensic accountant."

Harry remained absolutely still. "Yes?"

Frost swallowed hard. "He's reviewed the accounting in the estate and prepared a report, which I find very shocking." Frost's face was sheet white, and his hands trembled. "I couldn't find any record of the Elixicorp shares I gave you."

"I'll have to examine the file, but why didn't you raise any questions with me?" He nodded in Brackley's direction. "It might have saved the estate some money."

"Under the circumstances, I thought we should have an independent review," Frost replied. "According to Mr. Brackley, there's a lot of funny business going on with these Elixicorp shares."

"Funny business? Are you suggesting fraud?"

Brackley snickered.

Harry stared at him. Ugly and beefy, he thought. More of a henchman than an accountant.

Brackley began, "Let's get the cards on the table, Mr. Jenkins. "I'm gonna spell it out for you. Frost brought you shares in Elixicorp. Then you sold them under some other name, and now millions of dollars are missing."

"That's ridiculous. I'm sure there were no shares by that name." Harry reached for the phone to buzz Jeremy. No answer. He called his secretary. "Miss Giveny, do you have the accounting records for the Parrish estate?"

"No. Jeremy has them, and he's at the library."

"Can you run them off the computer?"

"All fifty pages?"

"Yes, and let me know when they're ready." Harry said.

Frost averted his eyes, and Brackley stared belligerently at him. Something was fishy.

"I'll need until the morning to review this. But I can tell you right now, *nothing* is missing. The estate was worth about two million." He shoved his chair back. "Give me a copy of your report, please, sir."

"I'll bring it tomorrow." Brackley shouldered past him.

Harry held the door open. "Shall we meet here at eleven thirty, tomorrow?"

Frost nodded gravely at him.

On the way out, Brackley chuckled, "Don't disappoint us, Jenkins."

Brian Frost looked even more pale and sickly than before. To Harry, Frost resembled a crane wavering above a fat quail, Brackley.

Frost and Brackley sat at the bar. Frost asked, "How do you think it went, Ross?"

Brackley paused to peel the cellophane from his cigar. "You religious, Brian?"

"No. Not particularly. Why?"

Brackley grinned. 'If I was you, I'd start praying. Mr. Pappas don't like excuses, so I wouldn't stop until he has those shares back."

Frost's voice was a croak. "Me? I don't know a thing about any shares. The certificate was just a crumpled up copy I found in David's desk."

Brackley gazed on Frost with pity. "You don't get it, do you Brian? Pappas gets real mean when you disappoint him. Just pray to God those shares show up fast."

Reams of computer sheets curled across Harry's coffee table. Examining the initial inventory sheet, he found no mention of Elixicorp in the list of capital receipts or disbursements. If Frost had never given him the certificates, what was he supposed to do? He jabbed at the intercom for Jeremy. Still no answer.

Perhaps the shares had been recorded under a similar name. He found the list of stocks. There it was! The third item was close enough for confusion. 'Elazacor Holdings' [nominal value].

"Hi, Harry." His junior stood in the doorway. "Gladys said you needed me?" Loosening his tie, Jeremy sauntered in and sat down. "What's up?"

"Do you know anything about some missing shares in the Parrish estate?"

The boy shoved a lock of hair from his forehead. "Haven't looked at anything except the accounting summary for a while.

"Where's the rest of the file?" Harry asked.

Jeremy shrugged. "Probably Gladys has it. I'll go look for it."

Within moments, Jeremy was back with a thick file. "Right where I suspected," he grinned. "Gladys had it stacked on a chair. Ever think of letting her go, Harry?"

Harry did not answer.

After several moments of rooting about, Jeremy pulled out a dog-eared photocopy of a share certificate, marked Elixicorp. "Got it, Harry. What's the problem?"

"Elixicorp? Frost and Brackley say the original is worth millions."

"Holy shit!" Jeremy gave a low whistle. "That's crazy." He leafed through the file. "Here's my letter to the Stock Exchange. Says the shares have never been publicly traded."

Harry spoke sharply. "That's not the same as having a nominal value, as you said in the accounts. Besides, the name on the certificate is Elixicorp, not Elazacor. You have to pay attention to detail."

"Sorry, Harry…" The boy gave a shrug of contrition.

Harry felt as if he were already sliding down a slippery slope. "We discussed the procedure. You have to track the shares until you come up with the principals, the real owners." Annoyed, he fingered the front and back of the photocopied share. "Where's the original?"

"It must be in the bank safety deposit box." Jeremy rose to his feet. "Look, Harry. I'm really sorry. I should have known better. I'll go first thing in the morning to find it."

Harry sighed and waved him off. "I'm in a tight spot. So you'll have to get me out of it."

Jeremy turned in the doorway. "By the way, did Mrs. Dinnick sign her new will?"

"Why do you ask?" Harry looked up and caught that damned calculating glint in his eye.

Jeremy shrugged and smiled. "Just thought it was a good one for a precedent…that's all." With a wave, he turned to go. "Well, good night. See you in the morning after the bank."

"Just a minute, Jeremy. Are you absolutely sure Bronwyn Saunderson—your Aunt—hasn't seen the will?"

"Of course not!" The boy sounded injured. "I'd never do something like that."

Harry watched him saunter down the hallway to Miss Giveny's office.

"'Night Gladys. You'll have that agreement ready in the morning?" Jeremy asked.

The secretary's only reply was a burst of typing.

Five minutes later, she appeared in Harry's doorway. "I just want you to know that the Parrish file was not on my chair. He got it from his own office."

Before Harry could reply, Miss Giveny trundled back to her office and closed the door. She sat before her typewriter for a long moment. Then she took a clean sheet of paper and began to type her letter of resignation.

CHAPTER 7

▼

When Bronwyn found the phone number on her dresser, excitement coursed through her. She rushed to call. The phone was answered on the second ring.

"Yes?" The man's voice was raspy.

"Is this 789-0909?"

"Yes, Madame."

"A friend gave me this number." Wondering how to proceed, she paused. "I have a project for you."

"Project? This is a limousine service."

Bronwyn was uncertain. "Should I make an appointment to come in?"

"If you want a limousine, you need not come in. Otherwise, you should."

"Then I'll come in."

"This is a cash business, lady."

A tremor of excitement passed through her. "How much?"

"I do not yet know. Come to 1223 Amoco Drive at four o'clock, and we will talk."

Once she put Norma's check in her purse, she hurried from the house. Just enough time to deposit it in the bank and get some cash. How convenient. A nice sum of money just at the right time.

She pulled into the Canon Club parking lot next to a line of BMWs and Mercedes. Lunch with Allison would be the first step in damage control of Meredith's version of the Holt's story.

Allison was hovering over a tray of veggies and Perrier water in the dining room.

"Allison, darling! You're looking marvelously svelte." She gave her a quick peck on the cheek. "You must be going to exercise classes religiously."

Smiling, Allison adjusted the zipper on her velvet tracksuit. "Well, I do try to keep up a regimen."

"I admire your dedication, dear." Poor Allison. Everything she ate went straight to her hips. "I hear Brad has just made partner. Is he liking his new responsibilities?"

"Oh, he just loves it. Working late every night."

Far too gushy, thought Bronwyn. "Yes, we must watch they don't over-do it." Smiling sweetly, Bronwyn continued, "Have you met his new secretary? She's an absolute wonder. She'll have Brad organized in no time."

"Brad didn't mention…"

"No, I'm sure he hasn't had a minute to talk. Partnership at Blackburn and Swanson does have its price. Home late at night: believe me, I know."

"Is Meredith joining us?" Allison asked.

Bronwyn looked heavenward then smiled sadly. "No, the poor dear's been having such trouble in the mornings."

"Trouble?" Allison frowned.

"You must keep this under your hat, dear. Meredith is in therapy at the Lawrence Clinic. They have all sorts of innovative treatments for a host of psychological problems." Bronwyn forged on with her plan. "Seems Meredith has difficulty distinguishing reality from fiction. The trouble started last year when she took up novel writing. I hear there's wonderful therapy for someone with such an active imagination."

"Really?" Allison had never heard of such an ailment.

"Why last week, she was even making up some crazy story about you and Brad." Bronwyn shook her head violently. "Don't worry. I didn't believe a word! Next she'll be fabricating stories about Peter and me."

Bronwyn was certain she had struck home. After all, Allison was not that bright. She picked at her spinach salad and watched Allison tackle an immense club sandwich.

"You and Brad must join us for dinner soon. Your husband has such a bright future at the firm."

The mission had been accomplished. She concluded the lunch as soon as decently possible.

Finally, she found 1223 Amoco, a low rambling warehouse in a desolate industrial subdivision. The orange sun dropped low in the sky, casting long dark shadows of the transport trucks at the loading dock. One white limousine was parked near a wrought iron staircase snaking up the side of the building to a small door. She cursed as she caught her heels in the slats of the stairs.

Inside, a thin, blonde woman pointed to another door. Bronwyn entered a dark corridor, lit only by a red exit sign at the far end. Bulky shapes of boxes rose up on either side of her as she stumbled along. A light flashed on, and Bronwyn shielded her eyes. A grinning face loomed up before her. An arm thrust outward, blocking her way. Transfixed by the scrawling serpent tattooed on the man's arm, Bronwyn shrank back.

"I'm looking for the limousine service," she managed to say.

The man stepped back and muttered, "Third door on the left."

When no one answered her knock, she pushed the door open. A huge man sat behind a small desk. His face was broad, smooth, and hairless. He wore a white short-sleeved shirt. His several chins hung over his collar and rested on a blue and white polka-dot bow tie. His narrowly set eyes gave him a piggish appearance, but they danced with merriment. Bronwyn concluded his general appearance was benign.

"Welcome, Mrs. Saunderson." He did not rise or offer his hand.

"How did you know my name?" she asked as she sat down.

"Forgive the mess. We do not often have a lady in here." He spoke shyly.

She opened her purse. "I brought the money, Mr....?"

"Call me Mr. Prince, my dear," he breathed. "Before we discuss monetary matters, I need certain information."

"Such as?" Bronwyn felt the first tremor of nerves. In theory, it had seemed so simple.

"Would you prefer to write the individual's name down?" Mr. Prince asked solicitously.

Bronwyn nodded and accepted his pad and pen. Quickly, she scrawled the name *Archibald Brinks.*

Mr. Prince looked grave as he examined the name. "Ah, Mrs. Saunderson, that could be rather expensive."

Bronwyn felt more secure talking price. "How much for such a project?" She felt in her purse for her wallet, hefty with cash.

Mr. Prince chuckled; soon his whole mass was silently shaking. After a few moments, he regained control. "My dear lady! We do not do projects. If Mr. Pappas agrees, I take care of the details." His face grew unpleasant. "We call such matters—arrangements."

"Call it whatever you like. Will you look after this business for me?"

"I will consult with Mr. Pappas, and if he agrees, I will call you back."

"Who is Mr. Pappas?" The name was vaguely familiar to her.

"You do not need to know," Prince said flatly.

Unused to being thwarted, Bronwyn felt her anger rise. "Perhaps I should speak with this Mr. Pappas directly."

Spreading his hands flat on the desk, Mr. Prince rose. "You do not speak with Mr. Pappas, lady."

"Obviously I've wasted my time." She stood and turned for the door.

Mr. Prince scurried from behind the desk. He laid his soft hand on her arm. Bronwyn recoiled. "When I have spoken with Mr. Pappas, I will call you, dear lady. Surely you did not think such a serious matter could be arranged so lightly. At that time, we will discuss price."

"All right." Bronwyn hesitated. "So nothing will happen until I hear from you?"

With a gallant flourish, Mr. Prince held the door open for her. "We must await the decision patiently, madam. You will hear from me at the very earliest moment."

Threading her way through the hallways and past the loading dock, Bronwyn met no one. In her car, she locked the doors and found a cigarette. Her hand shook violently as she tried to light it.

CHAPTER 8

▼

That evening, Harry spread the Parrish file on his kitchen table. After his divorce from Laura, he couldn't bear to remain in their suburban backsplit house, and so he had moved downtown, where he could start again.

He never understood how his marriage had silently unraveled. Nor could he comprehend how Katrina had grown cool and distant. But he was convinced Peter had something to do with it. Although he had no specific reason, he feared he might lose Natasha if they could not plan for the future. Something nagged at the back of his mind. One moment she was close and intimate and at another, she seemed cool and remote. If only he could convince her to move into his downtown brownstone! After all, why waste time?

The knocker crashed at the front door. Opening the door, he saw a young man with long, scruffy hair standing under the porch light.

"You Harry Jenkins?" the man demanded.

Harry nodded.

"Got an old lady in my cab who wants to see you. She's pretty strange." The cabbie leapt from the front porch and was at his car in a few strides. From the backseat emerged a small, decrepit figure clad only in a red velvet dressing gown and slippers.

"Good grief, Norma! Come in." Inside, she collapsed onto the chesterfield.

"Norma?"

"Don't hurt me!" Harry caught her hand, which flew up like a tiny, frightened bird.

"Norma, it's me, Harry. Your lawyer."

She sat up. "Is it really you, Harry?" She began to weep. "How kind of you to come."

"What happened?" He held her hands in his. "What do you need?"

"Those pills make me sick—I can't think right."

"What pills?" he asked softly, fearing she might slip beyond his reach.

"The red ones."

"Who gave you the pills?"

"The doctor. Archie took me to him for my arthritis."

"Where are they now?"

She smiled proudly. "Flushed them down the toilet."

"Do you have the bottle?"

"Gone! I threw it out the window of the taxi." Then she slumped back and closed her eyes.

Harry phoned 911. When the ambulance entered his street, the siren cut to a low growl.

In the hospital, several hours later, he was still waiting for Norma's tests from the lab. When he entered her cubicle, she slithered from the bed.

"Norma! What are you doing?" Harry tried to steady her, but she pushed past him and hobbled to the washroom. From behind the closed door, he heard retching and then the roar of the toilet. At last, she reappeared and announced, "I want to go home now."

"I know, but we need to wait until the doctor returns," he said, putting his arm around her. As he helped her onto the bed, he was shocked at the bony pallor of her legs. Fortunately, she fell asleep promptly. Close to midnight, she was admitted. According to the doctor's notes, she suffered from senile dementia, paranoia and a host of other conditions usually blamed on old age.

She slept peacefully until about 2:30 AM, when she began to toss about. Norma had escaped in her dreams, back to Monaco and Florence.

Arthur was to address the Juridical Council of European Countries on proposed procedures for the International Court at The Hague. All expenses were paid at the Hotel de Paris in Monaco, and if his recommendations were accepted, they would have a year at The Hague to oversee their implementation.

Overcome by the grandeur of the hotel, Norma gawked at the gold-leaf ceilings and crystal chandeliers until her neck grew sore. Endless broad corridors led off the foyer to ballrooms and stone patios yet to be discovered. Checking in, Arthur looked pale and sickly.

Their room was large, with white double French doors open to the sea. Sheer curtains stirred in the soft breeze. Arthur stretched out on the huge bed, and Norma went to soak in the tub. Half an hour later, she emerged in a billow of steam to find Arthur rifling through a briefcase while speaking in low, rapid tones on the telephone. His glance was furtive. Then he slammed down the phone.

"Who was that, Arthur?"

"Nobody."

From the tightening of the corners of his mouth, she dared not inquire further. The next day, Norma was shocked to see Archie Brinks down a distant corridor, angrily jabbing his finger at Arthur. He had nothing to do with the conference. When George Pappas appeared at breakfast in the cavernous dining room, Arthur nearly spilled his coffee. She could not fathom his presence. On a tour, she found Arthur kneeling in prayer in a small church on a hillside. In thirty-five years of marriage, he could not have said more than a hundred words on the subject of religion. Dread settled upon her as her eyes slid from his slumped form to the gaudy crucifix.

The following morning, Arthur gave his paper, which was greeted with great acclaim. A year in The Hague seemed very likely. Afterwards, they boarded the train for Italy.

In Florence, their dark and narrow hotel room overlooked the River Arno. Arthur had scarcely spoken all day, and now he lay in a wordless trance upon the bed.

The room was stifling. She opened the leaded glass doors to a private garden. Tendrils, thick and rank, wound around the legs of the wrought iron table. Their progress unchecked, they had advanced across the stone patio to a murky, green pond of vegetation.

Norma turned into the room. His back to her, Arthur slowly unpacked. "Arthur? We need to talk." she said.

With a sickly smile, he said, "Of course, my dear, it looks lovely out in the garden. Perhaps we should sit there after dinner."

Later that night in the garden, they talked of The Hague. Norma tried to push the climbing vines to one side.

Arthur attempted some joviality. He said, "You know, my love, we've had many wonderful years of marriage. Now there will always be enough money as we both move on to other things."

Disturbed by his tone, she said, "Arthur, you talk as if we're at an end. This is a new beginning for us."

Smiling at her sadly, he reached across the open space between their chairs for her hand. In silence, they watched the sun sink below the burnt orange roofs, leaving the garden in darkness.

Next day, Arthur remained in bed, complaining of a headache. Restless, Norma roved the Ponte Vecchio, arching across the River Arno. She poked about in the dark and crowded jewelry shops and straw markets. She tried to read over a cappuccino, but could not concentrate.

By two o'clock, the fierce sun was too hot to bear. Seized with a desire to see Arthur, she rushed back to the hotel. The room clerk was dozing. When she banged on the bell, he startled then handed over the heavy metal room key.

She rested her head against the cool brass bars of the elevator cage and waited for the lift to rise. As she inserted the key in the lock, she noticed the transom was open. Arthur must have wanted to get a breeze.

It was dim, hot, and still in the room. Arthur lay inert under a single sheet. Dread seeped into her. When she opened the curtains, the pale afternoon light illuminated his face. She saw the empty pill bottle in his hand and a note on the nightstand. She knew he was not breathing. She could not bear to touch him.

Betrayal was the first word that leapt to her mind as she picked up his note and began to read.

My Dearest Norma,

I am so ashamed. I have been involved in business with Archie, David Parrish and George Pappas. The money was raised by fraud and so I have decided it will be put beyond the reach of the perpetrators. There is almost five million dollars in an account under the code name Elixicorp Holdings. With my passport, you will find a share certificate, which you will need to access the funds. The account number is on the reverse side of the certificate. I thought the money was raised for legitimate medical research, but it is now clear that the scheme was fraudulent. They were peddling a wonder drug, which does not exist. I have hidden the money and I want you to keep half for yourself and donate the other half to a worthy medical cause, which does real research. I trust you to make the right decision. That way, perhaps some good can come of this fraud.

I have taken my own life because Pappas will kill me in an excruciatingly brutal fashion. He is no more than an animal. I know I cause you great sorrow, but in time I know you will forgive me.

With all my love,

Arthur

Norma was amazed at her control. She burned the letter and flushed the ashes down the toilet. She retrieved the share certificate from Arthur's passport and tucked it safely in her purse. From the bedside, she removed the pill bottle, and then called the front desk. Only after the police and undertaker left did she wonder what emotion would overtake her first.

Anger boiled up in her. George Pappas had murdered her husband by forcing him into suicide. The little room suffocated her. For the next four hours, she blindly strode the cobblestone streets of Florence. Finally exhausted, she collapsed in her hotel room and did not emerge until late the next day. By then, her plan was made.

Harry was at the hospital the next morning before seven o'clock. He strode down myriad green and yellow tiled hallways until he came to his father's room on the fifth floor. Willing him to wake up, Harry took his hand and spoke close to his ear. He turned away in frustration. His father remained locked in another world.

In her tenth-floor room, Harry found Norma sitting up in bed and chasing the last of a scrambled egg around her plate.

"Norma?"

She looked up curiously in the direction of his voice. "Harry? You're here?"

"Yes it's me," he smiled, relieved she was not off in some mysterious world. "Are you feeling all right? Last night, you were talking about some pills."

"Archie made me take too many."

"What kind of pills were they?"

"The red ones. They're supposed to be for arthritis."

"Do you have any left?"

"I don't know," she said uncertainly. "There might be some at home, under the bed." Norma's frail shoulders poked from beneath her hospital gown as she sighed. "He's trying to kill me, Harry." She spoke with such solemnity, Harry had to believe her

"Then we must call the police."

Norma shook her head vigorously. "The police can't stop people like Archie. He'll just say that's what happens when you help a crazy old lady. I can't prove a thing."

"But if we find the pills…"

"I really don't think there's any left."

"If you give me the keys, I'll look for them."

Norma rummaged through her purse and handed him the keys.

"It's really important to have them analyzed."

Norma nibbled on her toast. "Harry, I want you to sue Archie Brinks."

"Sue him for what?" Harry took out his legal pad. "I suppose you could get an injunction to keep him away from you."

"Yes, but something else." She looked at him thoughtfully. "To return a share certificate he took from Arthur and me."

She seemed very clear in her mind. Harry took down a note.

"And George Pappas."

Slowly Harry set down his pen. "You mentioned him the day I was at your apartment. How is he involved?"

If Archie doesn't have the shares, Pappas does. They were business partners years ago."

"Whose name is on these shares?"

"Arthur's and mine. They stole them from us." Norma fiddled with her coffee pot. Harry poured for her. "The company is called Elixicorp. Arthur and I had control of it.

The same shares Brackley's after in the Parrish estate, he thought. "Norma, they must think they have some claim to them. Most people aren't out-and-out crooks."

"Ha! Pappas is. And Archie will make up any kind of story. He'll tell you Arthur promised him all sorts of things, which he didn't. But now he's dead, he can't deny anything." She measured Harry's sympathy in a glance. "Please help me, Harry."

"If we're going to sue them, I'll have to ask you a lot of questions, and you must be very clear."

Norma grinned like a small child. "Shoot, Harry."

After half an hour of questioning, Harry set down his pad. "It's pretty thin, Norma. I doubt you'll be successful."

She looked at him as if he were a backward law student. "I was married to Arthur for thirty-five years. I know there's not a lot to go on, but I've given you enough to make some real trouble."

Norma was right about the legal action. If he made an application to court, Archie and Pappas would have to produce lengthy affidavits refuting the accusations, which could be rigorously tested on cross-examination. Provided it was not an obvious 'fishing expedition,' very interesting information could be revealed. He packed up to leave.

Back at his office, Harry spent the next few hours dictating a Statement of Claim and supporting affidavit for Norma. The trick was to reduce several centuries of legal doctrine regarding the tracing of assets from one hand to another into one or two relevant principles.

Norma insisted that the shares, and the money they represented, belonged to Arthur and her. Any increase in the value of the shares was due to Arthur's genius at investing. With Arthur dead, the shares passed automatically to Norma by joint ownership. Either Archie, Pappas, or the two of them working together had taken them without color of right—a legal euphemism for theft. Simple enough, thought Harry. But then the waters became murky. Archie and Pappas would claim they were perfectly entitled to at least a sizeable interest in the shares. It would be tough to exclude any claim by Arthur's former business partners.

Norma's mental status was enough to send him into a tailspin of panic. As soon as he filed her affidavit in court, she would be subject to cross-examination. She would make a poor impression if she began picking at tiny, invisible creatures inhabiting the courtrooms of Osgoode Hall.

Although Harry grumbled at the increasing difficulty of protecting clients, he decided to involve the Public Guardian from the outset. A civil servant, who knew nothing of Norma, would interview her and check off boxes on his Assessment of Competency Form. If Archie really were pushing pills on Norma, that might explain her lurching between clarity of mind and madness.

Later in the day, Harry was back at Norma's bedside. She read her affidavit with great care and signed it with a flourish.

"Norma? At five o'clock today, someone from the Public Guardian's Office will be here. I want them to assess your competence so we can launch this lawsuit.

"Don't worry." She patted his hand. "I'll pass with flying colors."

"Good. I'll have these papers served on Archie and Pappas immediately."

Harry gathered his case up and headed down the hallway. He stopped off again at his father's room. For an instant, he thought his father's eye-lids flickered, but it must have been a trick of light. Harry sighed. *Still comatose!*

CHAPTER 9

▼

Peter Saunderson clutched a raft of bills and stared out his office window. Jesus Christ! Bronwyn was out to crucify him. Fifteen thousand dollars spent in one goddamned afternoon on Bloor Street.

Divorce was a ridiculously expensive venture. It would be a fifty-fifty division, straight down the middle, just to get rid of a dead weight. Slowly, calm began to settle over his face. He smiled and jingled the change in his pocket. Since she was nearly on the verge of a nervous breakdown, there were many ways to deal with Bronwyn. By now, she would have seen Mr. Prince and given her instructions.

His secretary buzzed through. "Mr. Pappas on the line, sir."

Peter groaned, then braced himself. "Good morning, Mr. Pappas."

"Did you know your wife wants a contract on Archie Brinks?"

"Yes, sir."

"Have you seen the Dinnick will?"

"No, sir."

"With Archie gone, no doubt, she'll get the whole thing."

"Probably sir." Peter commenced doodling dark, concentric circles on his pad.

"Jesus Christ, man! You're wife's smarter than you. Why else would she want the contract?" His voice filled with disgust. "Maybe I should hire her to find the shares."

Peter glowered and sank further into the chair. "Do you want me to set it up?"

"Yes. Tell Prince to go ahead."

"Right away, Mr. Pappas."

Peter hung up and dialed Mr. Prince. "You have the go ahead on the Brinks matter from Mr. Pappas."

"Oh, wonderful," chortled Mr. Prince. "Do you have any specific instructions as to the manner?"

"Yes," said Peter thoughtfully. "I'll call you back by the end of the day."

"I await your call with pleasure."

Peter continued the review of his bank statements. The bleeding had to stop. Roger, too, was a serious drain. However, Peter's eyes grew blank as he imagined Roxanna, in leather, beckoning him to the divan. For Peter, the act itself was exhilarating, but tinged with self-loathing.

At Paramour Antiques, Roger shifted from one foot to another. The women from the Garden Club were becoming extremely tiresome. They weren't buying today—or probably any day—but Roger, desperate for cash, maintained his sweet expression and cajoled the old biddies in hopes of clinching a sale. In the past hour, they had sunk from serious consideration of a twelve-piece dinner setting of his finest china to passing interest in a lowly soup tureen. His patience with pleasantries had worn thin. As soon as possible, he whisked their blue-blooded fannies out the door. Time for his unannounced visit to Peter, the prick, who wasn't returning his calls.

The thought of money made Roger break into a sweat. He could not bear another embarrassing yellow notice from the landlord tacked up on his shop door for arrears of rent. The bank and suppliers were calling. Mrs. Wotherspoon had been back twice to see the Mary Wrinch painting in the Group of Seven style which, if sold, would clear off his most pressing payables and give him some breathing room. Why couldn't the old bag, who had tons of money, make up her mind? Peter had to be brought into line and persuaded to see him through this cash-flow crunch.

An hour later, Roger stepped off the elevator at Blackburn and Swanson. Dressed in black leather pants and his midnight blue silk shirt, he was ready to shock Peter into lending him more money. The loans were a perfectly safe bet. His inventory at the shop was worth at least two million. And Peter knew all business experienced cash flow problems. Peter would turn that ghastly shade of green, trying to get him off the premises and to sweep his dirty little secret under the rug.

Amazed, he stopped to consider an entirely new idea. It wasn't just the money. And for sure, it wasn't the sex. Peter was far too conventional for any *real* fun. Roger saw it as his calling to free Peter from his suffocating life, and, in exchange, Peter brought stability to his. They needed each other, and if that wasn't love, what was? For the first time, he saw himself as an old fart in a nursing home. Nobody except Peter would visit. Funny, but he actually cared about the little jerk.

In a leather case, he carried the pair of silver Gautier flintlock pistols. If Peter became stubborn, he would offer them as security. Tight fisted Peter had to be brought to heel.

At the reception desk, Roger said, "Mr. Peter Saunderson, please."

"Is he expecting you, sir?"

"No, dear, but he's always enormously pleased to see me." Roger smiled brilliantly down on her. "Just tell him his friend Roger is here to see him."

The receptionist put the message through to Peter's secretary. After a long pause, she said to Roger, "He'll see you in ten minutes. Please have a seat."

Ten minutes grew into fifteen, then twenty. Roger was delighted. Lots of time to pace the foyer in mincing steps. Time to sigh and whisper Peter's name. Big mistake, Roger chuckled. Finally, he was ushered into a boardroom.

Peter barreled through the door with his secretary at his heel. "Roger, this is a terrible day for you to come." Breathing heavily, he remained standing at the head of the table. Roger, with his long legs stretched out, looked to Peter like a portrait of indolence.

"My dear boy," Roger began with a smile, "you are going to have a heart attack if you keep racing through life at this pace."

"What can I do for you, Roger?"

"Don't be so stuffy, old chap. Pour us a drink, won't you?"

Peter sighed and then said to his secretary, "Pour us each a sherry, Susan. Then leave us for ten minutes, please."

Both men remained silent as Susan served the sherry and left.

"All right, Roger. What is it?"

"First of all, darling, why don't you return my phone calls? Don't I deserve the common courtesies?"

"I suppose you need more money," Peter said sullenly.

"Don't be such a stick in the mud." Roger's smile was beatific. "It's the pleasure of your company I seek. Besides, my dear, I believe I've fallen in love with you. Such a novel experience for me."

"You? Don't be ridiculous. Besides, I'm out of money." Peter studied his sherry glass.

"You *do* underestimate yourself. You're a very resourceful man." Roger crossed his legs and sipped his sherry daintily.

"Listen, Roger," he spluttered, "I've ploughed a ton of money into your little venture and gotten nothing in return. I was stupid to lend it without a scrap of security, not even a written agreement." Peter's face flushed. The lack of security bothered him the most.

"What security do you want? My soul? My body?"

"Don't be ridiculous!" Peter shouted. "I'm talking about good, hard security."

"Oh my, Peter!" Roger chuckled. "Such vigor!"

"Look," Peter hissed. "I'm sick to death of always paying out. Your demands are endless, and I'm just throwing money into a black pit. I'm in way over my head. It *has* to stop now!"

Roger waited quietly for the end of the tirade. Looking like he might have a stroke, Peter lowered himself unsteadily into the chair beside Roger.

"Peter?" Roger opened his case. "I have a little gift for you. Perhaps it can be the security you so desperately need." He withdrew the two gleaming dueling pistols and set them on the table. I want you to have them. Actually, they're worth quite a bit of money."

"Jesus, Roger." Peter covered his eyes for a moment. "What good are they to me? You owe me several hundred thousand dollars."

"I know to the penny. Don't think I haven't kept proper records." Roger said snippily. "But you have to understand how it is. You can continue to be your usual sweet, generous self. Or you can have it all come down on your head." Roger smiled brilliantly at Peter. "I can cause you more trouble than you can imagine. But darling, where's the fun in that, when I'm in love with you?"

In Roger's estimation, Peter was turning a very satisfactory shade of green. Waving his hand dramatically, he said, "Around here, they pretend to tolerate people like us. But only if you look and act straight. If you act queer, you're dead."

Roger stretched, and added in a playful tone, "You know how Roxanna loves to strut her stuff, darling. Just help this one time. The very minute I've made the obscene profits from the business, we'll cover that shortfall in the trust accounts."

Peter had sat in silence throughout Roger's speech, staring at the two pistols on the table. "Actually, I will accept your gift." He smiled benignly. "It's very good of you. Thank you, Roger."

Roger put the guns in the case and shoved them over to Peter. "So, my dear boy, we have an understanding?"

"All right. I'll write one more check, but that's it."

Peter wrote a check for twenty thousand dollars and handed it to him.

"Thank you, darling. That will do very nicely."

"I'll see you out," said Peter.

Peter's next clients, the partners of Wexler Insurance Brokers, sat in the foyer waiting for him. Nodding to them, he said, "Be with you shortly, gentlemen."

As they stood at the elevators, Peter saw his clients eyeing Roger. When the elevator door opened, Roger turned to Peter. "Thanks again, darling." He raised his hand to Peter's cheek and gently kissed his lips.

Blackness swiftly cloaked Peter's peripheral vision. His stomach lurched, and stars appeared from nowhere. He rushed to the washroom to avoid the foyer.

His face burned as he stood before the sink. He splashed cold water on his cheeks, but he could not control his trembling. Back in his office, he told Susan to show the Wexlers into the boardroom. Settling in his chair, he forced his breathing to slow. He dialed the phone.

"Mr. Prince," he murmured. "The arrangements are settled. We need to meet in person as soon as possible."

"How very exciting," purred Mr. Prince. "Do we have a time and place yet?"

"Yes. Eight o'clock as usual?"

"Certainly, Mr. Saunderson, I shall be at your disposal."

Peter hung up. Gathering up the Wexler files, he headed for the boardroom.

CHAPTER 10

▼

Norma was back home under the supervision of the hospital home care services. Harry called to say that the papers had been served on Archie, but there was trouble finding Pappas.

Archie's car skidded on the gravel as he pulled in front of her place. Stomping up the steps, he opened her door with his key.

Smiling vacantly, she said, "Do come in, dear. Are you from the Home Services?"

"What?" Archie stopped dead in his tracks. "Don't play games with me, Norma," he shouted, waving a sheaf of papers under her nose. "Goddamn it, woman! You sued me."

Norma smiled sweetly. "Would you like some tea, Archie?"

"Tea?" he bellowed, raising his hand.

She cringed. "Please don't hurt me!"

He shoved the papers under her nose. "Did you sign this?"

Squinting at the page, she said, "It does look like my signature. Is it for the Home Services?"

Nearly overcome with rage, Archie shouted, "No, it's your sworn affidavit. You say I've stolen the shares from you and that I'm drugging you."

"I did? But Arthur, what's it all about?"

"You know damned well I'm not Arthur. You must have told Jenkins all this stuff. He didn't make it up."

"Are you with the Home Services, then?"

"Listen, you conniving bitch! Do you know what you've done?"

"Oh, dear. Have I done something wrong?"

"Wrong! Stupid and deadly! You've sued George Pappas."

"Who is this Pappas?" asked Norma.

"Who is Pappas?" Archie was incredulous. "He raised the money in the first place. Now he's going to finish both of us off if he doesn't get it back."

Norma brightened. "You mean that big man with the deep voice?"

"Yes. And now, because of you, both of us are dead."

"I've been a good girl, Archie. I've been taking the pills."

Archie rose swiftly. "Where in hell are they?" he demanded.

"I think," she began uncertainly, "they're at the back of the night table drawer."

Archie rummaged through all the drawers he could find in Norma's room. At last he found the bottle of pills sitting right on the dressing table. Returning to the living room, bottle in hand, he asked, "How many have you taken?"

Norma shrugged. "Can't tell. My eyesight's poor."

"Don't take any more. You understand?"

"But why not? You said I had to take them to get better."

"Not any more!" he shouted. "You accused me of poisoning you, when I've only tried to help."

"I don't know where the shares are. Did you check with David?"

Archie slumped onto the chesterfield. "Oh, sure. David your lover. But he's long since dead. Or had you forgotten?" Archie's lips curled in disgust. "Damned convenient, Norma!"

Norma smiled in recollection of past years. "David was such a handsome man. After Arthur died, I was so lonely."

Archie's head was throbbing. "If neither of us has the share certificate, and it never showed up in David's estate, Pappas *must* have it." Then he asked himself, "But why has he been after us all the time?"

"Won't you stay for tea, Archie?"

"No! Can't you get it through your thick skull, I don't want any tea?" At the door, he turned on her. "I'll see you in court, Norma. I'm not having some stupid old woman maligning my reputation. I'm asking the judge to declare you incompetent."

Outside, Archie slammed the car door shut. He patted his pocket. Getting the pills was the only good thing accomplished.

Watching him as he drove off, Norma took the original medicine bottle with two pills remaining from her pocket. Archie only had the refill.

CHAPTER 11

▼

A thrill coursed through Peter as he shot up the ramp of the underground parking garage. He laughed, remembering the pursed lips and darting eyes of the Wexler brothers. Throughout their meeting, an unspoken question hung over the boardroom. *Do we want a flaming faggot advising us?* Peter craved Roger's sly, vicious streak like a drug. And then there were the masks! First the obligatory dinner with Bronwyn, and then a visit to Roger. It was payback time.

As Bronwyn lay back in her tub, the image of Mr. Prince, with his merry, pig-like eyes danced before her. Sinking beneath a mound of soap bubbles, she wondered who Mr. Pappas was and when someone would call. With her mind floating, she began to soap her left breast. It was smooth and unblemished, but then, just near the armpit, she felt something hard. Sitting up, she pressed again.

"Jesus, no!" she shrieked. Stifling her cry, she tried to think calmly. Was it trouble if it was hard? Bad or good if it hurt? She felt no pain or tenderness, just a lump, like a hard, perfectly rounded pebble. Instantly, she visualized spidery tentacles reaching throughout her body. Struggling into her robe, she phoned the doctor to find his office closed.. On the bed, she frantically searched her breasts until they were red and sore. When she could find no lump, she feared the paranoia was starting up. She could not afford to lose herself in those dead tunnels where no light shone. Maybe she should get back to the Lawrence Clinic where they treated her depression and the bouts of paranoia.

"Cancer or madness?" she laughed bitterly and then began to moan.

Finally her tears subsided and she was reduced to dry sobbing. She determined to dress for dinner. Biting her lip, she examined her face in the mirror. Foundation and powder could not hide her blotchy cheeks. Where was the real Bronwyn; the one who had always hoped for love? Her parents had first adopted her, then abandoned her to a long string of boarding schools. In desperation, she had settled for Peter, his prospects, and security. Some bargain!

She needed that money to get away—and now, to get well. Archie would have to go. Hire Prince or Pappas and be done with it. Then she could go away with Jeremy. Where the fuck was love, she wondered, dragging a comb through her hair and putting on her lipstick?

At dinner, Peter and Bronwyn sat at opposite ends of the twelve foot mahogany table. He was determined to enjoy his meal. The prospect of watching his wife squirm gave him immense pleasure.

In silence, the maid served a thick, rich clam chowder. Bronwyn poked at the floating masses in her bowl. Peter ate quickly and was soon tipping his bowl to scoop the last few drops.

At her end, Bronwyn looked speculatively about the dining room. The mahogany paneling gleamed. The crystal chandelier cast a glow over the delicate oriental carpets and gumwood paneling. Always surrounded by finery, she thought. Plenty of money everywhere, but none of it was really hers. What had she ever earned?

Jeremy had said that Norma was in the hospital. Surely it would not be long. She was determined to ensure Peter's cooperation.

Soon the bowls were cleared away and lamb was set before them. Peter heaped mint jelly on the side of his plate. Waves of nausea swept over Bronwyn as she stared at the rind of fat on her meat.

After sipping her water, she said, "I saw a Mr. Prince today."

Peter looked up. "Who is he, my dear?"

Bronwyn set her crystal goblet down with a smack. "He answered the phone at the number you gave me."

"Oh, I see," said Peter mildly. "I don't know the name."

"He said Mr. Pappas has to approve the contract."

"Really?" he said amiably and began munching on a buttered roll.

"Who is this Mr. Pappas?" Bronwyn twisted her napkin.

Peter shrugged. "I guess he's the boss, dear."

Bronwyn shoved back her chair. "Don't give me that shit!"

Peter looked shocked. "Really, Bronwyn."

"You know these people. Are they going to do the job or not?"

Peter smiled patiently. "Did you pay him?"

"I took the cash from the bank and had it with me, but he wouldn't take it until this Pappas approved."

Peter set down his knife and fork. Smiling, he said, "An excellent dinner." Concern flitted over his face. "But you haven't touched yours."

"I'm not hungry." She pushed away her plate.

"Darling," he began solicitously, "Are you up to date on your meds? Have you seen Dr. Lawrence lately? I'm just a little concerned about how you're feeling."

"I'm *fine*, you bastard. If I didn't have to worry about where we stand, I'd be perfect."

"Do you still have the cash and the withdrawal slip from the bank?"

"Yes. In my purse."

"Good lord! The cash is in your purse?"

"Yes. I didn't have time to get back to the bank."

"The money is drawn out of your account?"

"Yes. I'm not expecting you to pay."

"I understand that, dear. But that's not the issue. You'd better destroy the withdrawal slip, because you don't want to leave any trail."

Apprehension stirred Bronwyn like a chill breeze. She had not thought about bank records. The project seemed less like a game. "All right. I'll do it right after dinner."

"Where is your purse now, Bronwyn?" he asked quietly.

"Upstairs in my room, on the bed."

"With all that cash in it?"

"Yes."

"Heavens, Bronwyn! I'll put the cash in my safe and destroy the slip right now."

Before she could object, Peter went upstairs. Alone, she slipped her hand into her blouse and felt for the lump. Something was there. Shivering, she withdrew her hand. Would Jeremy still be attracted?

Upstairs, Peter extracted the cash and the withdrawal slip from her wallet and transferred it safely into his own. In her bathroom, he opened the medicine chest and emptied the bottles of antidepressants and sleeping pills. After flushing the capsules down the toilet, he filled each bottle with other pills, identical in appearance, and went downstairs.

Harry was delighted. Norma's application to Court would be heard in the morning. The request for a restraining order by an elderly woman warranted speedy attention.

Natasha called. "Harry, could we see each other tonight?"

"Sure," he said eagerly. Then something in her tone registered with him. He spoke cautiously. "Is something up?"

"Well, yes. I think we should talk."

"Yes?"

He heard the hesitation in her voice. "I know, Harry, that you're wanting me to move in with you, but really…"

Fearful, he cut her off. "Sure. Why don't we talk tonight around seven?"

"Good. I'll see you at my place?"

"Yes." Harry hung up and sighed. Always so intimate and immediate, but when he tried to move to the next logical step, she frustrated him.

At six o'clock, he set out across City Hall Square, which was dotted with stairwells to the cavernous underground parking lot. Wind funneled through the square, making newspapers and leaves swirl skyward. Bordering the north side of the square, the two tall towers curved protectively around the city council chambers, housed in a structure resembling a clamshell. Harry hurried down the poorly lit stairwell, which stank of urine. He was relieved to find his own parking level well lit, although it was almost deserted.

Tires squealed behind him. He turned swiftly. A gray van shot down the ramp to block the path to his car. All the windows were darkly tinted. Two men emerged from the far side.

"Mr. Jenkins?"

Harry nodded, thinking how clean-cut they looked.

"We have a matter of mutual interest to discuss."

"What?"

"Mrs. Dinnick, sir. My name is Victor Smith. My employer, Mr. George Pappas, is taking considerable interest in the case."

"Considering he's a party, he should," Harry replied.

Victor leaned in toward Harry, forcing him to step closer to the other man.

"Mr. Pappas should have his lawyer call me if he wants to discuss the case."

Victor smiled patiently. "Mr. Jenkins, my employer does not believe lawyers are necessary. Mr. Pappas is good to his friends. In fact, he is a very generous man. If you dropped the case, you would be well compensated. Otherwise, matters could become most unpleasant for you."

Sickened, Harry started for his car. With the men following closely at either side, he could neither speak nor breathe.

Victor held his car door open and smiled. "We will await your decision. You have until midnight."

As Harry got in the car, Victor said. "Have a pleasant evening, sir."

From behind the wheel, Harry managed to ask, "How will I find you?"

"Don't worry. We'll find you."

For more than an hour, Harry drove a circuitous path through the city streets, hoping he could lose them. After an hour, he was in the far eastern end of the city. Deciding not to use his cell, he stopped at a pay phone.

"Natasha?"

"Where are you, darling? I've been expecting you."

"Listen. Something's come up, and I can't make it tonight. I'll explain later."

"Are you all right, Harry?"

"Yes. Fine. I'll call you tomorrow."

Back in the car, Harry drove further eastward until he reached a row of neglected motels lining Kingston Road. He parked the car on a side street and registered at the reception desk. As he opened the door to his room, the red neon vacancy sign flashed on and off, illuminating the shabby furniture in a sickly glow. Wearily, he tossed down his case and stretched out on the bed. An old television, with antennae, stared at him bug-like from the dresser. He closed his eyes against visions of Pappas' men. Twice in the night, he startled awake to the sounds of heavy rain and tree branches scraping the roof.

That night, Mr. Justice Reginald Forfar brought home the Dinnick file. The judge, a widower, lived with his housekeeper on South Drive in Rosedale, surrounded by wooded ravines. With his wife dead almost five years, his union with the law was complete and undisturbed.

After dinner, the judge squeezed into his desk chair and switched on a single lamp in his study. One glance at the file told him it was an important case. He was proud of his record of thirty years on the bench. Almost one hundred of his cases had been published in the law digests. Perhaps this one might become another precedent for the courts to follow.

Holy Mother of God! Harold Jenkins had taken on George Pappas. Almost nothing ever stuck to Pappas.

The judge knew Jenkins only slightly. A good, solid lawyer, but his practice was mostly solicitor's deskwork with few court appearances. Well did he remember his deceased law partner, Richard Crawford. "Old goat!" he chuckled. "An unrepentant womanizer."

The Statement of Claim and supporting affidavit showed that Jenkins possessed a fine appreciation of the law. Perhaps the law of tracing money in and out of trusts could be clarified. Even if Jenkins were successful, he would never find the assets in Pappas' hands. The man had the resources to set up schemes devious enough to hide Mount Olympus.

Forfar worked through the file. Brinks had filed a lengthy affidavit, but there was no response from Pappas. Brinks was well known on Bay Street as fast and lucky. But someday the Securities Commission would catch up with him, thought the judge.

But what on earth was he doing with this Dinnick woman? Brinks' response to the allegations of drugging, isolating, and starving her was predictable: have the woman declared incompetent.

His housekeeper knocked on the door. "An urgent call for you, Judge Forfar."

Because Reginald abhorred interruptions while working, the telephone was in the back hallway. In the narrow passage, he picked up the phone. "Yes. Reginald Forfar speaking."

A hearty voice boomed in his ear. "Reg! Sorry to disturb you at home. It's Dennis Latham."

Dennis Latham? The deputy attorney general?" Reginald Forfar stood up from his stool. Could this be the call to the Appellate Court?

"Yes, Mr. Latham. No trouble at all. Good to hear from you."

The Deputy Attorney's tone dropped to a confidential level. "Wanted to speak with you, old chap. Strictly between the two of us, you understand."

"Yes, of course. I understand." Reginald began to gnaw a thumbnail. Although the back hallway was chilly, he dabbed his forehead with his handkerchief." "Is it about the court, Dennis?

"Yes, Reg."

"If I am to be considered…"

The deputy attorney general rushed on in low tones. "There is a matter on you docket in the morning."

Forfar had to strain to hear. "I would be most honored…"

"It's the Dinnick matter, Reg." The voice became soft and sibilant. "Once you've read the material—and, of course, heard the arguments— I'm sure you'll agree it should be dismissed very quickly."

Reginald Forfar began to breathe heavily. Had he heard the name 'Dinnick'? The Deputy Attorney General must know what was on his docket.

"Dennis, are you calling about the vacancy on the Appeals Court?"

There was a lengthy pause. "Appeals?" The telephone receiver was briefly covered, but he could hear a muffled voice exclaim, "Christ! Is that his price?" Latham came back on the line. His voice was hearty. "Reg, old man. Let's talk about that appointment soon, but in the meantime, just glance through that Dinnick matter. Lots of interest in the case. You catch my drift, of course?"

Standing stiffly at attention, Mr. Justice Forfar grasped the windowsill. As he spoke, he clearly enunciated each syllable. "Mr. Latham? Are you, as the deputy attorney general of this province, attempting to influence me?"

The laugh was high-pitched and angry. "Of course not! We'll have lunch soon. I think I heard you're short-listed." The line went dead.

Mr. Justice Forfar was suffused with fury. How dare they tamper with the judiciary!

Back in his study, his anger subsided slowly as he lost himself in the file. The case would get the most fair and considered hearing possible. By midnight, he was finished. Pouring himself a cognac, he permitted his thoughts to stray to Mr. Dennis Latham, the corrupt deputy attorney general.

Archibald Brinks rose at six AM. Today, Norma Dinnick would be declared incompetent—or so his counsel, Roddy Sams had assured him. He decided on breakfast at Shea's Restaurant. If he got her committed, she'd never make another will, and as her executor he would find those fucking shares. Their value ought to be close to fifty million by now.

Marble counters and mirrored walls set the interior of Shea's aglow. He slid onto a stool and ordered breakfast. When it arrived, Archie munched his way through the sausages and eggs. He had a momentary pang of guilt. Arthur wasn't *all* bad. He had saved the consortium from a whole pile of legal trouble. But that didn't mean he could run off with all the proceeds. With his stomach churning, he set down his fork. Why in God's name had Norma brought Pappas into the case? He could crush both of them on a whim. He paid the bill and hurried up the street to Osgoode Hall.

With determination, Archie flung open the heavy oak doors of the courthouse. Inside, he stopped and gaped up at the ornately scrolled ceiling and portraits of dead chief justices of the province. The royal blue carpeting and the marble staircases made him set his briefcase down and slowly remove his overcoat. Not since he was a child in church had Archie felt so small, yet oddly safe. Perhaps the trappings of the judiciary contributed to his sense of protection.

At last, he inquired at the desk for directions to Courtroom Four. Stumbling only once, he made his way up the grand staircase to the black-and-white tiled foyer above. Even the washrooms were opulent, dwarfing him with their high ceilings and mirrored walls.

While washing his hands, Archie saw shadows passing in the mirror. Dark figures materialized behind his right shoulder. Two of them tore back his arms. He cried out when a blunt, metal instrument was stabbed into the small of his back. His arms were pinned back. A gloved hand grasped his throat, cutting off his air. A silver razor flashed in the light.

The voice was pleasant. "Mr. Brinks, my employer Mr. Pappas wishes you to drop the Dinnick case. Go into court this morning, and tell your lawyer to withdraw the case." The gloved fingers dug into Archie's windpipe. Cold steel grazed his throat. He felt himself sinking, but then the hand released him, and he took greedy gasps of air. Archie clung to the sink until the men left. Then he rushed into a stall and retched into the toilet bowl. His legs kept buckling underneath him, but at least he could walk.

When Harry left the motel that morning, he checked the backseat and the trunk of his car. His imagination could not shake the shadowy presence of the men in the garage. At nine thirty, he entered Courtroom Four at Osgoode Hall. Sunlight flickered through the stained glass windows, casting dancing shadows throughout the room. As in a lecture hall, a tiered semicircle of desks and seats led downward to the floor of the court. Soon his lordship would preside from the raised oak dais. Harry looked upward to see cherubs and other winged creatures circling a brilliant sun painted on the vaulted ceiling, perhaps as a warning to the overreaching litigant.

He had lined up his legal texts and notes on the desk near the foot of the stairs. Two elderly clerks chatted beneath the dais. Harry was always concerned that his arguments might be punctuated by the snore of a dozing clerk.

"Which matter are you on, sir?" asked one of the clerks. Before Harry could reply, the clerk was seized with a racking, rheumy cough.

Harry waited until the fit was silenced with a noisy drink of water. "The Dinnick case."

"His lordship's moved that one to the top of the list, sir."

"Mr. Justice Forfar is sitting?" asked Harry.

Nodding, the clerk smiled a ghastly smile. Harry took his seat.

Within moments, the courtroom door at the top of the stairs flew open. Roddy Sams surveyed the entire room with magisterial calm. With his black robes flowing behind him, he descended the staircase. His entourage followed at an appropriate distance. Harry smiled. Three law students to carry his books and two juniors to feed him the argument. The bill would kill Brinks.

"Harry!" Sams grinned ear to ear. "Where's Mrs. D?" He dumped his briefcase on the desk. "Or wouldn't they let her out today?"

Harry peered over the tops of his reading glasses and said quietly, "Roddy, good to see you've brought your minions. You'll need them today. But where's Mr. Brinks?"

Sams chuckled. "Not to worry. My client will be here. He's very upset about the libel in Mrs. D's affidavit." Sams rested his elbows on his knees and leaned over to Harry, speaking in confidential tones. "All kidding aside, Harry, what's going on with Pappas? He's been served, but no lawyer has filed anything in court for him. Tony McKeown at Cheney, Arpin used to act for him, but now that he's dead I don't know who acts for Pappas."

Harry shook his head. From his experience on the Deighton estate, he knew plenty. Tony McKeown had been a high profile lawyer with several clients who had tentacles deep in the underworld.

Harry said, "I'm not surprised. Pappas is not a conventional litigant. I'm sure he'll make his presence known somehow."

The door at the top of the stairs opened. Roddy swiveled around to see Brinks enter. "Jesus!" Roddy swore under his breath.

Harry turned to look. Brinks, gripping each desk for support, slowly descended the broad stairs. His usually ruddy complexion was now a pasty gray. His normally robust movements now verged on the decrepit. At last Brinks stood before Sams.

"Archie, what happened?" Sams' mouth hung open. "Sorry to say, but you look like shit."

Archie slumped beside his counsel and hissed, "Get me out of this!"

"What?" Sams was bug-eyed. Harry turned to his books.

"I want out of this lawsuit," Archie persisted.

Roddy began to stammer. "Listen, Arch, I can't call it off, just like that." He snapped his fingers under client's nose. "Mrs. Dinnick brought the lawsuit. Not you. If you want to try to settle something, then maybe I can talk to Mr. Jenkins."

"I've been threatened, Mr. Sams. Do whatever you have to do," said Brinks.

"Who's threatening you?"

"Idiot! Can't you figure it out?"

Sams turned ashen. He tapped Harry on his arm. "Listen, old friend…"

Harry's eyebrows shot up. Desperation wafted from Sams. As a negotiator, he was bright as a bag of hammers.

"Could we talk? My client and I have some terms to…"

"Such as?"

"Well, I need time to confer with Mr. Brinks." Sams coughed discretely. "But I'm sure we can work something out."

"I'm not wasting my morning, Mr. Sams. At the very least, I want a restraining order against Mr. Brinks."

The door to the left of the dais banged open. A stout, elderly man entered and intoned, "All rise!"

Everyone in Courtroom Four clambered to their feet. Mr. Justice Forfar entered and ascended to the bench. All remained standing.

"Hear yea…Hear yea…Hear…yea. Motions Chambers is now in session, the Honorable Mr. Justice Forfar presiding," the clerk called out.

In unison, all present bowed and resumed their seats. Forfar scanned the court. Peering down at counsel, he said sternly, "Gentlemen, I have moved the Dinnick matter to the top of the list. Counsel on other matters are dismissed until further notice."

Settling back in his chair, his lordship continued, "It appears that exceptional interest has been taken in this case, and I intend to give it my most diligent and thorough scrutiny." He perched his reading glasses on his nose and opened the file. "Further, it is my sworn duty to protect the freedom and integrity of the judiciary."

Harry frowned. Such statements from the bench were rare. Forfar was a highly principled man—with a rebellious streak. Harry had been threatened. Brinks had been threatened. Had someone gotten to the judge?

"Mr. Jenkins, you represent Mrs. Dinnick. Is she present today?"

Harry was on his feet. "If it please your lordship, Mrs. Dinnick is not in court today. Given her state of health and the allegations of intimidation and medicating, I believe no useful purpose would be served in having her attend these preliminary proceedings."

"Very wise, Mr. Jenkins," the judge nodded. Turning to opposing counsel, he said, "Mr. Sams? Is Mr. Brinks present?"

Sams leapt to his feet. "Yes, your lordship, Mr. Brinks is here beside me." Brinks stood unsteadily.

"Is anyone representing the defendant, Mr. George Pappas?" The judge scanned the courtroom.

Both counsel shook their heads. Harry rose. "My lord, Mr. Pappas was personally served yesterday at his residence. I checked with the court office half an hour ago, and nothing had been filed on his behalf."

"Gentlemen," said Forfar, "I am issuing an order for contempt against Mr. George Pappas, and I will adjourn the hearing until he is brought before this court. At that time, I will hear argument from all parties as to the issues to be set down for trial."

"My lord," began Harry, "I ask that in the meantime a restraining order be issued against Mr. Brinks. I submit that the allegations are sufficiently serious to warrant such an interim order."

"Mr. Sams?" The judge glanced at opposing counsel.

Sams rose swiftly. "My lord, we have no objection to such an order, except that it is unnecessary. Mr. Brinks has no intention of contacting Mrs. Dinnick in any fashion."

"Very good. Then you consent to my making such an order?"

"Yes, sir. Of course, we would prefer not to have it on the court record." Under Forfar's icy stare, Sams' voice trailed off.

The judge then bent to the task of recording the order for contempt against Pappas and the restraining order against Brinks. Both Harry and Sams were busy scrawling their own notes. As they wrote, the courtroom was silent. The clerk nodded off, eyelids drooping and mouth open.

The judge and counsel were so absorbed that no one heard the rear courtroom door creak open. No one saw a very portly gentleman enter. Although it was late November, the man was dressed in a powder blue suit and white shirt. A blue and white polka-dot tie waggled under his chins. He wore soft, black leather gloves.

With delicate steps, he descended the stairs and stopped less than ten paces from the bench. He unzipped a slim leather case and extracted some papers. Giving a slight cough, he spoke in a high, quavering voice. "My lord, if it please the court…"

Mr. Justice Forfar was the first to look up. "Who are you, sir?"

"I am Mr. Prince, my lord."

"Are you counsel on the Dinnick matter?"

"No, my lord." The man smiled merrily as he gave a little skip downward to the bench.

"Do you have some involvement in the Dinnick case?"

"Oh, yes sir. Indeed I do."

The elderly Clerk shook himself awake as Mr. Prince drew closer. With a tentative smile, he rose to take the papers from the man.

"I wish to file these papers on behalf of the defendant, Mr. George Pappas." Prince stepped back as the Clerk took the papers.

Roddy Sams sprang to his feet in protest. The judge waved him off and began to read.

Prince began rummaging through his pockets. Harry knew the wisdom of letting the judge read in peace. He bent to a study of his notes.

Prince pivoted and marched toward Brinks' counsel table. A small silver pistol flashed in his hand.

Waving his arms, Archie struggled to stand up. "No! Please don't!" he shouted.

Roddy Sams dove under the desk.

There was a sharp crack, just like a whip. Archie clawed at the air. He clutched the desk, as his eyes grew wild and then began to darken. Blood gushed down the side of his face.

Prince had danced halfway up the steps. Harry lunged at him. From out of nowhere, Prince smashed a small metal club against Harry's knee. White-hot pain shot up his leg, but he tried to limp after the man.

Grinning, Mr. Prince held the pistol high in the air. For a stunned instant, Harry gaped at the tiny, elegantly scrolled silver pistol, which gleamed in the sunlight. With surprising agility, the man gained the last few steps to the door. He turned and bowed formally to the court, as was the custom of departing counsel.

"Somebody call an ambulance!" shouted Harry. With almost no sensation in his leg, he turned to Archie's sprawled form and saw that his entire right side was soaked in blood. Sinking to the floor, Harry took off his robe and folded it around Archie's head to staunch the blood still spilling from the wound.

Soon the paramedics and police arrived and loaded Archie onto a stretcher. Roddy Sams slouched at his desk, staring vacantly into space. Mr. Justice Forfar remained on his hands and knees behind the dais.

Suddenly, a police officer was at Harry's side.

"Did he get away?" asked Harry.

"They've closed off the building. They'll find him. Can you give us a description?"

Harry nodded. His leg began to buckle underneath him.

"Better get that knee looked at, sir."

"Is Brinks still alive?" asked Harry, looking over the officer's shoulder.

"Barely."

"May I ride in the ambulance?"

The policeman nodded and guided Harry out through the judge's chambers at the rear. In the ambulance, the paramedics thought Brinks might have a chance. Harry strained to understand as words tumbled from Archie's mouth. Something about Venice and a hawk and shares. The paramedics shrugged. Nothing made sense. Archie's eyes darkened, then closed. Despite their valiant efforts, they were unable to revive him.

CHAPTER 12

▼

Archie's murder was not the sort of news to be delivered on the phone. Bandaged up and limping only slightly, Harry arrived at Norma's. Who could believe such blood and mayhem would result from her lawsuit over shares? The violence of righting ancient wrongs.

She answered the door on his first knock, her face filled with expectation. "I've been waiting for you, Harry."

He took her hands in his and said, "Sit down, Norma. Something dreadful has happened. I'm sorry to tell you, but Archie was murdered in court this morning."

Tears welled up in her eyes, and he felt her tremble. "But who would do such a thing?" She searched his face for answers. "It's only about money."

"Someone named Prince filed some documents for George Pappas. Then he turned around and shot Archie right in the courtroom."

"So, Pappas really did kill Archie!" she said, her breath coming in short stabs.

"Why?"

"George knows Archie has those shares. That's why he killed him."

"Pappas may have them and wants to eliminate Archie's claim."

"Maybe. But others are involved. Pappas is just a hit man. He takes orders from higher-ups."

Harry spoke mildly. "You seem to know a lot more about Pappas than you originally said. And if you're right, then you're in grave trouble. He won't stop at Archie."

"George knows I don't have the shares."

"Why are you so sure?"

"Because he would have gotten rid of me years ago." Norma sagged back in her chair, seemingly exhausted.

"Do you want to continue with the litigation?" Harry asked.

"Can I?"

"Certainly. And it makes good sense. Once we know Archie's executor, we can go after him for an accounting of all the estate assets."

Norma smiled with satisfaction. "So it's settled then?"

"Yes. I'll have to get an order from court continuing the suit against Archie's estate."

"What about finding out who really murdered Archie? I mean the higher-ups."

"That's up to the police."

"But you'll keep me posted, won't you?"

"Of course, Norma."

She showed him to the door. "By the way, Harry, thank you. I haven't heard those tenants. You must have gotten them out."

Harry waved good-bye and then got into his car. Tiny and hunched over, Norma waved and then rubbed her hands together as if for warmth. George Pappas, he thought, could finish her off with a flick of his finger.

As soon as Norma entered her apartment, she heard the banging upstairs. With Archie gone, the trouble should be gone. Shaking her head in dismay, clinging to the banister, she hoisted herself to the second floor and into the long hallway filled with gray light. When she opened the door, a cold draught cut at her ankles. She no longer saw Arthur's study, only the barren apartment.

Back in memories of her childhood, she shivered from within. Mama used to leave her alone in the big house outside of the town where she worked as a waitress. The land was stony and barren, and the wind swept down from the hills behind the house and made the windows rattle. The loneliness and the gray twilight, waiting for mama, seemed endless. Fear overcame her as darkness fell, listening for mama. She crawled under the bedcovers and waited, sometimes all night.

As she stood at the door of the upstairs apartment, she wished once again that the unremitting silence would be broken by a human voice. She wandered through the empty rooms until she reached the far bedroom at the back. She sank into the white wicker chair by the window. How did they get in? Why did they come in? Suddenly she was aware of a low whistling sound, like a furious wind.

"Arthur, is that you?" Her smile was tentative as she strained to listen.

"David?" She tapped her foot on the hardwood floor.

"Surely not you, Archie? Not so soon!" She heard a swishing sound, like tires on a wet road.

"Who is it, please?" She began to rise from the chair, but then stopped. Her face was wreathed with smiles.

"David, darling! How wonderful to see you and looking so well." Her David smiled graciously and sat beside her.

"Now we can chat over old times and have a cup of tea." She patted his hand and smiled. Norma's mind had returned to the Toronto of the 1940's.

She was eighteen when she escaped her childhood of silence. The traffic, the motion, the lights, sounds, and colors of the city almost overwhelmed her. Her first job was as a clerk in the haberdashery department of Eaton's Department store. The ceilings rose up like in a church, and Norma reveled in the atmosphere of class and breeding.

She shared a small room in the Willard Residence for Ladies with a clerk from cosmetics, Heather Hartwick. In the winter, the hotel was overheated and noisy, and the radiator next to Norma's cot clanged all night.

Norma hurried past the lounge, a depressingly dusty room off the lobby, which was filled with overstuffed chesterfields. From within came sounds she had never heard before. It was the only place a young lady could say good night to her gentlemen friend.

Her roommate, Heather, had *big* ideas. She was a dreamy, blowsy sort of girl who spent most evenings either out with boys or reading stacks of movie magazines.

Heather said, "Norma, the only way to get ahead in this town is to find a rich husband."

"And how do you think you'll do that?" Norma murmured from behind a novel.

"Well, they don't have to be rich right at the start. But they got to have prospects and good manners."

Norma lay down her book and said, "I want someone intelligent and ambitious. But he has to be *very* kind. I want him to make me safe and secure."

Several weeks later, Arthur Dinnick appeared at the haberdashery counter. He was thin, almost gaunt, but Norma knew the minute he looked over the top of his spectacles at her.

"May I help you, sir?" Norma smiled sweetly.

Touching a blue and green silk tie, he said, "No, thank you. I'm really just looking."

Was he really blushing, Norma wondered? He had such a refined and cultured tone.

"What kind of suit do you have?"

"Pardon?"

"You know, to match the tie with."

Smiling, he looked straight at her. "Why, a blue one, miss."

For Heather it was much more difficult. One night she returned home with her blouse was ripped and her stockings torn. In the morning there was a large bruise under her right eye. The man's name was Lenny, and he lived on the east side of the city.

Several months later, when Heather returned from the bathroom down the hall, her face was red from crying. "I'm pregnant," she whispered. Lenny was long since gone.

Norma asked another friend, Doris, over coffee break where to get an abortion. Doris had that worldly look about her; she would know. Norma was aghast at her friend's news. The doctor in Buffalo charged *three hundred dollars!*

"Where's Lenny?" Norma asked Heather.

"Maybe it isn't Lenny. I don't know."

Norma was aghast. "How can you *not* know?" It took her some time to understand.

"I can get the money," Arthur offered one night. But by that time, it was too late. Heather continued to grow bigger until, at last, her mother arrived and took her away. Much later, Norma received Heather's letter. A seven-and-a-half-pound baby, named Bronwyn, had been born and put up for adoption. Heather was sent to a convent.

Sometimes Arthur would look at her *that* way. Norma liked it well enough when he kissed her, but she felt almost nothing. When he tried to touch her breast or put his hand under her skirt, she moved away. That sort of thing was for marriage. Puzzling over Arthur's longing and the passion in his kisses, she finally realized her power. Sex was a woman's most valuable coinage. Throw that away, and you had absolutely nothing. Because she hadn't understood that, Heather was now stuck in a convent with the nuns.

"David? Did you ever know Peter and Bronwyn Saunderson?"

David shook his head.

"Poor Bronwyn!" Norma continued. "I have no idea why Heather gave her such an ugly name." She shook her head in amazement. "Almost as if she wanted to curse the poor child! Anyway, despite all that, Bronwyn's done very well for herself. Fine people, a couple who could afford the best nannies and the best boarding schools, raised her. Granted, her adoptive parents were often away, but she was well cared for. And then, she found herself a young man, Peter. He's a fine and respected corporate lawyer with lots of wealthy clients."

David nodded and sipped his tea.

Norma rocked in her wicker chair in the apartment, "Do you remember what a fine man Arthur was?"

David only smiled.

"I only mention it, dear, to explain why I never left him for you." Then she added coyly, "Although I was greatly tempted. But Arthur was almost everything I could ever want. He loved me, and I could always rely upon him." Norma looked sadly at David. "I know it wasn't perfect. Not every life is filled with love, sex, and passion. But there was deep affection."

David seemed to nod ever so slightly.

"And, of course, there are times when I have regretted that decision." she sighed.

David grimaced. "What's done is done." But then, he brightened. "Didn't we have a lovely time in New York?"

Norma smiled broadly. "New York was wonderful, darling. But it's too bad you forgot your heart medication before we climbed to the top of the Statue of Liberty. It was so terribly sad, when you died in my arms."

David hung his head.

"But just so you understand why I stayed with Arthur, I want to tell you about after we moved to Barclay Street."

After five years of marriage, they had moved into the house high up on the hill overlooking the Rosedale ravine. They accumulated far more money, Norma realized later, than anyone could on a just professor's salary. But no matter how much they had, Norma never lost that empty hollow feeling. The sound of wind sweeping over the scrubby meadows and rocks of the northland was always with her.

One morning, shortly after moving in, Norma went up to the attic. Under the little dormer window sat a small desk and a filing cabinet. Curious, she knelt down and tried to open the drawers. Except for one, all were tightly locked. Inside, Norma found a folder filled with reams of paper covered with penciled columns of figures. Why would Arthur work up here, with a comfortable study on the second floor? She turned around. There was Arthur. His face was somber.

"You must *never* come up here, Norma." Snatching the file from her hand, he locked it in the cabinet. "Do you understand me?" His face was ashen.

"But Arthur, what is it?"

"Nothing. Just personal papers." He led her down the stairs.

Once in the Barclay Street house, the Dinnicks began to entertain. On the back lawn, the string quartet played for the bankers, stockbrokers, lawyers, and their wives. Chinese lanterns cast a warm peach-colored glow. The women drifted languidly about the stone terrace discussing dress designers and the best private schools for their children. The men congregated at the foot of the garden considering weighty business matters. Norma would break away from the women's chatter, never admitting that envy drove her off. She found herself wandering past the azaleas and roses to join the men. She could not resist their talk, hushed and energetic in the soft, night air, or the way it mingled business with the dark underside of politics. But Norma did not fit with them either.

She talked with one wife, Samantha, whom she had gotten to know. "Don't you just hate this, Norma?" Samantha had drunk a bit too much wine.

"Hate what?"

Samantha flung her arm out to encompass all the guests. "Men."

Norma was cautious. "How do you mean?'

Sam gazed at her intently. "C'mon, honey. I know you're different. You've got a brain. Really, it's the women, you know."

"I thought we were talking about the men," Norma said uncertainly.

Sam shrugged as if there were no distinction. "It's all the same. The men make the women crazy. Ever notice how all of them are so goddamned perky? All these hollow women with smiles pasted on, running around with their charity work and their kids' private schools. Living their lives only for their men: they've got nothing inside them."

Norma did not understand Samantha. She felt honored to be a professor's wife. She had won Arthur by making him wait until marriage. Arthur was her security. Look at the house, the furnishings, and the two servants. It was a good bargain.

"Norma? Ever thought of doing it with another man?"

"Samantha! What's got into you?" Norma stepped back. "Why?"

"Just for the hell of it. To shake things up and see the look on the ladies' faces. You don't fit in unless you put on the smiley party face and play the loyal wife. If you don't, they call you a slut. But men do it all the time. They've got the best of both worlds."

Norma patted Samantha's hand. "Very interesting, dear. But I really must attend to my other guests." She was aware of an audible stir of excitement from the wives on the terrace.

"He came after all?" someone said.

"Is his wife here too?"

"Wife? He's not married, I hope."

The string quartet began to play again.

"You mean he's out of jail, already?"

"No! He wasn't in jail. They never got a thing on him."

Norma turned and, for the first time, glimpsed George Pappas, surrounded by many women. His head was thrown back in laughter, long fair hair flowing down to his collar. When she heard his gravely, languorous voice like a rough caress, she shivered in the night air.

"Where is my hostess?" he called out.

Norma stood before him. "Mr. Pappas? I'm Norma Dinnick, your hostess," she said proudly. "I'm delighted you could come."

He did not reply at first, but stood perfectly still and appraised her. Arthur never looked at her that way. She felt intimately aware of every cell in her body. Her cheeks burned, and she caught her breath. For the first time, she understood—as clearly as if she had stepped into another world. This was sex. This was the attraction that made you lose all sense.

With a flourish, he took her hand and bent to kiss it. "Mrs. Dinnick," he caressed her name. "I am charmed."

Immediately, Norma knew what she had been missing. Arthur brought security and love, but never once had he instilled the passion she now felt rising in her. Blushing, she murmured, "So pleased to make your acquaintance, Mr. Pappas."

Arthur was at her side. Under the lights, he looked worn and faded. Taking Pappas by the arm, he guided him to the bar set down at the foot of the garden. Norma knew she had to see him again.

CHAPTER 13

▼

"Mr. Jenkins? Your father is out of his coma and asking to see you."

"Wonderful! I'll be there as soon as possible." Harry hung up and tossed on his coat.

Thank God! Relief flooded through him.

Within half an hour, he was striding through the noontime crowds in the underground maze of corridors at Toronto General Hospital.

Now he's awake, we'd better start talking, especially about the gun. That's been the trouble all my life. I've never been able to have a real conversation with him. Always putting each other off and ending up in arguments. You don't get a second chance every day. So now that it's here, you are damn well going to make the most of it.

As he passed by the cafeteria, the aroma of lunch wafted out to him, reminding him he was hungry. A sea of faces met him as he looked at the line-up at the cash register. One elderly man's face bore no trace of his thoughts, seemingly focused entirely on his inner world. The woman behind him was open and laughing as she talked with a friend. Another was ravaged with worry. Perhaps he had desperate concern about a wife, a child, himself. It was hard to imagine what others bore and to understand that everyone had as murky depths as he did. But then, you could only see the outside. Only by what people said or did could you ever know much about them.

Poor Dad! I can only imagine what it's been like for him, buried inside himself, unable to talk. When Anna died, he just disappeared. It seemed like he hated Mother and me, and of course, himself. Good God! How I resented him for that. Probably still do. But now's the time to straighten things out, starting with this damned gun.

Suddenly, Harry realized he had made a wrong turn. The elevators to the Eaton Wing were down the other corridor. He shouldered past a woman pushing a little boy in a stroller, who clutched a teddy bear. Whining, he lurched back and forth to break free of the straps. At last, Harry arrived at the glass elevators.

But what about the gun? Jesus, was he trying to kill himself? And why? You just don't know what's going on inside somebody, even your own father. Maybe, he's gotten so depressed, there's nowhere else left for him to go. But goddamn it, why does he have to be so hard to reach? Most of the time, it's like talking to a brick wall.

Harry pushed past the laundry cart parked in the hallway near the nursing station.

One of us has to figure this out and make some rational decisions. And of course, it'll be me. The gun business shows he can't be trusted to make the right ones. How can you find a safe place for a man who wants to kill himself?

Harry marched into the room. His father's head was turned on the pillow toward the door. Struck by the glimmering intensity in his eyes, Harry grasped his hand.

"Dad, thank goodness you're back in the land of the living." He was depressed by his own forced joviality. "You sure had me worried the last few days." His father's eyes bore into his. His arm reached up to draw him closer.

"Son!" His father's voice was little more than a gurgle.

"Yes, Dad?" Ready for another demand for freedom to live on his own, he bent closer. His father pulled him down to his chest.

Stanley's eyes were fierce. "I want to apologize, son."

Harry jerked back. "You've nothing to apologize for Dad."

His father shook his head violently. "Listen! You've been a good son."

Harry grimaced and patted his hand. "You've been a good father."

"Bullshit!"

"What?" Harry reared back. He didn't want to argue, but his father seemed determined to start. "You want some water?" Harry looked frantically about for a glass. "Where the hell is the nurse?"

"I don't want water."

"Some juice, coffee?"

"I want to apologize."

"What? You've nothing to apologize for."

"Why won't you let me?" he demanded angrily.

Steeling himself against old arguments, Harry stared into his father's weak and watery blue eyes, and he saw the pain and frailty of an old man. Relenting, he sighed. "All right. I'm listening."

"When Anna died, I abandoned both you and your mother. I know I withdrew into myself and did nothing for you."

Harry was shocked. Tears stung his eyes. Such an bald admission from his father, a taciturn man at best, was incredible. He turned away, hating his own suspicion and wanting desperately to open himself to the man. But he found it hard to speak.

Dad was always closed off and unreachable. And now, only when *he* needed something, did he start talking. Childhood was not shrouded in some dark and distant past. The eight-year-old Harry jumped out filled with recrimination. The child saw his father weeping before Anna's grave and wondered why he was not enough. Shamed at his own thoughts, he stared out the window.

His father's head lolled on the pillow, and his voice was hoarse. "I am asking for your forgiveness, son."

Harry turned back. Here lay his father nearly dead but somehow come back to him. So much time had been wasted in silent misunderstanding. He remembered his mother at the window as his father slammed the door and marched down the front walk, leaving silence in his wake. They never touched or spoke, laughed or cried. Every year, Harry tried harder at school. His report cards showed all As. But nothing ever drew more than a grunt or a wan smile.

"Why do you want my forgiveness now?" he asked.

"Because I'm still alive, so maybe it's not too late."

Harry was stunned by the simplicity of his father's words. *Not too late. Not until you're dead.*

"Dad?" Harry began. "Tell me about the gun."

His father looked away. "So you heard about that."

"It was in your hand when they found you unconscious in the cellar."

"Are you asking if I was going to kill myself?"

"Yes."

"Well, I was thinking of it."

"But why?"

His father shrugged. "So I decided, since I didn't die, I had a chance to ask you."

"You didn't answer my question." Harry's throat ached, and he blinked away a tear.

"No, I didn't. I don't know how to answer it. What do you want to hear?"

"The truth."

Stanley's gaze slid from Harry's to his own hands, and then he began to weep silently. "I don't know. I don't fit anywhere anymore. I never did. I'm only trouble to you."

"Please, Dad, don't say it's my fault!". Harry gritted his teeth. "It was only after Anna died that the trouble started. You really were a good father until then."

Suddenly, Harry recalled his father coming home from work and, with shouts of laughter, hoisting him high up over his shoulders. There *had* to be more good memories.

His father did not answer, but turned to stare out the window. Finally, he said simply, "I want to go home."

"Home? You mean back to the house?" Harry steeled himself for an argument.

"No. I just want to be gone. I am *so* sick of the pain and the suffering I've caused. I can see it in your eyes."

Harry shied away from such blatant honesty. "Dad, look! You're depressed and can't think straight. I'm going to talk to the doctor about some medication."

His father's bright blue eyes clouded over. "Will you forgive me, son?"

"Sure, Dad…" Harry said without conviction. Tears blurred his vision as he rose from the bed and found his way to the nursing station to locate the doctor.

CHAPTER 14

▼

Bronwyn, feeing strangely unwell after her massage with Ricardo at the club, decided to return home early. Just thinking about the lump made her sick. Her appointment with the gynecologist wasn't until tomorrow.

The gravel road to the house wound down into the ravine and past the pond. With the temperature dropping rapidly, the light drizzle became freezing rain, which ticked noisily on the windshield. She turned on the wipers and strained to see ahead in the dark.

Abruptly, the music on the radio was interrupted by a news bulletin. Suddenly the steering wheel dragged sharply to the right and spun out of her hands. The Mercedes slid on the gravel toward the shoulder. Jamming the brakes, she brought the car to a stop, wavering at the edge of the ravine.

In shock, she rested her head on the steering wheel. And then she heard the report. *Mr. Archibald Brinks, a wealthy stock promoter, was fatally shot in open court at Osgoode Hall this morning. Witnesses describe his assailant, who escaped, as a white middle-aged male, approximately five foot eight inches and weighing approximately three hundred pounds. Police are asking for any help from the public.*

Pain stabbed into her heaving chest. She clutched the wheel. "Impossible! Not so soon!" she cried. Then she whispered, "I never paid."

She buried her head and did not see that the car, pitched on a sharp angle, threatened to teeter down the steep embankment. Unaware, Bronwyn eased her foot from the brake. The Mercedes rolled swiftly downward. Immobilized, she watched bushes and trees sweep past. Braking was useless, and the wheel spun in her hands. At last, the car clipped the side of a tree and came to rest on the floor of the ravine.

A primitive wail came from Bronwyn, followed by a low, keening sound. She scrabbled and scraped at the door until it opened. She dragged herself from the car. Wrapping her long, black mink around her, she gazed up at the night sky. Fine, cold rain stung her face. Unsteady in her heels, she stumbled over small, sharp stones.

"Dear God! I didn't do it," she wailed, trying to scale the embankment. She made it up about ten feet, then started to slide back down in the mud. "No! I only inquired." Her mind clung to this mantra, and she clutched at the underbrush to pull herself up. Finally, the road was at eye level.

Shivering, she stumbled for another ten minutes along the road to the house. *How can we live in such a godforsaken place when we're in the middle of the city?*

"I never paid. I didn't do it," she gasped, inserting the key in the door. The house was silent when she entered. Cynthia's note was on the hall table. It said something about not working in the home any longer. Didn't matter. It wasn't a home anymore.

Bronwyn sat wearily at the bottom of the staircase and began peeling her filthy stockings off. She stared at the splotches of mud making a trail across the black-and-white tiled floor. Tossing her mink coat onto the hall settee, she poured a glass of wine in the kitchen. Her bare feet slapped on the floor as she carried her glass and the bottle into Peter's study.

Mechanically, she rocked back and forth in his desk chair. The red light on the phone flashed angrily at her. She retrieved the message, but did not immediately recognize the friendly, seductive voice.

"Mrs. Saunderson," The breathing became raspy. "I am so sorry you are not in at this time. I wanted to deliver the good news to you in person. But I know you are an important lady with a very busy schedule." The voice sighed pleasantly, causing a chill to run through her. "The task which you assigned to me has been completed with efficiency, dispatch, and the utmost discretion. I will contact you in a few days to arrange for payment. Have a pleasant evening, Mrs. Saunderson."

Bronwyn was very cold as she tucked her feet underneath her in Peter's immense leather chair. She stared at the telephone, then replaced the receiver.

Frozen in place for the past ten minutes, Bronwyn felt her feet begin to sting and tingle. She wiggled her toes. At last, she stood up and carried her glass and the bottle upstairs. In the bathroom, she ran the tub as hot as possible.

She sank under the suds. Involuntarily, her hand returned to her left breast to hunt for the lump. With her mind dancing around the memory of the voice, she circled the lump with her finger. "I never paid," she repeated under her breath. She jumped when the front door banged open.

"Bronwyn, darling! Are you all right?" Peter shouted, racing up the stairs.

She struggled out of the tub and wound a robe around herself. "For God's sake, Peter. What is it? I'm in the bath."

"You're not hurt, are you? I saw the car in the ravine. What happened?" he shouted through the door.

Shit! I completely forgot about the car.

"Stop yelling. I'll be out in an minute." She wound a towel around her, taking time to examine her face in the mirror. Time to think.

Calm now, she entered the bedroom. "It was dreadful, Peter!" she began tearfully. "The wheel just wrenched out of my hands. The next thing I knew, I was at the bottom of the ravine."

Peter gently touched her cheek. Bronwyn lurched backward as if struck. Awkwardly, he reached out and drew her into his arms. Woodenly, she consented to his embrace.

"Darling," he whispered in her ear, "I saw the car at the bottom of the hill, and I was so frightened for you. For us."

Suspicious of his sympathy, she pushed him away.

"I know. It's been a long time since we've even been civil to each other." He sank to the bed and covered his face with his hands. When I saw the car, I thought the very worst might have happened. When I was running down the hill, I realized how much you really mean to me and how much we have together."

Bronwyn was disgusted by his act. *The little bugger is out to screw me.* She sat at near him on the bed.

He patted her hand. "Are you absolutely sure you're okay. Nothing banged or bumped?" He smiled. "How did it happen?"

Bronwyn, stunned by his new solicitude, groped for words. "The wheel just wrenched out of my hands. Something terrible must have gone wrong with the steering."

"You likely just had a flat tire. But to be absolutely sure, I'll have the mechanic check it over first thing in the morning."

"But the brakes didn't work either."

"Don't worry. We'll check everything. I won't have you exposed to any danger."

Bronwyn stared at her husband. Something was very wrong.

Peter laughed. "I know what you're thinking. Wondering why I'm suddenly so concerned about you. Honestly, you needn't be so alarmed. I really do love you." He gave her a peck on the cheek.

Her eyes grew hard, and she backed away. "What are you up to, Peter?"

He spoke quietly. "Darling, I have so much to tell you. I want us to start again. I've given up Roger, for good, and I'm seeing a psychiatrist. She thinks I might respond well to behavior modification. If there's a real desire to change there may be a chance. No guarantees, of course, but I want to try if you will."

Peter bowed with a flourish and kissed her hand, leaving Bronwyn speechless. His finger flew to his lips. "No. Please don't answer now. Let me prove myself and then we'll talk." He stood with his hand on the door knob. "Let me try to win you back." He smiled broadly, then continued. "I'm going to phone the mechanic right now. Have him tow the car out of the ditch and take it to the shop. Then I'll bring you up some dinner."

"Cynthia's given her notice."

Peter shrugged and said, "Then I shall scramble us up some eggs, pronto."

Bronwyn lay on the bed. The merry, piggish eyes of Mr. Prince danced before her. "I didn't pay a cent," she whispered before she drifted off.

An hour later Peter knocked, then backed through the doorway carrying a tray laden with steaming plates of eggs, bacon, and toast. "Breakfast or dinner, whichever you prefer." He set the tray down on a side table and began to serve her. At first, Bronwyn poked suspiciously at the food, but then she found she was hungry. After she had finished, Peter poured the coffee from a silver carafe.

"Did you see on the news about Archie?" he asked mildly.

Bronwyn sat up, her face rigid. "I don't understand. I didn't tell them to do it. I never paid for it." She started rocking slightly to and fro, rubbing her hands. "Jesus! What do we do now?"

"Absolutely nothing, darling." He bent to kiss her forehead.

She pushed him away. "Fuck! Leave me alone, Peter. Pappas must have ordered it. I thought they would ask for the money first."

He stroked her hand. "Listen, Bronwyn. The police are looking for Mr. Prince, not you."

"But what if they find him? He'll tell." Her face grew blotchy as she tried to hold back her tears. "I *never* told them to go ahead. I never *paid*."

"We'll meet that problem together," he assured her. "I'll do my best to protect you."

Bronwyn was unconvinced. "You better. Because if they find me, they'll find you. Don't forget, you gave me the phone number."

Peter smiled tenderly. "Darling, you *do* look sleepy. With what you've been through, I'm not surprised." He cleared away the dishes and cups. "Have you had your meds yet?"

Bronwyn shook her head.

"I'll get them for you." In a minute he was back with the two bottles of pills and a glass of water. "These are the right ones, aren't they?"

Bronwyn nodded and took one capsule from each bottle.

"They'll help you get a good night's sleep," he said as he handed her the water.

After she swallowed the pills, she went to the bathroom and put on a nightgown. When she got into bed, he bent to kiss her forehead. "Poor

Bronwyn," he smiled. "You'll feel much better in the morning. Good-night."

As she lay in bed, her hand crept to her breast. She expected to see visions of Mr. Prince and Archie Brinks. Instead she was soundly asleep within minutes.

CHAPTER 15

▼

When Harry arrived at Natasha's, she was on the phone. With the receiver tucked under her chin, she beckoned him in. Hanging up his coat, he poured himself a scotch and a glass of wine for her. First, he sat on the chesterfield and occupied himself with some of her magazines. Smiling, she moved off into the den, leaving the door only slightly ajar. He heard murmurs of conversation and then her low and intimate laugh. He stood up and gazed out onto the harbor, which shimmered with a myriad of tiny lights.

He checked his watch. Ten minutes had passed. He amused himself by examining the photographs on the lamp tables. A man and woman, arms around each other's waists, squinted in the bright sunlight. *Must be her parents*, he thought. Another photograph, set in an ornate gold frame, was of a young man dressed in jeans and a T-shirt. That was her brother Josef, murdered at twenty, of whom she rarely spoke. He tipped the next picture into the light to for a better look. There was Natasha with a girlfriend, sitting on the hood of a car. Natasha wore a man's hat at a rakish angle, and the other woman sat demurely next to her wearing a broad straw hat. Harry set the photograph down and returned to the magazines.

At last she emerged from the den. "I *am* sorry, Harry. Just my friend Sheila. Sometimes it's hard to get her off the line." She accepted the glass of wine and kissed him. "What happened to you last night? You sounded so mysterious on the phone."

Harry stared into his glass. "I couldn't talk then, but now I can. Natasha, a lot's been going on." He told her about the threats in the parking garage and the shooting in court. "I didn't come last night because I thought I might be followed."

She nodded slowly.

"And then I got a call from the hospital saying Dad was out of his coma."

"Oh, Harry. That's wonderful." She set down her wine glass. "Is he going to be all right?"

With frustration in his voice, he said, "Yes, I think so, but he's so damned difficult sometimes."

"What do you mean?"

Harry jumped to his feet and began to pace. "He asked me to forgive him."

"What's wrong with that?" she asked.

"What's wrong? Why has he never asked before? It might have helped me, years ago. Not now." The situation seemed self-evident to him.

Natasha shrugged. "What did he want you to forgive?"

"*Everything*, I guess. Turning his back on us after Anna died."

Natasha sipped her wine.

"But what about me?" Harry continued, hearing the bitterness in his voice. "There was always such a silence in that house." He rubbed the back of his neck.

The telephone rang. Natasha answered. She waved at Harry to hand her a pen.

Obviously a business call, he thought.

"There aren't really any comparables for that property, Doug." She listened for several moments, then said warmly, "Let's talk it over at breakfast tomorrow."

In a flash, he saw Natasha differently. Even after almost a year, he did not know her that well. She was a highly successful realtor, with hundreds of contacts, living in a world he knew little about. Feeling marooned, he got up and looked out on the balcony.

She hung up. He sat down again.

"Who's Doug?" he asked lightly, as he flipped through a magazine.

"Just another realtor. We're working on a deal together." She came and sat beside him. "How did you answer your father?"

He tossed the magazine down. "I said I forgave him."

"Well, that's good. You could hardly refuse."

"No, but what about me. Don't I count?" he asked.

"What are you wanting from him?"

"I don't know. He won't talk about the gun, for instance."

"It's likely a very emotional topic for him," she suggested mildly. "What do you think the gun means?"

"That he was going to kill himself. What else?"

"Why?"

Harry stopped. "A thousand reasons, I suppose."

"Such as?"

"Loneliness, depression, exhaustion?"

"Exactly! Can you do anything about that?"

"But he won't let me! He just says I'm meddling and trying to control him."

"Are you?"

Harry and Natasha had never argued. It frightened him that they might. He settled in beside her, taking her hand. "So what do you think I should do?"

"Talk to him. Earn his trust. Maybe if he feels he can confide in you without being taken over, it will get better. Why don't you wait until he's ready?"

"Because I need to get this settled. I can't just pretend my whole life with him can be swept away, that his behavior had no effect on me. Now he wants *my* understanding. When did I ever have his?"

Natasha studied her glass. "No, I suppose it's hard to get beyond those feelings, Harry," she sighed. She hesitated, then smiled and reached for his hand.

"You remember my story about my brother, Josef?" She reached for his photograph on the table. "And how he was left to die after being stabbed?" She shook her head. "He was trying to protect someone he didn't even know. A Good Samaritan, you might say." Gazing at the photograph, she spoke slowly. "It took me years to learn anything from such a useless, random event, but I did."

"And?" he asked. "What did you learn?"

"I learned that if you permit such tragedies to destroy you, then the madness fomenting them has claimed another victim."

"Of course." He looked confused.

She smiled patiently. "Your sister's death destroyed your father. If you let the pain from his abandonment continue to hurt you, then the horrible event never loses its power. Things like that can go on *forever*."

Harry finished his scotch in silence.

She laughed gently. "You've had a difficult time. Can you stay tonight?"

Harry sighed. "Yes. I'd love to."

She led him down the hall to the bedroom, where she drew back the covers in the dark. He took off his shirt and came to stand behind her, kissing her neck and shoulders.

"Shall we turn on the light?" she asked. She kissed him slowly.

"No. Let's leave it off."

But I want to see you," she whispered.

He shook his head. Any other time, he would have reveled in the sight of them naked together. Tonight, he needed the darkness.

"All right," she said carefully.

Harry lay beside her in the dark. She stroked his naked chest and undid his belt and zipper. He reached for her and drew her close. To her, his caress seemed abstracted, as if he were elsewhere. Fifteen minutes later, he sat up in frustration. He had never been impotent with Natasha before.

Harry? Never mind. Just lie back and relax for a bit. Maybe you need to talk some more."

He could think of nothing to say. Of course, she was right about his father, whose problems prevented his concentration. He was seeing the situation only from his own viewpoint.

Too many years had passed in silence between him and his father to suddenly start talking as if there were no hurt or pain. But he got her point. Glimpsing the depths of his own loneliness and frustration, he thought that love, security, and happiness always seemed to drift beyond his grasp. And, as always, it came back to Dad.

Staring at the shadows flitting on the ceiling, he said quietly, "No. Not really, Natasha. I think I'd better go." He swung his feet to the floor and started to dress.

"Why do you have to go so suddenly, Harry?" She sat up beside him as he struggled with his shoes.

He sighed. "I'm afraid I've got too much on my mind right now."

Although he worried her, she did not try to dissuade him. Wrapping her robe around herself, she saw him to the door. When they kissed good night, she felt the trembling in his shoulders.

"May I call you tomorrow?" he asked.

She smiled sadly. "Of course, Harry. Call me anytime you like." She closed the door.

Feeling like a grotesque fool, he waited for the elevator. He could not believe he had just walked out on the woman he loved.

CHAPTER 16

▼

Enraged, Roger Blenheim leaned over the counter at the bank. "That can't be! Of course there's money in the account."

The teller shook her head and handed Peter's check back to him. "I'm sorry, sir, but there are insufficient funds in Mr. Saunderson's account."

Motherfucker, Roger whispered thought to himself. "When was the money transferred out?"

"I'm sorry, sir. I'm not at liberty to divulge that information about another customer's account."

Roger turned on his heel and marched from the bank. *That conniving little bastard will pay! But not until I've got the right plan.*

Roger's fury came in waves. In the cab to the doctor's appointment, he whistled tunelessly through his teeth and rapped his fist on the door. Peter had deliberately deceived him. He devised numerous retaliatory strategies, but none seemed sufficiently gruesome. First, he had to arrange a meeting with Mr. Saunderson.

At the clinic, Roger waited in a darkened room for almost fifteen minutes. At last Dr. Feinstein, who looked as young as a high school student, stepped in and shook his hand. Roger thought the slides on the screen looked like a modern art exhibit. A loose, random shape in violet and yellow was illuminated. Next, a patch of pale pink was smeared over with a colony of black ants. In the third slide, wild purple and green light emanated from a brilliant cosmos of blue.

"What are these, Doctor Feinstein?" Roger asked.

"Cultures and tissue samples back from the lab."

Roger stood to examine the explosions of light and color. "You mean, all of this is me?" Feeling weak and light-headed, he sank onto a stool. "What do I have?"

The doctor shook his head. "Have you had nausea, vomiting, night sweats."

"Some chills."

The doctor frowned. "Weight loss?"

"Maybe a little, but I've not been eating too well lately."

"I assume you're sexually active, Mr. Blenheim. Are your partners male or female?"

"Male."

"We need the blood tests first, but I suspect you may have gonorrhea."

"That's it?" Roger left thinking an antibiotic would fix him up. But what a dirty little trick! He had been completely faithful to Peter. He must have gotten something from his bitchy little wife, who was probably fucking the milkman or the mailman.

At home, Roger sat at his dressing table. Peter would think he had three or four days before the check bounced. Plenty of time for him to plot his strategy. His hand trembled as he snapped on the two tiny crystal lamps. His reflection in the mirror, at first a sickly green, was bathed in a soft rose hue. He examined the bottles, jars, and brushes before him. "Not much time left, old girl," he whispered. Leaning forward, he examined his brows, then tweezed the rebellious hairs.

Rising to his full height before the mirror, he removed his shirt and undid his ponytail holder, letting his hair fall free. His chest was a mass of dark, tangled hair. *Fucking virile!* he thought. Its furious re-growth might be evidence of his good health. Stepping out of his jeans, he padded into the bathroom and stepped on the scale. Not long ago, he had weighed himself every day to ensure that he remained lithe and trim. After all, no one wanted a fat fag. Silently praying, he stepped onto the scales. *Shit! Two fourteen. Four pounds gone in less than a week.*

He wiped the beads of perspiration from his brow and turned on the basin faucet to hot. He shaved his face twice. Any sign of growth would spoil the effect. Then he piled gobs of shaving cream in his palm and lathered his chest.

Gazing into the mirror he knew Roxanna was hiding in there somewhere, waiting to be coaxed out. After two blades and twenty minutes, his chest was hairless, smooth, and glistening with oil.

Georgette, the Pekingese, was yapping outside the door. He emerged from the bathroom and scooped the dog into his arms. "There…there, precious. Come to see Mama?" Holding the dog close, he buried his face in the white ball of fur. Peter would pay dearly for his actions, which Roger considered to be the worst kind of betrayal. Georgette nuzzled and licked at his ear, then bit the lobe hard enough to puncture it.

"Fucking little bitch!" he screamed. "How could you do that to Mama?" Roger's motion was swift and sure. With one hand, he flung the small animal against the mirrored wall. Stunned, the dog lay still on the floor.

Roger, stricken with his own violence, cuddled the animal to his chest and collapsed on the bed. "Georgette. Please forgive me," he whimpered. "If I lost you, my life would be over." He curled himself about the quivering mass of fur. "But, sweetums, you must never, ever bite Mama again." The dog heard the menacing tone and remained still, blinking its eyes open.

Roger drifted off for half an hour, with images of Peter flashing through his dreams. When he awoke, he thought about the doctor's visit. Something was terribly wrong with him. His stomach lurched as he wiped the perspiration from his forehead. A good dose of antibiotics would probably do the trick…but what if it didn't? It must be Peter's fault. He began to sob, but there were no tears. Georgette licked his face. He stopped. Tears would make it harder to beckon Roxanna.

Roger sat at the dressing table again. "Put on your face, darling. Can't go about like an old frump." He started with his best foundation cream. With expert strokes, he quickly applied the makeup. His hand hovered over the pencils and brushes. Better tart up tonight. Peter would need a firm hand.

Suddenly, he stopped. How strange, he thought. In putting on the mask, he was revealing the truth. Finishing the eye shadow and lipstick, he smiled, "There you are, Roxanna. Time to get dressed."

In the cab to Roger's, Peter checked the case containing the Gautier Flintlock pistols. Time to return them. Mesmerized by the windshield wipers, he almost drifted off. The rain was sharp and biting on his neck as he paid the driver. Looking up at Paramour Antiques, he knew the end was coming. Thank God. He would soon be bankrupt if he kept paying out. And then there was George Pappas breathing down his neck. Maybe he should just walk out on everything, but where could he hide?

As soon as he knocked, the door opened. Peter shrank back and clutched the railing to right himself. "Jesus, Roger!"

"Do come in, Peter. Roxanna's all ready for you."

Peter gawked at Roger dressed in tight pants, a silk blouse, and heels. "For Christ's sake, Roger, I don't have much time tonight."

"Silly boy!" Roger laughed. "Come out of the rain." Roger almost lifted him inside.

"I don't have time for your games tonight. We have to discuss business. I brought a plan with me."

Roger was deadpan. "What good is a business plan, without money, Peter?"

Peter turned on him. "Listen, I can't keep shoveling money into this place." He waved his arm to encompass the shop, as if to point out the whole sorrowful mess. Then he stopped. It was ridiculous shouting at an adult male dressed up as a hooker, and a cheap one at that. But his face grew hot as Roger undid the buttons of his gold blouse, revealing the black lace beneath.

"I have something to show you downstairs in my darkroom," said Roger, taking his wrist so tightly he winced.

"All right. But just for a moment." Peter could never resist Roger's power. He trotted obediently behind him down the basement stairs.

From the bottom of the steps, Roger turned to beckon him further downward. His face, a pale white mask, seemed to float disembodied in the darkness.

Unsure of the terrain, Peter shuffled like an old man to the bottom of the stairs, where he had never ventured before. Roger led him by the hand.

"You must see my creatures from the watery depths, Peter. They stopped in front of two massive aquariums against the wall. In the first one, Peter saw only a tangle of vegetation in stagnant yellow water.

His stomach churned. "What's that?" He pointed at a charcoal-colored coil pulsating on the floor of the tank.

"A huge eel."

Peter could not conceal his revulsion. In the next aquarium, a dim light penetrated the murky water to reveal claws slowly opening on the gravel bottom. Bulbous antennae waved upwards through the depths.

Peter recoiled. "Why are you showing me this?"

Roger did not answer, but took his arm leading him farther along the corridor. At last there was light. "I have a slide show for you in my darkroom."

"Well, hurry up. I can't stay for long."

Roger giggled in the dark. "After you see the show, you will *want* to stay." He turned on the light and fiddled with the projector. "Sit on the stool," he commanded.

At first the photos were only grainy shadows and light. But when Roger focused the lens, Peter saw himself and Roger, naked and entwined.

"Oh my God!" Peter groaned. He was swamped with revulsion at the detail. Yet the familiar swell of passion was almost immediate.

Roger touched his shoulder. "Aren't they fabulous, Peter? A little memento for you. I'll give you a set of prints tonight. I can, of course, reproduce any number of them at any time."

Peter's voice was harsh. "You son of a bitch! I didn't think you'd stoop to blackmail."

Roger sighed. "Peter, you were very cruel to me. There was no money in your account. I tried to deal with the cash problem in a civilized fashion, and you betrayed me."

"What could I do? I didn't have as much as I thought. I'm nearly bankrupt. I've given you hundreds of thousands of dollars." Peter collapsed on the stool. "Where will it end, Roger?"

Roger took him by the wrist. "You always underestimate yourself. If I can get some decent sales, I'll pay you back with exorbitant interest. Let's have a drink and talk this over sensibly." Peter retrieved his case containing the guns from the main hallway and followed Roger to the bedrooms upstairs.

Peter cleared his throat. "As a gesture of goodwill, I want you to have the Gautier pistols back. Maybe you can sell them, and we can start a repayment plan."

Roger was surprised. "Why, thank you, darling. They really are my favorites."

"Good. I'm glad you're happy with the arrangement. Can I do anything to help you sell some of your art? Advertising? Whatever?"

"Advertising's expensive."

Peter shrugged. "Well, just a thought. We need to make a plan."

"Of course. But now that you're up here, would you like to see my new acquisitions?"

Acquisitions? Peter thought.

Roger handed him an Indian mask that he had never seen before. It was painted a brilliant sea green and deep red.

"Fascinating story behind this one. It's a Haida Indian mask called a Gagiid, meaning one who has almost drowned in the depths of the watery ocean."

He touched Peter's shoulder lightly. "Because he is so strong, he drags himself to shore and lives off snappers and sea urchins."

Roger set the mask on the display case. "See? That's why he has all those ugly spines sticking out of his lips."

Roger caressed the brow of the mask with his fingertip. "His dance is so frenzied that he frightens the audience, who finally captures him and returns him to his human form."

Peter reached out to touch the spines.

Roger spoke sadly. "It's very strange, but it's as if this mask tells us we all must adapt or perish." He handed Peter a scotch. "Just like you and me."

Peter took a gulp of his drink. "Very interesting. I suppose it cost a pretty penny."

Roger drew back. "Don't be such a testy ogre! Must it always be about money? Surely you can feel the power of the mask."

He lifted down another mask, made of finely detailed copper, and handed it to Peter. Mesmerized, he traced the wide opening of the lips. Caught between the rows of broken and crooked teeth was a tiny face expressing extreme agony. Two more faces, desperate souls, were molded into the eye sockets.

"It's called the Nisgaa, the keeper of drowned souls," said Roger softly.

"He entices the soul down to the ocean floor where he sucks up its very spirit. The man in the mouth is alive, but the ones in the eyes are dead souls. It makes me think: if we leave our deepest thoughts and secrets safely buried, they come out later to destroy us and those around us."

Roger donned the mask. The voice from within was deep and sonorous. "The Gagiid and the Nisgaa are inextricably linked, just like us."

"I have to go soon, Roger." The copper mask bore down on him.

"Put on the Gagiid!" Roger commanded.

In silence, Peter complied. After his first flash of panic, he began to breath more slowly. The knot in his gut loosened, and his habit of worry and fussing fell away. Then he felt the surging power of the mask.

The keeper of lost souls bore down on him. "Come to the mirrors, Gagiid."

Wordlessly, Peter followed.

Before the mirrors, Peter watched in dumb fascination. The bright green and red mask swayed from side to side atop his shoulders. From behind, the copper mask bore down on him.

"Take off your shirt, Gagiid," the Nisgaa commanded.

Peter sought to bargain with the power of the masks. He tore at the sharp spines sticking from his mouth. "Don't Roger. This is ridiculous. Let's just forget it."

Roger was strong. His mask glimmered in the light, exposing each hellish, suffering face.

The devourer of souls, thought Peter.

Their images entwined into infinity in the triptych of mirrors.

The Nisgaa forced him to the bed. Fear clutched Peter as the copper mask swayed above him. Unable to breathe, he was entered with such brutal force that he cried out in pain. At last, Roger removed the masks and Peter lay on the bed, drawing greedy breaths of cool air.

Roger lay beside him smoking a cigarette. "The clinic tells me that the blood tests should be back by the end of the week."

Slowly, Peter's consciousness moved from his pain to Roger's words. "Tests for what?"

Roger shrugged. "I expect they think I have some nasty social disease, which I could only have gotten from you. You see, I've been entirely faithful, darling, which is more than you can say."

Peter sat up against the pillow. "But so have I."

"Have you forgotten about wifey?"

Peter got up and began dressing. "Jesus, Roger! I wish you wouldn't smoke in bed."

Roger put out his cigarette. "Don't worry. I'm sure some antibiotics will do the trick. You should see your own doctor."

CHAPTER 17

▼

Next morning, the brilliant winter sun cut the city skyline into frozen, jagged shapes. Waiting for his car, Mr. Pappas stood on the crunching snow and breathed sharply inward. Puffing and stamping for warmth, his men waited with him on the driveway for the car.

With the door held open for him, Pappas settled into the leathery warmth of the white stretch limousine. He smoked his cigar as his men sat in silence. They knew better than to speak on such a mission.

Only Victor dared. "Sir?"

Pappas nodded to signify permission to speak.

"Are you certain you want to accompany us? We could drop you at your office and take care of the matter." Victor looked very worried.

Momentarily Pappas' lips relaxed into a smile. "Definitely not, Victor. I wouldn't miss this for all the world."

Knowing any further attempts to dissuade the old man were useless, he murmured, "Very well, Mr. Pappas."

In his office, four or five miles away, Mr. Prince stirred his tea and prepared for his day. He fussed with piles of paper and ensured that the voice mail system was on.

The white limo pulled off the ramp and headed west to the industrial park. Mr. Pappas whistled tunelessly. Caught in the sunlight, he appeared vigorous for his almost eighty years. Although his skin was wrinkled, it was not too loose.

"I have been more than patient with Mrs. Dinnick. Don't you think so, Victor?"

"Definitely, sir."

Gazing out on the barren industrial park, the old man smoothed his leather gloves on his knee. "By the way, call Saunderson. Tell him to be in his lobby in half an hour. We'll pick him up after we get Mr. Prince. I want the little queer to see how we deal with incompetence."

At his desk, Mr. Prince adjusted his floppy bow tie and then slurped his tea. Jimmy, his assistant, stood in the doorway fretting over the paperwork. He thought Mr. Prince was a bookkeeper, who should be far better organized.

Mr. Pappas' limo sped into the parking lot. The sun's rays ricocheted off the aluminum roofs, almost blinding the driver.

Just as Mr. Prince was brewing a second pot of tea, Pappas' men brushed past the receptionist for the trucking firm. His face turned white when they told him Mr. Pappas was waiting in the car. He was permitted his jacket, but there was no time to get his gloves or galoshes. Outside, on the iron staircase, the wind bit fiercely into him.

"Hurry up, Mr. Prince," said George Pappas as he pulled him in. One of the men had to shove from behind to force his bulk inside. The tires squealed on the pavement as the limo sped back to the highway. They drove southward along the river. Abandoned warehouses stood starkly against the sky.

"You have failed me miserably." Pappas stared at Prince with red-rimmed, angry eyes.

Prince choked, "But sir…"

"Do you recall the penalties?"

Panic overwhelmed Prince. His hand struggled with the door handle.

"Stupidly, you've gotten your pictures all over the newspapers, when you were supposed to be discreet."

"Please, Mr. Pappas."

The old man's tone was chilling. "You are a serious liability."

Once downtown, the limo pulled to the curb at Bay and King. Victor ushered Peter into the front seat, where he was wedged between him and the driver. Peter could not turn around at the sound of George Pappas' voice.

"Well Saunderson, Mr. Prince has become a serious liability to the organization. How do you think we should deal with him?"

Peter's voice was little more than a squeak. "Mr. Pappas? I think Mr. Prince carried out his duties…"

"Really?" Pappas cut in. "You know our standards, Peter. I do not tolerate incompetence. Mr. Prince has failed us miserably. Surely you do not disagree?"

"Oh no, sir! His name is all over the papers, but…"

Pappas chuckled.

The stench of urine fouled the air. Mr. Prince had wet himself and was now crying softly.

"You're a lawyer, Saunderson. What case can you make for this incompetent."

Peter tried to twist around. "Until now, sir, he has served loyally…"

"I disagree, Saunderson. You're going to see how we deal with incompetents."

By now, they were at the foot of Bay Street. The white limo shot up a ramp from the shadows under the bridge to the expressway high above the glistening lake.

The road was still partly under construction and entirely desolate. It ended abruptly a quarter of a mile east, jutting into space high above railway lines and warehouses. When the car stopped, Victor and the driver got out and removed the barricades. Then they opened the rear door and assisted Mr. Prince into the brilliant winter sunshine.

The huge man blinked and tried to pull his coat around him for protection from the bitter wind. Victor took his arm and gently led him beyond the barricades. The driver returned to the car and remained at the wheel with the engine running.

Peter, in the front seat, began to shake convulsively. "What are you going to do, Mr. Pappas?"

"Get out, Saunderson, and stand back. *This* time, you are only a witness."

Peter slid from the car and stood to one side. Pappas emerged from the backseat and accompanied Victor and Mr. Prince.

The rotund man was so disoriented that he stumbled over his own feet. Victor took him to within a few paces of the edge of the roadway. The endlessly stretching city and lake spun out at least two hundred feet below.

"Take off your shoes and socks," said Mr. Pappas.

The immense man gazed at Pappas without comprehension. Then one of the men stepped forward to assist him. Prince bent to undo his laces. The howling wind cut into his bare fingers and ankles. He did not notice the white limo edging closer toward him.

About to retch, Peter stood to one side, his hands stuffed in his pockets.

Tears flowed down Prince's broad, flaccid cheeks as he removed his socks and shoes.

"Admire the view, Mr. Prince. It is indeed a beautiful city," said Pappas. "Then set your shoes together at the very edge."

Peter was rooted to the spot.

Once more, Prince bent down. He could only hear the screaming wind at his ears, not the limo behind him. The bumper gently touched the backs of his knees, just as he was straightening up. Frantically, he clawed at the frigid air for balance. He was tilting downward, desperately shrieking into the wind.

Peter, faint, sank to his knees but said nothing.

In life, Mr. Prince's body had always been an awkward burden to him. Now, Pappas and his men admired the gracefulness with which such great bulk arced outward, downward, and out of sight. Pappas flicked his cigar over the edge and nodded to his men.

"Mr. Saunderson," said Pappas, "take note. *That* is how we deal with incompetents in this organization."

The doors thudded shut, and the limo sped back to the ramp and into the city, leaving Peter stranded at the top of the expressway.

Mr. Prince's shoes sat neatly together, toes pointing over the edge. His socks were stuffed inside, much as a child might have left them. The fierce wind caught the edge of one sock and hurled it far out into space above the lake. Tears froze on Peter's cheeks as he started the long walk back to the up-ramp.

CHAPTER 18

▼

Above Norma's apartment the banging was accompanied by low moaning sounds, as frightening to her as the wind behind Mama's house. Up the dark stairwell, she climbed to find the safety of Arthur's study within the empty apartment. Lowering herself onto the purple velvet sofa, she waited.

David stepped out of the kitchen, looking very angry.

"David, you've come," she began.

"Why did you do it, Norma?"

He looked so fierce, she cringed. "What do you mean, darling?"

"Archie! You had him executed, all because of those cursed shares."

"But David!" she cried. "I had absolutely nothing to do with it. You must believe me."

With a disgusted expression, he flopped down beside her. "You pitted Archie and George against each other in the litigation. What other result could there be?"

"Please, David, you must believe me. I did not intend that. I thought that court would be a safe and proper place to settle the matter," she sniffed. "Can I help it if George went overboard?"

David appeared to relent. "George sometimes goes a little crazy." He chuckled, then kissed her cheek. "Anyway, no great harm done."

Relieved, Norma squeezed his hand. "Let's have a really *nice* visit, David."

He seemed to catch her mood. "All right. Let's talk about our time in London, just after Arthur died. I was terribly in love with you, but I guess I was a bit premature."

David always puzzled Norma. She could not understand his enduring protestations of love. But she enjoyed his company immensely, and he was very handsome. Was that love, she wondered?

Somewhere, in a cemetery on a sunny hill overlooking Florence, she had buried Arthur. Then, after a brief trip to Venice, she left for London. Her small hotel in Kensington was light and airy, not like the Hotel Ponte Vecchio in Florence. The carnations, mums, and azaleas cramming every corner of the lobby and dining room had sickened her. Flowers were for funerals.

Her tension eased slightly in the warm glow of her room, decorated in gold and white. She set her suitcase on the bed and telephoned the concierge to find the nearest photocopy shop. Her plan was sound. She ordered tea and began hanging her two suits, two dresses, and a raincoat in the closet. When the tea arrived, she sipped it as she looked out onto the drizzle of Plimpton Close. She could not eat the tiny sandwiches and cakes.

When the rain cleared, she walked to the photocopy service two blocks away and requested three copies of all the documents Arthur had left her. Back in her room, she telephoned David.

"Hello?" he answered on the first ring.

"I'm in London," she said.

"You poor darling! What an awful time you've been through."

She could not bear his heartiness. After a lengthy silence she said, "Yes. Thank you. He should not have died."

"I want to see you. I'll come to your hotel right away."

"No, please, David. Not now. I'm terribly tired and just want to sleep."

"Of course you do. Why not have a nap, and I'll pick you up for dinner?"

He was hard to resist. She longed for company, but she had work to do. "I think I'll just turn in early, David."

"All right," he said carefully.

She rushed in when he hesitated. "Let's meet tomorrow around noon. I was thinking of Trafalgar Square."

There was a lengthy pause. David's tone was injured. "Couldn't we find a more private spot?"

"Perhaps later on. Tomorrow at noon, just by Nelson's Column on the St. Martin's side."

"If you say so."

"Please understand, David. This has been a terrible strain, and I'm exhausted."

"Yes, of course, my darling. See you then."

Norma was relieved to hear his briskness return. She had won a tiny skirmish in a very long war. Her sleep was dreamless and uninterrupted for the first time since Arthur's death.

In the morning, she entered Barclay's Bank in Cromwell Road and opened a safety deposit box, where she put the originals of all Arthur's documents. She put the key in her purse along with her passport. Now she was ready to meet David.

Flocks of pigeons in Trafalgar Square descended upon her as she waited in the rain for David. At last, he appeared at her side.

"Let's get inside." He kissed her cheek and took her arm as if no time had passed since they last met. "There's a tea room over there."

They sat at the table next to the window. Norma pushed back the lace curtains to see a young woman outside dressed entirely in white, with a plume of pink and yellow feathers sprouting from her shoulders like angel wings. The woman waved at Norma then drifted off toward the square. A good omen, she thought.

Norma looked at David closely as he polished his misted glasses. He was about five years younger than Arthur, Archie, and George. His blond hair was slicked back, curling slightly behind his ears. He had an innocent, cherubic air about him.

"How did it happen, darling?" he asked with genuine concern.

"Arthur died of a heart attack asleep in bed." Her eyes flitted about the tearoom. "In Florence."

"There was no warning?"

"He was very tired." She bent her head and stifled a sob. "Oh, David. We had everything ahead of us." He reached for her hand. "The whole conference was very impressed with his paper, and we were looking forward to a year at The Hague."

Fearing she would soon be lost in tears, David decided to get the business matters out of the way. "I know it's difficult to think, darling, but did Arthur leave anything with you to give me? He wrote a month ago to say he'd bring some papers with him."

She tried to compose herself. "Yes. He gave me an envelope." She fished it from her purse.

David slit it open to find only a single piece of paper. "But it's only a copy of the share certificate. Where's the original?"

Tears came to Norma's eyes. "Original? I don't know. Arthur never told me about his business affairs." She reached for a napkin to dab her cheek. "It's just beginning to hit me." Red-eyed, she looked up at David. "How will I ever live without him?"

David looked about the tearoom in panic. "I'm *so* sorry, Norma. I shouldn't be troubling you about business now."

The waitress took their orders. Norma hid behind the menu.

"I'll help in anyway I can," he continued.

They sat in silence until lunch arrived. Hungry, David munched on his chicken salad sandwich, while she poked at her salad.

"Arthur said the business was worth a great deal of money," she said.

"Almost five million."

Norma set down her fork. "How did the three of you ever make so much?"

He became business like. "We made some very good investments, and we sold off assets at the right moment. Timing is everything."

"I've never seen the original certificate. That's all Arthur gave me. When I get home, I'll look in his box, where he kept all his important papers."

When lunch was finished, they strolled about Trafalgar Square. Norma kept an eye out for the strange woman with the feathery plumes, but she was nowhere in sight.

"Why don't you stay at my flat? We could pick up your things at the hotel…" His voice trailed off under her gaze. They walked in the direction of St Martin's in the Fields.

He gave her a brave smile. "You know I'm in love with you, Norma."

She took his hand. "I don't really understand, David."

"Understand what?"

She almost said *about love*. Instead she said, "Arthur's just gone. I need time."

He gazed up at the leaden sky "Very well. May I see you again?" He spoke stiffly.

"I've decided to leave tonight, but I'll see you back in Toronto."

"All right. I'll be home in about three months, once business is finished. He tried to draw her into his arms, but she eluded him. He kissed her cheek, and she gave him a brief hug.

Going back to her hotel, Norma tried to understand. She knew about affection and caring from Arthur, who kept her safe from the emptiness. But she did not understand this business of love, which David talked about. But she did know that such emotions gave her a sense of power. The sheer lust she experienced in the presence of George made her feel weak and vulnerable.

Norma shifted on the purple velvet sofa in Arthur's study. "What a lovely time we've had reminiscing about the past, dear!" She took David's hand. "Please come for another visit soon."

When she showed him to the door, he looked longingly at her. "I could stay, if you'd like."

"At my age, I get very tired, David." She smiled sadly. "Not like the old days."

David kissed her cheek, and then he was gone. Looking out the window, she noticed the heavy snow falling. Then she locked up and hobbled down the stairs into the gloom.

CHAPTER 19

▼

Harry stared at his father's unloaded gun on the kitchen table. Willing himself to pick it up, he cradled it in his palm. Its pleasing heft and coolness amazed him, filling him with a seductive sense of power. What were his father's thoughts, gun in hand, on the cellar steps?

He stood up and aimed it, through the doorway, at the dining room chandelier. Gently, he pressed the trigger. With the satisfying snap of the gun, energy rushed through him; he sensed, if only for a moment, what his father must have felt. Shuffling on the basement stairs, Harry touched the barrel to his temple. Nearing death, his father must have struggled desperately to maintain *some* sense of command over his body and mind. So very ironic! Only by snuffing life out could he end the pain and gain control.

If his Dad had not tripped, he would be arranging his funeral. Instead, he had to find a way for both of them to live. As he neared the bottom step, he caught a flash of his father's regret and his need for forgiveness.

Back in the kitchen, he put the gun in its case and checked his watch. Almost five thirty. Time to shower and shave before seeing Dad. The telephone rang.

"Hello, Harry. I haven't heard from you for a few days."

"Hi, Natasha. No, I've been trying to deal with my father."

"Is he all right?"

"He's staying awake and beginning to eat a bit. I'm going to see him in about an hour." He lay back on the pillows.

"Do you want to get together later?"

He hesitated. "All right. Say about seven thirty?"

She agreed and they hung up.

When he entered the hospital room, his father turned away to stare out the window.

"I brought you some flowers, Dad." Carnations hung down from his hand. He looked about for a vase, but finding none, he set the wilting flowers on the bed and left for the nursing station to find a container. After five minutes, he returned empty-handed. His father was still staring out the window.

"When the nurse comes, I'll ask for a vase."

Stanley did not reply.

"Can I get you anything?" asked Harry.

"No."

Harry moved to the window and stood in front of his father. "We need to talk."

"What about?"

"Everything."

"I asked for your forgiveness," his father said quietly.

"And I gave it to you."

"Only to shut me up. I was hoping for a little understanding."

Immediately, Harry recalled holding his catcher's mitt and asking Dad to pitch. From behind his newspaper, his father had muttered something, just to shut him up.

"So I learned well from you." Harry was startled at his harsh speech.

"It's all *my* fault?" his father whispered.

Harry could not stop himself. "I was the kid, Dad."

Cursed by their old arguments, he thought. *How strange to be driven to hurt the one you love! How hard to stop.*

"Dad, was the gun loaded?"

His father turned his head to face him. His eyes were clear and cold. "Yes, it was loaded."

At least he's telling the truth, thought Harry. "Dad? I held the gun myself tonight. I was trying to understand what you were thinking...feeling."

His father said nothing and looked out the window.

"And I thought *what a way to control life—by ending it.*"

Stanley's lips tightened. "That's a brilliant thought."

A nurse appeared at the door, vase in hand. "Look at those poor, wilting flowers." Quickly, she filled the vase with water and put the carnations in it. She asked Harry, "You're his son?"

Harry nodded.

"I'm glad you're here. He needs visitors."

They remained silent until she left.

"I'm sorry, Dad. We have to look ahead and plan what's best."

Stanley said nothing.

"We have to talk about the gun."

His father shrugged. "There's nothing more to say."

"There's plenty!" Harry's voice peaked in frustration. "How can I let you alone, live my life without worrying about you?"

His father gazed at him, then said, "It's *all* about *you*, is it? That I might interfere in your life?"

Harry bit his lip. "That's not what I meant. I only want to help. But, goddamn it, you won't let me." He recalled Natasha's words. *If you let the pain from his abandonment continue to hurt you, then the horrible event never loses its power.* Fine for her to give advice. She wasn't responsible for such an obstinate old man. But how could he ever break the cycle? Only by deciding to step beyond the eight-year-old boy.

His father grimaced and turned away.

Harry could see the old wall going up. "Okay, Dad. Let's leave it for now. Can I get you anything from downstairs? Something to read?"

His father shook his head. When Harry turned to go, his father spoke in a hoarse whisper. "Come back soon, son."

Going down in the elevator, Harry leaned heavily against the mirrored wall. He could scarcely believe his childhood was only a moment away.

Harry had more than an hour to kill. Not hungry, he drove westward along Bloor Street and stopped for a coffee. Lights from shops spilled onto the crowded sidewalks. He picked the first restaurant he saw. In a mirror, his reflection caught him by surprise. How like Stanley he looked. He moved to another booth. Imagining Natasha with him, he wondered what explanation he might give for the other night. He finished his coffee and went outside. Passing several fruit and vegetable stores, he stopped to buy a bunch of flowers, then headed back for his car.

When he pulled into the driveway of Natasha's place, he was surprised to see her waiting in the lobby.

"Let's get something to eat," she said as she slid in beside him and kissed his cheek.

He turned to her. "But I thought…"

"I've got a big day tomorrow, so I shouldn't be long. But I *am* hungry."

They drove off in silence.

"Damn. I forgot. I bought you some flowers," he said, glancing in the rearview mirror to see the bouquet lying on the backseat.

"Really? Thank you, Harry."

"They won't wilt?" he asked.

I'm sure they'll keep for an hour or so. What kind are they?"

"Yellow and white. A mixture."

She smiled at him. "Carnations?"

He shrugged. "Guess so."

They drove slowly up Yonge Street past the clutter of electronics stores and shops selling leather. Only a few people walked the windy streets and some huddled in doorways.

"Let's eat somewhere that won't take forever." she said.

So much for a romantic dinner! He nodded and turned eastward along Bloor Street.

Natasha broke the silence. "How is your father, Harry?"

He had trouble organizing his thoughts into words. "Pretty much the same as the last time." He gripped the steering wheel. "But we keep shutting each other out. As usual."

"Did you ask him about the gun?"

"I tried, but we really just danced around the topic. But he admitted it was loaded.

Glancing at her, he caught the light of the street lamps on her face. She was so soft and beautiful, he thought. And yet, tonight, she seemed in another world.

"I keep thinking about when I was a kid. And that gets in the way of any adult conversation." He parked the car on the street. Despite the dropping temperature, people still walked along with coats flapping open. He took her arm as they hurried into the restaurant. With a flourish of menus, the maitre'd seated them near the back, where it was quiet.

Reaching across the table, he took her hands in his. "I got his gun back from the hospital, and when I was holding it, I could almost understand." He let go of her hands and sat back. "The sense of freedom, the power and control."

"Good God, Harry! It wasn't loaded, I hope."

"No, of course not. I was only trying to understand..." Harry examined the wine list and ordered from the hovering waiter. "I was trying to imagine what he felt like. That's all."

"Can you talk to him about it?" asked Natasha.

Harry shook his head. "Every time I try, he shuts me out. For example, I told him that it was odd to try to gain control of life by ending it."

"You said *that?*" She set down her menu and gazed evenly at him. "Harry, don't you think the business of the gun is a cry for love and attention? He's asking for your forgiveness."

As if he hadn't heard her, he continued. "I keep remembering the stupidest things. The summer Anna died, my father nearly went nuts. You know, one day he took me for this long drive out in the country. I thought he wanted to spend time with me. Maybe talk. We drove and drove, until suddenly we stopped on this empty country road. He reached across me and opened the door, and told me to get out. I asked why, but he wouldn't answer. I was scared he would drive off and leave me."

Taking a deep breath, he continued. "Then he just sat in the car by himself with his head on the steering wheel for almost an hour. I didn't know what else to do, so I played in the ditch by the road, making little castles with stones, sand, and twigs. I remember the sky was so huge above me, the sun was so hot, and I just wished we were back in the city. I was only eight."

"So, what happened?"

"Nothing! Not a damned thing happened. Finally, he opened the door and let me back in. And we went home." Harry shoved his hands in his pockets. Neither of them spoke, until the waiter poured the wine.

"You know, Natasha," he said, twirling the stem of his wine glass. "I doubt I ever heard him say more than five words together after that."

Natasha smiled sadly. "You're in such pain, Harry. Remember, your father's an old man. He *needs* you now. You have to find a way."

Harry was wrapped up in recollection. Suddenly, he said, "But what about me? How do I just pretend everything's okay when it's not?"

"You're not the child anymore. You know, you're very lucky to have this chance. You may regret it if you don't straighten things out."

Harry fell silent and sipped his wine. At last, the waiter took their orders. Unable to think of anything more to say, he fiddled with the salt and pepper shakers.

She reached out and touched his hand. "Harry, what do you think love is?" She saw the wary look in his eye and decided to tread carefully.

He shrugged. "I don't know. It's about wanting someone as part of your life. Wanting them always with you." He looked into her eyes. "Why? What do you think?"

"I think it's about getting outside yourself and seeing another person's life from their point of view. At least that's a start."

Harry heard his father's words. *It's all about you, is it?* Would he always be the kid, he wondered?

Natasha spoke gently. "I hope you can stop torturing yourself, Harry. Do you really want that kind of life? Your father's a tired old man who feels he's been given a second chance to make amends. That's why he wants your *real* forgiveness. Unless you let the wound heal, how can you ever really forgive him?"

"I guess you're right," he muttered. They ate in silence until he asked hesitantly, "Natasha? About the other night…"

She looked into his eyes. "You shouldn't be so troubled, Harry. I'm not."

"I know, but I shouldn't have walked out on you."

"Listen, you had a lot on your mind."

"When we go back to your place…"

"Harry, I've got a big day tomorrow. We can spend the weekend together."

As they drove down Yonge Street, the lights cast an eerie pallor in the fog gathering in doorways, where people lay curled up in sleeping bags.

At her place, she kissed his cheek and asked, "Come up Friday night, all right?"

Harry nodded, then glanced in the rearview mirror. "Oh, the flowers." He jumped from the car and held out the package. "I hope they're not all wilted."

She drew him close to her. Her breath was warm in his ear. "I'll see you then." She kissed him and took the flowers. "I'll put them in water right away."

When Harry drove off, he caught her figure in the mirror as she entered her building. At first, he was enveloped in sadness. Then his anger surfaced. Was she seeing someone else? Doug?

CHAPTER 20

▼

Roddy Sams, Archie Brinks lawyer, shouted, "You released the Brinks file, Mr. Thompson?"

The junior lawyer nodded miserably. "We were sent an authorization form, sir."

Sams rounded his desk and descended upon Thompson. "I don't give a fuck if the Prime Minister authorized it." Sams' normally boyish face was a storm of gray fury. "Have you never heard of a solicitor's lien? Wouldn't it be nice if we had the goddamned file to bill?"

"Sir? We received an authorization from a George Pappas to turn it over to Blackburn, Swanson."

Sams stood with his arms dangling helplessly at his sides. His eyes darted about as if fasten upon a safe harbor of sanity. "You absolute moron! Pappas is the co-defendant. Do you understand nothing?"

White as a sheet, Thompson hurried for the door.

"If you want to save your ass around here, get that file back here by noon!" Roddy banged his fist on his desk. Thompson closed the door behind him.

Harry sat at his desk, staring up Bay Street at the old city hall clock. Earlier, he had received a call from an apoplectic Roddy Sams. After that, Harry had called Blackburn and Swanson to determine who was in charge of the Brinks estate. Peter Saunderson's firm—interesting.

Miss Giveny buzzed him on the intercom. "Mr. Frederick Hopkins returning your call."

He snatched up his pen and lifted the receiver. "Harold Jenkins here."

The voice was cold and formal. "I'm returning your call regarding the Brinks estate." Harry envisioned a tall, austere looking man seated at a highly polished desk with a single file on it.

"I act for Norma Dinnick in her action against Archibald Brinks and George Pappas," Harry he began.

"Yes?" The tone was measured.

Harry responded in kind. "I want to serve the executor of Mr. Brinks estate with a Notice of Continuance of her law suit."

Hopkins remained silent. Something odd was afoot. "Does your firm represent the Brinks Estate?"

"Yes."

"Should I send the Notice to your attention?"

"Yes."

Harry could imagine no reason for such extreme reticence. After all, his request was a mere procedural matter. "Who is the executor?"

"Mr. George Pappas."

"Pappas!" Harry dropped his pen. "That's some conflict."

The voice was impatient. "You may choose to view it in that fashion. Nevertheless, Mr. Jenkins, he is the executor named in the current will, predating your client's frivolous action by seven years."

"Kindly send me a copy of the will, Mr. Hopkins," Harry said quietly.

"No. We are not in a position to do so. If we apply to the court for Probate, then it will be a matter of public record for all to see."

Harry's mind raced over all possible situations in which Probate could be avoided, but none seemed to fit. "You know perfectly well I'm entitled to see the will and a list of assets when there is an ongoing legal action."

"You are at liberty to apply to court for the production of documents, but I put you on notice that you will be vigorously resisted. Good day, sir."

The line went dead. Harry spent the next few minutes making notes on their conversation. What in hell was going on?

Miss Giveny buzzed again. "That Mr. Brackley's on the line again. He won't get off until you speak with him."

Harry snatched up the receiver. "Yes, Mr. Brackley?"

"Find the shares yet?" the voice growled.

"No! Hire a lawyer, a good one, if you or Frost want to pursue this."

"Mr. Jenkins…"

Something in the man's tone made Harry hesitate. "What?"

"I gotta admire a guy like you. You look like a real little chicken shit, but you don't scare easy. I'll bet you'll cooperate, if we pay your little old lady client a visit."

Rage mounted swiftly in Harry. "You're threatening me and now an old woman?"

Then he remembered the men in the underground garage, and Mr. Prince. "We never had an original share certificate, only a crumpled up copy."

"Find those shares, asshole!" Brackley barked.

Harry slammed down the phone, then dialed Norma. He closed his eyes as her phone rang. A vision of her chill, shadowy apartment rose before him. After eight or nine rings, he pictured her heaped on the bathroom floor. A list of horrific possibilities tormented him. He struggled into his coat and rushed out the door to see for himself.

Norma sat in the white wicker chair in the far bedroom upstairs. Bathed in the cool late November light, her delicate skin looked white as alabaster. Ceaselessly, she rubbed her fingers for warmth. Her David sat in the armchair next to her, looking just like he had in New York City.

"What a wonderful time we had on that trip, David. Our only worry was how to keep Archie and George from those shares Arthur gave me in Florence."

Her David nodded agreeably.

"Arthur meant those shares for me," she said decisively, but then added, "and of course for you as well, darling."

Her David looked skeptically at her.

"Now don't you raise your eyebrow at me. You know very well that once Harry Jenkins gets those shares for me, I'll divide them right down the middle with you."

David folded his hands in his lap and smiled.

"Let's have some tea and reminisce about our lovely trip."

They had stayed for a whole week at the Plaza Hotel that hot and early spring.

The new buds on the trees turned Central Park into a lime-green haze, and the sounds of horses' hooves floated upward through the open windows of their room.

At breakfast on their last day, they sat in a café overlooking the park.

David, normally effusive and energetic, sat in silence. Before she spoke, she buttered the last fragments of toast and poured coffee for them both.

"Let's do something we've never done before." She looked at him with fond challenge. "Why don't we visit the Statue of Liberty this morning?"

"Rather touristy, isn't it?" David was feeling unwell.

Norma smiled, "That's just the point." Her tone was light and playful. "You mustn't be a snob, darling. If we're snobby about places just because they attract the masses, we'll miss out on the fun."

In the cool darkness of the café, she saw a thin line of perspiration forming on his upper lip. "Are you ill, David?" she asked anxiously.

David tried to smile convincingly. "Just a little tired, love. You did wear me out a bit last night."

Blushing, Norma lowered her eyes. "You were magnificent, David. You *will* recover. I just know it." She sipped her coffee. "Have you taken your heart medication yet?"

"No. But as soon as we go upstairs, I will."

He rose with determined cheeriness. She took his arm and led him to the elevators. "So it's settled then?"

David nodded. Upstairs in the bathroom, he filled a glass of water and took two painkillers. His headed pounded, and the roar of blood surged at his temples. Forcing lightness into his tone, he called out. "Sure you wouldn't prefer to spend the morning in bed with me?"

Appearing in the doorway, she wound her arms around him, feeling the dampness of his shirt. "There'll plenty of time for *that* later, David. Soon, it will be too hot to go out." His heart medication remained on the counter.

From the cab to Battery Park, they strolled slowly under the trees to the docks. Strung out in the bright sunshine was a line of people, at least two hundred yards long, waiting to board the ferry. David rested against the railing for support and shielded his eyes. After more than an hour's wait, they boarded the ferry.

On the upper deck, Norma sat in the breeze with her face raised to the sun. David clutched the railing and tried to control the heaving in his stomach. Black water swirled beneath him.

"Are you all right, David?" she asked. "Did you take your medication?"

He stopped short. "Damn. I forgot."

"Do you want to go back?"

He smiled bravely. "Not on your life. I'll be fine."

Once off the ferry, he felt much better, and they covered the distance to the Statue of Liberty without difficulty. The city loomed up close behind them.

"Let's go to the very top, darling," she laughed, pointing upward.

Expecting an elevator, he agreed.

Inside the base, Norma bought their tickets, and they edged their way along with the crowds up the first flight of stairs. David's breathing became labored. At the top of the first flight, they learned that the elevator only went to the pedestal and not the crown. They were trapped in the throng.

David turned down the stairs in hopes of finding escape. In the pale gray light, a sea of a thousand faces stared upward in expectation. He resigned himself to the trek but halfway up, his knees began to quiver. Norma guided him from behind as he hoisted himself along with the railing. Outside on the pedestal, David drew in deep gulps of air. At last, his breathing settled, and he grabbed her arm and started for the crown.

His left leg began to drag, and his hands trembled. When he slowed, angry voices from below urged him upward. Blackness surrounded his peripheral vision, and beautiful stars distracted him. He wondered at the loud rasping sounds, coming from his chest. His body sagged, but Norma supported him the last few steps. At the very top, he collapsed onto a bench. The air tore at his lungs. He was only fifty-five. Sitting beside him, Norma helped him off with jacket.

Patting her hand, he gasped, "Just a few moments rest, Norma, and I'll be fine."

Then he clutched his chest as the pain roared upward. His head hit the concrete floor, making a dull thud, and his body sprawled at her feet. The last sound he heard was her scream.

Half an hour later, David Parrish was pronounced dead at the hospital. Norma said he had forgotten his heart medication. The coroner quickly completed the paperwork when told of David's insistence on climbing to the crown. Norma remained in New York and made the arrangements. David had wanted cremation.

Harry's tires skidded on Norma's gravel driveway. Mounting the verandah steps two at a time, he wrenched open the outer door. All was quiet. He rapped hard on her apartment door. No answer. Just as he prepared to lunge at the door, he tried the knob. The door swung open.

"Norma?" he called.

The living room furniture was still covered in dirty bedsheets. Glancing about, he ensured she was not stuck between the chesterfield and chairs. He moved swiftly through the dining room and kitchen to the bathroom. He tore the shower curtain back. No Norma. In the bedroom, he checked the closet and under the bed. Had Brackley already been there?

Harry paused. An indistinct creaking sound came from the apartment above. Norma had complained bitterly about the noise from upstairs, right above her bed. In moments, he was racing upstairs. The door to the apartment stood open. Every floorboard snapped and groaned as he marched through the empty rooms and on into the far bedroom.

Norma sat slumped in a white wicker rocking chair. Harry approached her slowly and touched her shoulder. "Norma? Can you hear me?"

He tipped her back in the chair and smiled when she started to snore. He spoke again. With louder snorts and snuffles, her eyes flew open.

When she focused, she cried out, "Oh David! Thank God you've come."

"It's not David. It's me, Harry, your lawyer."

She grasped his hands. "Please, David. George is going to kill me. He thinks I have the shares."

Harry began to massage her fingers to get the circulation going. "Has George been here, Norma?"

"Don't be foolish, David Parrish. I don't have the shares. George has them."

He helped her to her feet, and very slowly they descended the stairs to her apartment, where he settled her in a chair propped up with cushions. "David? Let's have some tea, dear."

Knowing the futility of debating his identity with her, Harry hurried off to the kitchen. Her mind still came and went with alarming rapidity. Lucid one moment, and off into her own world the next.

When he gave her the tea, the cup and saucer clattered violently in her hand. With her eyes closed, she groaned. "Sometimes, they come to me, Harry."

"Who?" He took her hand and leaned closer.

"Arthur, David. Even Archie and George."

"Where?"

"Upstairs. Sometimes in the little bedroom, I wait for them, because it's no use to hide."

Harry remained silent. Now he would have to contend a host of spirits from the dead.

"I'm terrified."

"Of what?"

"George."

Harry frowned. Her danger was real, especially with Brackley around. "Has he been here yet?"

She shook her head. "No. But he will. He'll stop at nothing."

"We have to go to the police."

"There's no point. George always does just as he pleases. Besides, they'll just think I'm a demented old woman."

"You're tying my hands, Norma. Even without the police, I still have to try to protect you."

Mr. Justice Forfar was sympathetic, he mused. He had issued an order of committal against Pappas, who was required to appear in open court. Requesting the court to enforce its own order was the best strategy he could devise. If the judge made the order, the police would pick up Pappas and take him to jail. It was like trying to catch a lion with a butterfly net, but it was worth trying.

"Norma, I don't think you should stay here.

"This is my home, Harry."

"Just until we straighten this out. I'll find you a place in a retirement home for a few weeks."

Her shoulders slumped. "All right. Find me a place, and I'll go there for awhile."

Relieved, Harry smiled and patted her hand. "I'll have a spot for you this afternoon. I'll send a cab around to take you there." On the way out the door, he said, "Now, don't go back upstairs. Keep things locked up until a taxi driver comes for you. I'll call first."

As soon as Harry returned to the office, he had Miss Giveny phone all the retirement homes in the city. No vacancies until late the next afternoon. He phoned Norma and made her promise again to keep all her doors and windows locked until she could be moved.

"Miss Giveny? Please come in. I have some dictation," Harry said over the intercom.

She appeared in his doorway clutching several files, which were threatening to slip from her grasp. "Yes?" Her tone was not accommodating.

"I have to organize an exparte application to court for this afternoon. Will you see if Justice Forfar is sitting?"

He could ask for an immediate committal order. After all, Pappas had flouted Forfar's order to appear in court. Trying to catch a crook with a piece of paper could be futile, but it was all he had. Other than Norma's fears, he had no evidence that Pappas was intending to harm his client.

Brackley had threatened her, but Harry could not establish any connection between him and Pappas. The real hope was that Forfar would be angered by the failure to comply with his order.

Miss Giveny appeared. "Mr. Justice Forfar will be hearing exparte applications starting at four o'clock today."

A wave of uncertainty swept over him, but he began his dictation. *Pretty thin stuff*, he thought when he finished.

Miss Giveny nodded curtly and said, "Anything else, Mr. Jenkins?"

Her tone contained a strange note of finality. He looked up at her. "No. Why?"

She stood up and with great dignity, passed an envelope to him. A coolness crept into the office. "What's this?" he asked.

"Read it when you have time, Mr. Jenkins."

He looked closely at her. He saw her red rimmed eyes behind her reading glasses. Instead of her usual sharp and critical spirit, he saw exhaustion.

She sniffled into bunched-up Kleenex and hurried from the room.

Harry collapsed into his chair, but he was relieved to hear the clack of her typewriter from behind her closed door. He glanced at her envelope and decided to wait for a quiet moment to read it. After a quick trip to the coffee room an hour later, he saw the finished court application on his desk. He spent the next half hour reviewing the work and forgot about her letter.

Forfar was well known for his righteous indignation, Harry recalled as he threaded his way through the wrought iron gates of Osgoode Hall and up the steps to the courtrooms. Most practitioners of his vintage would chuckle at his naïveté, but whenever he mounted the staircase covered in royal blue carpet and passed the row of dark portraits of former chief justices, he felt he could draw from their strength and believe in an imperfect system.

Harry marched across the anteroom of Courtroom Four, which looked like an immense black and white chessboard. Forfar would understand the position of his client, an elderly lady surrounded by power brokers such as Archibald Brinks and George Pappas. As quietly as possible, he entered the courtroom.

From the top row, Harry had an unhindered view of the judge seated on the bench below. Only he and his clerk remained in the courtroom. Harry remembered Prince, after executing Brinks and leaving him in a pool of blood, gave the court the customary departing bow. Standing at his desk in the front row, Harry looked up at the judge, appearing hawk-like in his black robes.

"If it please your lordship," Harry began graciously.

"What's your application about, counsel? Not more on the Dinnick case, I hope."

Surprised, Harry hesitated but said. "It is about Dinnick, my lord…" He handed the court documents to the clerk.

When Forfar flipped through the affidavit, he grimaced and then glared down at Harry. "Mr. Jenkins…"

Harry knew from the caustic edge in the judge's tone that he was doomed.

"Now your client is accusing another person of intending her harm. First it's Mr. Brinks. Now it's Mr. Pappas?"

"Yes, my lord. I submit that there is sufficient evidence warranting concern for her safety."

"Really?" The judge's eyebrows shot up.

"And further, Mr. Pappas remains in breach of your court order to appear in this action and present himself in court. It's been almost ten days, sir, since your order. Under the circumstances of potential danger to my client, I submit that the enforcement of the committal order is well warranted."

Forfar peered down at Harry. His voice cut through the courtroom. "Has it not occurred to you, counsel, that Mr. Brinks might have been correct and that Mrs. Dinnick should be declared incompetent?"

"Before I took instructions, my client was examined by the Public Guardian's office, which found her to be competent for the purposes of this action." Harry handed the report up to the clerk.

The judge waved him off impatiently. "If that report was not filed in the original action, I'm not going to consider it on an exparte motion, where no one is here to dispute it."

"But my lord, it *was* filed in the original action." Harry knew he was dead.

"It was not brought to my attention in argument, counsel." Forfar spat out.

"Nonetheless sir, I submit that Mr. Pappas is in breach of your order and that he should be immediately brought to answer."

"Mr. Jenkins, I am not about to subject Mr. George Pappas, an eminent member of the business community, to being dragged into court by the Sheriff with this vague, cobbled-together affidavit material. This elderly woman makes fantastic allegations against Mr. Brinks, and when he's murdered, she cooks something else up about the co-defendant." Forfar tossed the file onto the clerk's desk.

Harry could not believe his ears, or his eyes. The learned Justice's face was, now a deep red, as glared down at him. Forfar's original moral outrage with Pappas had been diverted to his client.

"Have you anything else to say in support of your application, counsel?"

Harry rose to his full height. "My lord, it is my submission that the court is duty bound to enforce its own orders by committing Mr. Pappas." Harry knew the case was hopeless. Something was rotten in Forfar's courtroom.

Forfar scrawled on the file. "Application denied, Mr. Jenkins. If you come into my court again, be sure you have a case."

The clerk scrambled to his feet. "Court adjourned. All rise."

Forfar swept from the courtroom through the curtains behind the bench. Harry collected his files and hurried out.

There was no rational explanation for the judge's total reversal of attitude. Forfar was a maverick passionately devoted to the ideal of justice. Someone had influenced him, Harry concluded. He could not imagine the judge accepting a bribe; most likely, he had been threatened. Thinking of the men in the garage that night, his mind created numerous gruesome scenarios, which might have befallen the judge. Pappas was everywhere, he thought as he walked back to his office. Harry swung from bursts of anger and frustration to an all-pervasive sadness.

CHAPTER 21

▼

Back at the office, Harry found Miss Giveny fussing over the stalled fax machine.

Harry fiddled with buttons until the light flashed on, and they heard the appropriate whirring sound. The transmission of typed words on a page over a telephone wire baffled his secretary, who barely accepted the electric typewriter.

"I can hardly believe what happened in court. Forfar, who was very much on Norma's side the last time, threw me out. Something really stinks."

Miss Giveny collected her file and trundled into her office. "Mr. Crawford was very worried about Norma Dinnick," she said.

"How so?"

"I don't really know, but he spent a lot of time at her place just before he died."

"Really? Are there any files from his visits?"

"Not a one. Just her husband's old estate file."

"Any billings?"

She shook her head. "And he was there almost every day for several weeks before he died."

Harry knew Richard Crawford was incorrigible when it came to his female clients. Sometimes he caught glimmers of Norma as a young and attractive woman, but for him, Norma was all enigma and intrigue.

"I think he was helping her with a personal problem from way back, urging her to do something about it, and she kept refusing."

"He never said anything at all?"

His secretary pursed her lips. "Mr. Crawford never discussed his clients with me."

Harry shrugged and headed for his office. From his doorway, he called back to her, "Did you find a place for Norma to stay?"

"Yes. The Madrid Towers can take her tomorrow afternoon," she replied.

"Great. Give her a call and let her know, please."

"I already did."

"Was she all right when you spoke to her?"

"As far as I could tell."

Seated at his desk, he stared up Bay Street musing about Crawford's womanizing and his potential connection with Norma. Harry's thoughts shifted back to Natasha. He could put his finger on nothing troubling other than a growing coolness and her questions about his father. Longing for the uncomplicated passion of their first months, he dialed her office. After being told she was not in, he did not leave his name. Better let sleeping dogs lie until Friday night, he decided.

Just the simple intimacy of sharing life with someone was vitally important to him. In the first years of his marriage to Laura, he had probably most enjoyed the hours they spent talking in bed. And then the atmosphere changed. Not all at once, but slowly the distance grew and coolness penetrated their marriage. And of course there was Katrina, whose mysterious departure had left him hollow for years, which Laura filled for a time.

The telephone rang in the outer office. He stared at the red flashing light on his phone. Almost six o'clock. He hesitated, but then picked up the receiver in hopes it might be Natasha.

"Is that you, Harry?"

"Yes." The voice was strangely familiar.

"It's me, Peter."

Harry knew at once it was Saunderson, senior partner at Blackburn, Swanson and esteemed Bencher of the Law Society. Peter, with his barely detectable lisp. The one who used to pile his dirty socks and underwear in the bathroom sink. Vaguely, Harry wondered if he had improved in his personal habits over the years.

"Yes," he said.

"I suppose you're wondering why I'm calling you after so many years."

Harry picked up his pen and began doodling. "Well, yes. What can I do for you, Peter?"

"I need to see you." There was a lengthy pause, which Harry did not fill. "I need your advice."

Harry was incredulous. He had seen Peter on one or two social occasions over the years and only on a few legal matters. "My advice? What about?"

"That Dinnick case of yours."

Harry stopped his erratic doodling. "Seems all sorts of people know of it."

"Actually, I may have some information you should have. And," Peter hesitated, "I need some help on a personal matter."

"Listen, if you have threats to deliver on the Dinnick case, forget it. I've had enough."

"Threats?" Peter sounded genuinely surprised and mildly offended. "Of course not! I hoped I could count on an old friend…" After a moment's silence, Harry heard a deep sigh. "I need to meet with you tonight, as soon as possible. I wouldn't ask if I weren't desperate."

"Tonight? That's ridiculous. We haven't spoken in years, and now you want to meet at a moment's notice."

"Please, Harry."

"All right. I'll meet you for a drink at the Alton Club in an hour."

"No. We have to meet out in the open where no one can hear us."

"What the hell is this about?"

Peter ignored him. "Meet me at the footbridge at the end of Cecil Street at nine o'clock." The phone went dead.

Had Saunderson lost his mind? First, he called after twenty years of silence. Then, he demanded to meet at the old spot where his affair with Katrina had ended. Same old Peter.

Ten minutes before nine, Harry parked his car in front of Madame Odella's house. She must, Harry reflected, be long since dead, but where was Katrina? Probably married with four kids. He slammed the car door and locked it. Pulling his collar up against the sleet, he headed down the block to the bridge.

Katrina and he had always met at the footbridge. With Madame Odella and Peter lurking about, it was hard to find privacy. Up ahead, he saw the familiar entrance. Katrina used to wait for him at the very center of the bridge.

With the leaves gone, he could see the first lamppost casting its yellow light in the tangle of naked branches. He stepped onto the bridge. The view had the perfect perspective of a well-executed painting. The eye was gently but inexorably drawn up the cresting path to the very center of the suspension bridge, where railings of wrought iron appeared to converge in the drifting fog. On the farthest side of the footbridge there was a smudge of white light marking the entrance to the subway.

Deep in the ravine, the river coursed. Sounds floated up to him; the swish of tires from the snaking road, the splash of water on the jagged rocks. From his vantage point on the bridge, he felt suspended in time and space. Pulled in all directions at once, he sensed that he had rarely experienced this fine balance anywhere else. Any movement might instantly dispel it. Perhaps Katrina and he met here to keep that balance, somehow knowing how tenuous love could be.

On this spot, he had begged Katrina to return to him. With shocking immediacy, he saw her face, bravely hardened against him. From her few words, he knew Peter had something to do with it. But what? The loss left an unexplained gaping hole, which he had never filled up.

He turned to face the far end of the bridge where the bright light glowed. Instantly, he recognized the figure, even at two hundred yards. Peter always rolled slightly from one side to the other as if his feet hurt.

When he loomed out of the mist, they shook hands.

"Good of you to come, Harry."

Harry shrugged. "Interesting choice of places."

Peter looked away. "Well, yes. I have to talk to you in private. It was the best place I could think of."

"You mentioned the Dinnick case." Harry intended to get right to the point.

Peter withdrew a cigar from his vest pocket and puffed deeply to light it. Once the tip was smoldering, he stared in silence over the railing. Harry bided his time watching the cluster of rain drops run along the latticework of the bridge. At last Saunderson turned back to him, his face pale and sickly in the light.

"I know it's odd for me to approach you after this long, Harry. But you're the only person I know who'll understand my predicament, and," he laid his hand on Harry's arm, "I may be able to help you."

His words were so plainly and earnestly spoken that Harry finally said, "All right. What is it you want?"

"I've been seeing someone, a man. His name is Roger Blenheim. Bronwyn, my wife, doesn't know. In fact, no one knows, and I have to keep it that way."

"So? What's that got to do with me?"

"It doesn't. But you gave a description of the murder weapon in the Brinks shooting." Peter drew on his cigar and looked out over the ravine. "My friend is a collector of antique guns," he said quietly, then turned to gaze at Harry. "Your description of the weapon in the Brinks murder fits one in his collection."

"I see." Harry could not imagine Peter being involved with the likes of Mr. Prince. "But, obviously, your friend is not the Mr. Prince who came to court."

"No, of course not. But the gun is very old, a Gautier flintlock dueling pistol. Silver, very delicate looking, and *very* rare. It's also worth a good deal of money."

Harry shook his head. "I still don't see what you want from me. Why don't you just tell the police?"

Peter leaned out over the railing. "It's in a cabinet in his bedroom." He began to chuckle softly. "He likes to play games with it." He turned back to Harry. "Of course, I don't want anyone knowing I've been there."

"For God's sake, Peter! Do you think people care anymore about someone being gay?"

Peter's laugh was bitter. "If you're a senior partner and head of the commercial department at Blackburn, Swanson, they do. If you're on boards of directors of major corporations, they do. And if you're a Bencher of the Law Society, they damn well insist. No! According to them, you must be straight and happily married to the right woman—and, of course, to the law."

"That's ridiculous. Lots of people are entirely open these days."

Peter regarded him somberly. "You don't live the life, Harry. You don't know."

In the lamplight, Peter looked old and tired, but Harry could see his bruised and bloody face of years back. He didn't want to know how many times Peter had been beaten up. And after all, what did he, Harry, really know? He knew the pain of lost love, but he had never had to hide his fundamental identity from the world. Harry sighed. Peter undoubtedly had his reasons for his fears.

"How do you think Blenheim is involved?" he asked.

Peter shrugged. "I don't know, Harry. Roger's very secretive, but he seems to have a lot of connections I know nothing about. In any event, that gun is very unusual, and the description in the paper certainly matches it.

"So what do you want me to do?"

"Contact the police for me. If I'm your client, my identity is privileged. You can tell the police where the gun is."

Harry knew that, at least morally, he had to disclose any evidence, which came across his path. Now he knew about Blenheim, he had to act anyway. "All right. I'll act for you in this, but you said you could do something for me."

Peter tossed his cigar into the ravine. Harry watched the smoldering ember twirl into the darkness. "One of Blenheim's contacts is a man named Ross Brackley."

"Jesus! Brackley?"

"Yes. You know him?"

"Unfortunately, yes. But I thought he was connected with a George Pappas."

Peter frowned. "Pappas? I don't think I know that name, Harry. But the other night I heard Roger talking to Ross Brackley on the phone. Something about taking care of Dinnick."

"So Blenheim has been involved with Norma, George, and Archie?"

Peter tossed up his hands in frustration. "I don't know how, but I've heard about Brackley, and I think I can get some people to call him off. That's the best way to keep your client safe. After all, isn't she really an innocent bystander—and very elderly?"

Fat flakes of snow were drifting down so heavily that both men were coated in white. Harry stamped and brushed himself off. He had trouble believing Peter, but he felt compelled to act. "All right. I'll get in touch with the police in the morning. And you better do whatever you can about Brackley."

The two men shook hands. Without further words, Harry headed back across the bridge to his car. Peter walked in the opposite direction toward the lights at the subway entrance.

The police took almost twenty-four hours to respond to Harry's letter.

"I'm calling about your letter, Mr. Jenkins. About the murder weapon in the Brinks case."

"Who's speaking please?" For Harry, caution was the watchword when dealing with the cops.

"Officer Kilworthy," the voice continued.

"Yes. What are you going to do?"

"First of all, sir, we want to know how you can act for an unidentified person, when you're also a witness to the murder, and your client, Norma Dinnick, is the litigant?"

Harry knew the *hat* issue would be raised. Which one was he wearing now? Best to meet the problem straight on. In his most aggressive tone, he said, "Are you going to follow up on the tip, or are you going to fiddle around with it?"

"Of course we're following up on it." Kilworthy sounded appropriately defensive.

"Then get someone over to Blenheim's place and have a look."

"Got to get a search warrant first."

"Of course you do, Officer. I'll be happy to swear an affidavit to support the application. You have everything you need, and you don't have to reveal my client's name."

Within the hour, Harry was at the police station swearing out the warrant.

CHAPTER 22

▼

That evening, Harry received a call just as he was settling down to catch the ten o'clock news.

"Mr. Jenkins? This is Dr. Fairbourn speaking. I'm the resident on duty at the hospital."

"Yes?" Harry asked anxiously.

"Mr. Jenkins, I'm afraid your father is missing."

"How can that be? Wasn't anyone checking on him?"

Harry was at the hospital within twenty minutes.

"His clothes are gone, Mr. Jenkins. It seems he just got dressed and left. We're searching the hospital, just in case."

Harry leaned against the corridor wall and sighed. "He's probably gone home."

In the car, he counted the number of times his father had run away. Always back home. After all, what did he want most in life but to be there? When he let himself in, his father was eating a sandwich and watching the hockey game.

Harry stood in the front hall. "Dad, everyone at the hospital is looking for you. Why didn't you at least sign out?"

"For Christ's sake! I'm not that stupid. They'd have stopped me."

"At least you could have called me. I would have picked you up."

"Bullshit!"

Harry tossed his coat on the chair. "I'm going to call the hospital. Let them know you're safe, so they can stop looking for you."

"I'm not going back." Stanley drank his beer.

"Fine." He picked up the phone. After some moments, he reached the nursing station.

"They're not sending an ambulance, are they?" Stanley called out.

Harry shook his head and sank into a chair, positioning himself between his father and the television. "You have to listen to me, Dad. We can't keep this up."

"I'm not asking you to." His father stood up and snapped off the TV set. "I'm going away."

"What? Where?"

"I'm selling the house and getting out of here. We're too much trouble to each other." Slapping his fist into his palm, Stanley started to pace. "I've had it with retirement homes, which is where you want me to be."

"It's only because I want you to be safe."

"Look! Do you have any idea what it's like to live in one of those places? Doesn't matter which one. They're all the same. Bingo and moronic card games; pub nights with no beer; old biddies gibbering away about nothing. And the caretakers are either from Auschwitz or la-la land. It's no place for anyone with a brain. Jesus!" Stanley stifled a sob. "There's all these poor inmates, slumped over in wheelchairs, calling out for help, and nobody ever answers." The old man shivered. "I'd rather be dead than there."

"But Dad! You had a gun here in your own home. You were going to kill yourself right here, not in some retirement home."

"So?" Stanley sat on the chesterfield. "I don't want to be a burden to you, son. That's why I'm going away."

"Where?"

"Halifax. I have a second cousin there. I'll buy my own place with the money from this house."

"You've never talked about any relatives in Halifax."

"Well, I've never talked much about anything. That's the problem, isn't it?"

His father's face softened. The guarded old man faded for a moment.

"Why don't we start right now?" Harry said softly.

To his shock, Stanley buried his face in his hands. His shoulders shook violently.

Speechless, Harry reached out to touch him. His father turned and threw his arms around him. Harry felt him shaking.

"I don't know where to start, Harry," he whispered hoarsely.

"Start when Anna died and how you felt."

At last, his father looked at him and said, "It shouldn't have happened, but when we buried her, I was buried too. Your poor mother! She was so determined to keep on living, even though losing Anna just tore her apart. She was so much stronger than I was. She knew she had to live for you. But I just caved in." He grasped Harry's hand. "God forgive me," he whispered.

Harry felt his chest constrict and then he had a sense of letting go, letting the pain in his heart float off somewhere. It was now or never. Holding his father close was a strange sensation, for he had always feared to touch the man. "I *do* forgive you, Dad. I am so truly sorry for you." He was shocked at how frail and insubstantial his father felt in his arms, no longer the forbidding presence.

Harry sat apart from his him. "But you can't go away."

"Why not?"

"Because I want you here. So we can talk." Harry chuckled. "Aren't I more important than some second cousin?"

His father only nodded. "But I want to live here."

"Sure, Dad." Harry was surprised. He actually sounded as if he meant what he said. "So, have you got a beer for me? I'll watch the game with you."

Harry found a beer in the fridge. There wasn't much else in the cupboards. From the kitchen, he called out, "You'll need some food in the house. I'll help you shop in the morning, if you like." No answer. Rushing into the living room, Harry found his father snuffling into a Kleenex.

"Well, son," he said, trying to sound hearty, "We've talked enough about me and my life. Tell me about yours. You got anyone since Laura?"

Harry was surprised. Although he had never really discussed his divorce, his father had remembered. "Actually, yes. I do."

Stanley looked up with interest. "Really? That's great. Who's the lady?"

"Her name is Natasha."

"Russian?"

"Ukrainian."

"Good for you! I'm glad you've got someone, Harry. After Laura left, you weren't in good shape."

"You're right. I'm feeling much better now." Harry was surprised his father had noticed.

"Good woman?"

"Yes. Very good."

"What's she like?"

To speak to his father openly about his own life was a very new experience for him. Unsure of where to begin, he said, "She's a realtor, and a very successful one, too."

His father chuckled. "Good looking?"

Harry smiled slowly. "Very! She's beautiful." He felt himself blushing. "And *very* good for me."

"You sound like a man in love, Harry. I'm glad."

Harry shook his head. "This seems strange, Dad. I'm not used to talking like this with you. It feels good, though."

With a grin, his father said, "Well, that's great son! Now you get the hell on out of here until the morning. I want to get to bed."

Harry set his beer down. "You're sure you'll be all right?"

"Listen, son. If this is going to work between you and me, you've got to give me space. Lots of it."

His father stood up, only slightly unsteadily. Grasping the edge of the lamp table, he said, "I've lived here all my married life. I'll be just fine." He opened the front door and squinted at Harry.

"Why don't you bring that lady friend around sometime? Your mother and I would love to meet her. When you're ready, that is."

Harry frowned. "Dad? Mother's been gone almost ten years."

His father looked up at him sheepishly. "Yes, of course. What was I thinking about?"

"Okay, you get to bed, and I'll be here to go shopping at ten." Harry hated to leave him alone, but he knew he had to trust him.

"Don't worry, Harry, I can shop myself." Then he shrugged. "Oh, what the hell, it'd be nice to have the company."

Harry patted his father's arm. "I feel the same, Dad." As he got into his car, he felt as if an dam had burst. They were actually talking!

CHAPTER 23

▼

Feeling nauseated, Roger sat up on the edge of his bed and pushed the scrolls of paper onto the floor. Opening the curtains, he closed his eyes to the painful light. Swirls of color swam before his eyes. Shit! Snow everywhere outside. Fucking Toronto weather.

Last night, he had written the summary of his life. An obituary. It was, in fact, a pretty shitty life. No one would ever bother to read it. Then he wrote out what he considered to be his last will and testament. He estimated his worldly wealth to be in excess of two million. There would be plenty to pay off Peter, once everything was sold. But there was no one to leave the rest to, except Peter. He smiled wanly. Surely to God that would satisfy the little bugger. Sitting on the edge of the bed, he knew it wasn't just that. He actually loved him and so, he signed everything over to him.

The telephone rang. Weakness flooded his whole body.

"Mr. Roger Blenheim, please." It was the cheery voice from the clinic.

Suddenly, he didn't care much anymore. "Speaking," he whispered.

"Dr. Radlikov would like to see you today to discuss your blood work. Could you come at two o'clock?"

"Of course, my dear." His throat was dry and sore. "Am I going to die?"

There was a lengthy pause, a shoring up of bureaucracy. "I'm sure the doctor will discuss everything with you in detail."

Roger gently hung up the receiver and gazed once more at the scrolls of paper on the floor. Strange. His life had only filled four pages.

He jumped at the sound of the door-knocker crashing below. Light-headed and still disoriented, he rose and hunched over to keep his robe around him. Wobbling, he descended the stairs until he saw a blue hat through the glass of the front door. Yesterday, the police had been by selling tickets to a charity ball. Hell, he thought dimly, maybe Roxanna would like to go. He opened the door to see two uniformed officers and another man in plainclothes.

"Mr. Roger Blenheim?"

"Yes, gentlemen?"

"We have a search warrant."

"For what?" Roger tried to focus on the paper handed to him. "What's it about? I don't have my glasses."

"Read it to him!" growled the plainclothes cop, who was at least six inches shorter and much broader than the uniformed men.

"I don't have any stolen property here," said Roger indignantly.

The smaller man shouldered his way forward "I'm Detective McGee, and we're authorized to search for pistols."

Roger looked down on the bustling detective, who was squinting suspiciously about. Although he knew he had to concentrate, he could only think of sitting down.

"You want to show us where you keep them, or do we tear the place apart?" McGee demanded.

Roger recovered sufficiently to gesture the men upstairs. "I keep them in my bedroom, safely locked up, with the ammunition stored separately. All according to the letter of the law."

In his room, Roger strove to maintain a reasoned tone, although the men were beginning to swim before his eyes. He unlocked the cabinet and stood back.

McGee stood before the cabinet and extracted a photograph from his pocket. The other two officers moved toward the triptych of mirrors and kicked several pillows to one side.

"May I help you, officers?" Roger asked. They did not reply.

McGee, engrossed in a study of the photograph, whistled tunelessly through his front teeth. Standing patiently at his side, Roger, dazed, did not notice the uniformed officers making a slow circuit of his room. Now and then they paused to examine a vase, an ornament, or a book. Their voices were low, yet jovial. Detective McGee progressed to a detailed study of each pistol in the cabinet.

"May I help you, detective?" Roger finally asked. He was beginning to feel extremely ill, and was, in fact, swaying back and forth.

McGee shook his head and said quietly, "Are you attempting to influence me, Mr. Blenheim? Because if you are…"

"Pardon?" Roger could not believe his ears. The search was becoming incomprehensible. He needed a lawyer. Where was Peter? His head was throbbing, and he thought he might vomit. He sank to the bed.

"Well, lookie here!" With a broad grin on his face, one of the uniformed officers turned sharply to face the others. McGee stopped rummaging in the cabinets.

The second officer gave a low whistle. "Isn't this the prettiest little box for you-know-what?" He opened it to sniff inside.

Roger rose from the bed. "Please! Be careful of that. It's worth a lot of money."

"Put it down, boys. You heard Mr. Blenheim. Besides, I've found the pistol, so we're outta here." With a gloved hand, he carefully inserted the pistol into a plastic bag.

"Detective?" The officer was smiling broadly. "I think we should take this box for testing."

In confusion, Roger stood in the middle of the room gaping at the men. He could not understand why the officer was still sniffing the interior of the box. "Please, gentlemen. That's valuable property."

"Think our little faggot boy has some coke on the premises?"

"Now, officer," McGee continued in a teacherly fashion, "What does reasonable and probable belief entitle you to do?'

Roger was so overwhelmed with fear for his precious box that he failed to comprehend the words spoken. He did not understand why the two men were circling the bed and closing in on him.

"Sir," continued the officer still cradling the box, "that entitles us on reasonable and probable grounds to conduct further searches of the premises and the person for any illegal substances."

Both officers, grinning as if they would burst, were closing in behind Roger.

"Excellent, officers," smiled McGee. "You are definitely entitled to strip-search this suspect." The detective waved his cigar grandly in the air.

By the time the words reached Roger, it was too late. One officer had pinned his arms behind him and forced him onto his stomach on the bed.

Roger cried out. "I want my lawyer. I want Peter!"

"Only the finest silks for our pretty boy!" the first officer snickered as he tore Roger's robe away.

The other grabbed his ponytail and shoved his head into a pillow. Roger struggled for air, then writhed in pain as they wrenched his legs apart. The officer snapped latex gloves on his hands. A scarf was tied over Roger's mouth.

McGee said, "Proceed, men, but watch the old faggot doesn't enjoy it too much."

To keep from blacking out from the searing pain, Roger forced himself to concentrate on the Gagiid and Nisgaa masks in the cabinet.

After five minutes, McGee and the officers covered Roger up and left with the box and the pistol. Roger closed his eyes and did not move. Georgette, the Pekingese, licked his face. When he opened his eyes again, he saw the scrolls upon which he had written his life story. *Yes*, he thought, *a shitty life indeed*. For an instant, he hoped it would be over soon.

Finally, he got up, and saw the smears of blood on the bedspread. Walking gingerly to the bathroom, he examined his face in the mirror. Old, haggard, and ugly, he thought. Roxanna was gone forever.

Bronwyn lay on her bed, searching for the lump in her breast. She imagined a gray, glutinous mass with tentacles ready to reach throughout her body and cut off her life. The bedside table was strewn with crumpled Kleenex and bottles of medicine. She downed two more pills with a sip of water. The doctor had not called back to confirm her appointment. And Jeremy—where in hell was he?—had not called back yet.

She turned on the television. Oh God! More about Archie. "I gave no authorization. I never paid a cent," she muttered. Suddenly, she remembered the bank receipt for the withdrawal. Forgetting Peter's promise to keep it safe, she began a methodical search for the piece of paper, which might condemn her.

First, she emptied her purse and wallet. Nothing. She searched behind the jewelry box and under the gloves in the drawer. Where in God's name could it be? Her careful hunt rose to panicked frenzy. Underwear, nightgowns, sweaters, and stockings were strewn across the bedroom floor. Collapsing to her knees, she scrabbled about on all fours, searching. Fuck! Peter must have it.

Scarcely able to breathe, she swallowed two more pills to calm herself. Absently scratching her burning and tingling palms, she sat back with her knees drawn up to her chin and her back to the wall.

Goddamn Peter! With her bathrobe clutched about her, she raced down the cold and drafty staircase to his study. Rocking back and forth in his desk chair, she listened to the voice mail. The message from Prince had been deleted. Tucking her feet underneath her, she began to gnaw at her thumb. Peter's smirking image appeared, protesting his love and concern. What had he done with the receipt? Trying to concentrate, she absent-mindedly dragged her fingernails back and forth from her wrist to her elbow.

Her rocking motion became frenzied, and she began to tear at her leg with her nails. "I only inquired. I authorized no one." Splotches of blood appeared on her shin.

Back in her room, she snapped on the television to see a computer sketch showing the many chins and merry, piggish eyes of Mr. Prince. And then, oh Jesus! His body had been found at the bottom of the expressway. Dead from the two hundred foot fall. *Please God, keep them from looking any further!*

She rose and dressed in a pair of jeans and a sweatshirt. She did not brush her hair or apply makeup. In the front hall, she put on a light jacket and when she looked in the mirror she saw Archie swathed in bloody white bandages. She touched a red, scaly patch of skin on her neck, and digging her nails into it, opened the front door. Bronwyn welcomed the piercing cold like an anesthetic. Thank God Prince was gone.

Outside, she stumbled and squinted in the light. To her right, the lawn fell away to the ravine, where the sun illuminated black tree limbs against a washed-out sky. When she looked up toward the road, she saw a fine, hard rain spattering down. She drew up her collar and trudged along the driveway. Through the woods, close to the edge of the ravine, the sky turned black and threatening. Right there the steering wheel of the Mercedes had suddenly wrenched out of her hand. Probably Peter had tried to kill her in an accident. A deeper cold settled in her at the thought of him.

She stared into the ravine. The car was no longer there.

Shivering, she smiled, "I only inquired. I paid no one." Archie and Prince were gone, and only Peter knew. She turned and headed home. Undoing her jacket, she hurried into the house and locked the door.

Upstairs, in her bedroom, she lay on her bed until, hours later, she heard a key in the lock. The bedside lamp bathed Peter's smiling face in a rose hue.

"I got your medicine from the bathroom." He handed her two pills and a glass of water. "Take them now, then eat, so you'll have something in your tummy."

Twisting to the far side of the bed, Bronwyn jerked upright. "Where's the receipt and the car, you bastard?"

His voice was filled with concern. "Darling, I told you already. I have the receipt in my safe, and the mechanic checked out the car yesterday. Have you forgotten already?"

Bronwyn said, "You didn't tell me that before."

"But I did. You must have been too shocked and exhausted to take it in. Listen, I brought you some dinner. You need to eat to get your strength back."

She looked at Peter suspiciously. Finally, she broke the silence. "Mr. Prince is dead."

"Prince? Who is that, darling?" Peter set the tray on the bed.

"Who is that?" Kicking at the bed covers to untangle herself, she knocked over the teapot. "Goddamn it, Peter. You gave me his phone number."

"I think you're a bit confused, Bronwyn. Maybe the doctor should check you out. You did have a nasty accident."

"Don't give me that shit!" Bronwyn screeched, sweeping the pills to the floor. "You sent me to Prince. You put his phone number on my dresser."

"Honey, I don't know a Mr. Prince," he said quietly. "Remember? I said I didn't know anyone who could do something like that."

Bronwyn was on all fours on the bed. Grabbing his necktie, she pulled him close. As he jerked forward, all he could see was her inflamed red eyes bearing down on him.

"Listen, you little bastard! You set me up. You gave me the number," she shrieked.

Gasping for breath, he said, "You must calm yourself. Really, it's important, darling." He loosened his tie and moved away from her. When his breathing returned to normal, he continued, "I will destroy the receipt. There is not the remotest bit of evidence to tie you to the murder."

"You filthy, fucking bastard! You're trying to frame me."

"Frame you? Hardly! I'm your husband. I can't testify against you. After all, the marriage vows carry some weight. It's one of the few real privileges the law permits."

Her laugh was harsh. "You! Talking about the sanctity of marriage vows!" As a wave of nausea swept over her, she slumped onto the pillows.

Peter stood up. "I really think I'd better call the doctor, Bronwyn."

"No…" she groaned, turning her head away. "I don't trust you."

Peter sighed. "All right, carry on like this if you must. But remember, while you're lying here, I'm doing everything in my power to protect you and get you better." At the door, he turned back, saying, "I know you don't believe me, but I really *do* love you."

Bronwyn disappeared under the covers and began to scratch her leg.

At the office, Peter instructed his secretary to tell Roger Blenheim, if he called, that he was unavailable. The first call came shortly after eleven, when Peter was in the boardroom with the Sheffield Inc. directors.

"I want to speak to Peter," Roger said.

"He's out at meetings, Mr. Blenheim," said the secretary.

"Don't give me that shit! Stick a note under his nose and tell him to call me back now."

When she delivered coffee to the boardroom, she passed the note to Peter. He scrawled on it *Tell him I'll call back at the end of the day.*

At twenty to twelve, the second call came.

Roger's bellow was deafening. "You tell that little fucker to call me, or I'll come down and parade in his foyer."

When Peter emerged for lunch, Susan flagged him down and delivered the message. Peter told her to escort the directors to reception. Slamming his office door, he phoned Roger.

"What the hell is this about, Roger? I'm in meetings all day."

"I need a lawyer. I don't know who else to call."

"Why do you need a lawyer?"

"The police were here this morning with a search warrant."

Peter glanced at his watch, then said casually, "What were they looking for?"

"They went through my pistol collection and took the Gautier flint-lock."

"You've been keeping them locked up with the ammunition stored separately?"

"Yes, of course. But…"

"Listen Roger, I've got a lunch right now. Fax me the search warrant, and I'll have someone in criminal law look at it. You know that's not my field."

Peter heard a choking sound at the other end of the line. "What is it Roger?" He heard a sob. "Roger, what is it?" Impatiently, he looked at his watch. "Is there something else?"

"They took the pistol and something else. A scrolled box. They claimed I kept coke in it." Roger stifled another sob. "Then they—those vicious bastards—did…something I'm sure they weren't entitled to do."

"What did they do?" Peter asked softly, as he jingled some coins in his pocket.

"They said they had grounds to do a strip search, right in my own room. One of them held me down, and the other did it, and the third one just watched. By the time they were done, I was a bloody mess."

"That's totally outrageous! Look, I'll call Phil Gillespie right now. Get him on the case immediately. He'll get hold of the cops responsible. You didn't get their names, did you?"

Roger groaned. "No. I was feeling so rotten even before they came, that I had a hard time concentrating."

"One of us will get back to you before the end of the day. I promise, Roger. Got to go." With a slow smile, Peter gently set down the phone and strode out to meet his clients for lunch.

At noon, Bronwyn forced herself to go to the club. Her skin itched and burned, but she could see no rash anywhere. Every muscle in her body ached, and so she decided to book a massage.

At one o'clock, there was an opening with her favorite, Michel. She lay naked under a stiff white sheet on the massage table. Michel entered the room and approached her cheerily. "And how are we today, Mrs. Saunderson? I haven't seen you here for several weeks."

Bronwyn groaned. "My God, Michel, I feel absolutely horrible. Every part of me aches."

Michel, a devotee of bodybuilding, was reputed to be the most attentive masseuse at the club. His tone was light and teasing. "Everywhere?" He saw yet another middle-aged matron ignored by her husband and desperate for attention. "I'm sure we can remedy that, Mrs. Saunderson." He had to acknowledge that, for her age, she still had a pretty good body.

"Mmmmmh…yes, please." she murmured.

He turned to close the door. "Then you need the full treatment."

Almost drifting off, Bronwyn longed for him to begin. She imagined the sensation of his fingers working their way slowly down her neck, her shoulders, her back, and still lower. She could hear the clink of jars of lotion as he made his preparations. But, she admitted, it was a poor substitute for love—whatever that was.

She turned her head and said sleepily, "Will you lock the door, Michel?"

He lowered his eyelids and said, "Indeed. We must relax you completely." He touched her neck and shoulders. "I see…" he murmured. "You're extremely tense. Only the full treatment will do today."

Under his touch, Bronwyn floated off in fantasies of being someone else, somewhere else. Archie must be haunting her, she decided. More than anything, she wanted release from visions of his ugly, twisted face. Other thoughts floated into her brain, but just as they were almost formed, they dissipated like wisps of smoke. *What is love, anyway?* she wondered.

With the heat of the lamps, she was transported back in time to the island of Corfu, where she and Peter had spent their honeymoon. Then, she had actually thought she was in love. Sitting on the patio of the hotel, she had gazed out at the tiny white boats bobbing like corks on brilliant blue waters. Further out, she saw the sun caught behind rocks forming fantastic natural arches above the waters and hiding caves beneath. But where was Peter? She looked in the foyer and the hotel bar. She wandered the narrow beach of sand and stone where the boats ferried back and forth to the grottos. No Peter. But then she saw him at a distance on the beach, walking slowly with a younger man she did not know. Where had they come from? Right from the start, she had known. Of course the bargain was unspoken, but it was well understood. For money and security, Bronwyn had sacrificed any chance for love.

Michel drew down the sheet and gasped. "Oh my God, Mrs. Saunderson! What has happened to your back and your legs?" Displayed before Michel were angry, raised welts.

Bronwyn was jolted out her dream-like state.

"Mrs. Saunderson? Have you seen a doctor?"

She sat bolt upright. "What's wrong, Michel? She clutched the sheet around her.

"Look!" He grasped her shoulders and turned her toward the mirror on the white tiled wall. "You didn't know?"

Bronwyn craned her neck around to see. At first, she made no sound at all. She gaped over her shoulder to see the red and swollen skin. At that moment, she entered into another world. She tried to speak, but no words came. Madness? As if reality had dissolved before her eyes, she became captive in a foreign place no words could describe. But Archie and Peter were there.

She did not see the room or Michel, yet she could hear his voice at a distance. She no longer saw herself, but she felt his hand on her shoulder. She heard the crack of the gun. She saw Archie sprawled on the floor with blood spurting everywhere. When she looked down at her hands, she saw that she had no fingers.

The last Bronwyn heard was a female voice shrieking somewhere at an hysterical pitch. The same words, over and over, rebounded on the tiled walls of the massage room: "I only inquired! I didn't pay a cent!"

Shuddering from deep within, she cried out to her unseen accusers, Archibald Brinks and Mr. Prince, "I have no fingers! Must I pay such a terrible price?"

As if in another world, she dropped the sheet and took her robe from the hook on the wall. Michel hastened to cover her. Unseeing, she calmly walked from the room. The club faded from her vision to be replaced by a new world. In a dream of madness Bronwyn followed endless yellow hallways leading nowhere. She saw blood-spattered rooms and heard fantastical creatures making unearthly sounds. She dared not enter any one of them, for there she would find her accusers.

She tried to escape by running. Down the hall and past the change room she went, unaware of Michel and three other attendants. A woman dressing at the lockers backed away from her.

"Please! I will do anything!" But she had nothing with which to bargain. She wept in the knowledge that Archie would always be with her.

The second sitting for lunch had already begun in the crowded dining room. Allison, Meredith, and Sonia were among the first to be seated.

Over white wine and Perrier water, Meredith smoothed her snowy white napkin and asked brightly, "Has anyone seen Bronwyn lately?"

No one had.

"I hear she's having trouble with Peter," she continued, glancing significantly at her luncheon companions.

Sonia laughed. "Nothing new there, sweetie. Peter's had a love interest for years now. A gentleman antique dealer—isn't that perfect? And isn't she afraid she'll catch something nasty?"

Meredith was not to be outdone in telling tales. "Nothing to worry about there!" she laughed knowingly. "They haven't slept together in years." Leaning forward confidentially, she continued, "But I'll tell you the latest gossip. Last week in Holt's, our dear friend had a little trouble with the credit department. Apparently, Peter had been on a spending spree for the antique man. Poor Bronwyn was left high and dry."

Allison was disgusted by Meredith's gossip, but, being new to the club, she feared speaking up. Bronwyn had warned her about Meredith's stories. She sat back from the other two and let her eyes wander about the dining room. Then she gasped. Squinting in the brilliant winter light flooding the room, she saw a tall, slim figure, clad only in a white, terry cloth robe, wavering at the top of the stairs. The maitre d' rushed forward, but the figure, eluding his grasp, floated beyond him as if disconnected from its surroundings.

Allison clutched Meredith's hand. "My God! Look. It's Bronwyn!"

Bronwyn, her expression vacant, drifted blindly past the first set of tables. When she raised her arms, her robe threatened to drape open. The maitre d' rushed after her, accompanied by a string of waiters. No one knew what to do. Every woman in the dining room was silent

Every so often, Bronwyn stopped and drew back as if in fear. In her mind, she was avoiding the endless rooms of moaning creatures that threatened to escape and surround her. She raised her arms and clawed at the air.

The pale light accentuated the frailty of her bony hands. "Look," she began in a quiet, singsong voice, "I have paid the highest price." She held up her hands and cried out, "See, I have no fingers at all!" She shook her head. "No. Not a one." She became lost in a study of her hands and rings.

"Once upon a time, you see, I had my own life to live. But I sold it too cheaply." She laughed softly to herself. "Women often do. They make a bargain with a man. Expecting to be loved and cared for, they find themselves lost in a hollow shell of a life. They always hope that money will fill the void." A single tear rolled down her cheek. "But it never *does*, and for me, it is too late."

The women diners became quietly attentive. Bronwyn smiled at no one in particular. "Don't pay this terrible price. Or your fingers will be hacked off, one...by...one."

Unseeing, she threaded her way past tables and on toward the windows. "You must believe me," she said earnestly, stopping at one table. She reached out and took the hands of one of the oldest club members, Mrs. Monserrat, who tried to draw Bronwyn into a chair beside her.

"Dear, please!" the old woman urged. "Do not do this. You are ill, child."

Bronwyn smiled dreamily at her. "I authorized no one, you understand," she said in a hoarse whisper. "I never paid a cent." She moved on to the next table. "See? My fingers, all ten of them, are cut off and bloody." She held up her hands and asked, "Is that not a terrible price for one woman to pay?"

At the next table, Bronwyn began to claw at her arm until it was red and raw. "A woman must be able to stand on her own, beholden to no one. That is the mistake I made."

The women looked down at their hands in embarrassment. Yet each one was mesmerized by her words. "Truth in madness," said one to the other.

Stopping at the windows, Bronwyn shrieked, "But if I am set free, dear God, I will gladly pay the price!" She began to scratch her right leg just above her knee.

All the women were transfixed. Allison was the one who broke rank. Swiftly, she caught up with Bronwyn. Gently, she took her arm and led her toward her table. "Bronwyn? It's Allison. Can you hear me?" she asked.

Bronwyn resisted. Seeing nothing, she began to sway gently to and fro. "I only inquired, you see." She began to twist her arm from Allison. "I authorized nothing. And yet I have paid the very highest price." Again she held up her hands and examined her fingers. "All gone," she sighed.

"Bronwyn, please," Allison whispered. "Come sit with me and Meredith." Over Bronwyn's shoulder, she could see the paramedics advancing down the steps. Three men surrounded them. Bronwyn thought her accusers had escaped from the rooms where they did their unspeakable acts. Shrieking, she tore herself away. Throwing up her hands, her robe flew open. She tried to run. Allison rushed to cover her.

"Let me be! Dear God, please let me be," Bronwyn moaned, sinking to the floor. The dining room was silent as Bronwyn was shifted onto a stretcher and taken from the club.

Outside, Allison, Meredith, and Sonia watched dumbly as the ambulance drew away. Not until the paramedics pulled onto Bayview Avenue, did they turn on the siren.

Meredith eyes gleamed as she exclaimed, "My God! What a performance!"

Allison turned on her. "Meredith, don't say anything! Not one thing! Poor Bronwyn!"

Bronwyn was delivered immediately to The Brentview, a highly esteemed private clinic north east of the city. The ambulance darted north on the shoulder of the jammed superhighway, then turned off onto a township road. Following the road's twists and turns, it came to a wooded area and an old estate mansion surrounded by barbwire—the hospital. Here new and experimental treatments for old and broken spirits were devised under the auspices of Dr. John Larkin.

Bronwyn was immediately admitted for observation. Her first room did not resemble a hospital ward but rather, an elegant and sumptuous hotel room. Theoretically, Larkin and his staff believed patients like Bronwyn should respond positively to such surroundings. Two psychiatric nurses were assigned to her care, and Dr. Larkin himself made several visits. Upon being shown to her first room, Bronwyn sat on the floor rocking and moaning.

The creatures from her nightmarish rooms were snarling and nipping at her heels. When her straightjacket was removed, she fought for her life, striking one nurse so hard that she loosened her tooth. She snatched a lamp from the night table and smashed it on the floor, then huddled in a corner. At last she was restrained by two orderlies and moved to a Spartan-looking cell.

When they removed the safety jacket, she held her hands to her face and began a slow circle of the room, crying, "You see, I have no fingers. The bloodiest price has been extracted." Then she collapsed to the floor, and her sobbing was heard throughout the tiled corridors.

When Dr. Larkin arrived again, he ordered another injection of an anti-psychotic drug. After ordering her hands bandaged, he reassigned her to Room C, where she could be observed continuously and would not be able to hurt herself.

The room was eight by ten feet and contained a hospital bed with securely fastened rails. The walls and floor were padded in a soft green leather. Two cameras, camouflaged in the ceiling, transmitted grainy images of the room to the nursing station.

Twelve hours later, Bronwyn awoke. Lying very still, she tried to focus her eyes on the shiny rails surrounding her. When she attempted to lift up her hands, she tugged at the restraints. Only then did she see the binding on her wrists. The word 'shackles' drifted into her mind. Then she realized her feet were also bound. Bronwyn's cries went unheard at the nursing station; the sound on the monitors had been turned off.

Two floors above, in Dr. Larkin's office, Peter observed his wife on the silent screen. The doctor pressed a button, and the camera zoomed down to capture her silent cries. Peter thought her face looked grotesque on the black-and-white monitor, distorted and strangely disconnected from any reality. Another flick of the switch, and the camera panned to her hands, which were clawing upward against the restraints.

"You see, Mr. Saunderson, we have bandaged her hands."

"Why is that?"

"She thinks she has no fingers, that they have been cut off. Consequently, we are treating her as if this were true. With the bandaging, we hope to promote psychological healing."

"But why does she think that. Can't she see it's not true?"

Dr. Larkin, a large and ponderous man, shrugged. Sitting forward in his chair, he steepled his thick fingers. "The cutting off of fingers could be a symbolic clue to the distortion in her psyche. Perhaps when we feel helpless, impotent, or enraged, we may express that feeling to ourselves by imagining physical injury…" The doctor trailed off, but then added. "Of course, that is only speculation, Mr. Saunderson."

"Bronwyn has always been a very strong woman, doctor."

Dr. Larkin shrugged. "As I say, it's speculation. We must find a working hypothesis. From the very little she has said, it appears she has suffered a severe psychological trauma. Put more specifically, she is seems to be suffering from excruciating guilt, justified or not, caused by some event." Dr. Larkin examined Peter with curiosity. "Do you know what might have caused this?"

Peter shook his head and stared at the monitor for some moments. He could see two nurses enter Room C. One held Bronwyn's hand, and the other fitted a blood pressure cuff on her arm. As soon as one hand was freed, Bronwyn began to scratch and claw, first at her arm and then her leg.

"That's another matter," said the doctor. "Your wife cannot stop scratching herself." Consulting his notes, Dr. Larkin continued, "On examination, we observed red welts formed in a circular pattern on her shoulders, her back, and all down her legs. Have you noticed this condition before, Mr. Saunderson?"

"Bronwyn never complained about that," Peter began. He rose uncomfortably. "You see, my wife and I have not been…intimate for over two years."

"Really?"

"Yes, really." Peter was careful not to let his annoyance show. "Our marriage has had its share of troubles."

"So it would seem, Mr. Saunderson." The doctor sighed and snapped off the monitor. "Has she been taking any medications?"

"As far as I know, only the occasional sleeping pill—and she takes an estrogen replacement therapy."

"Any recent disturbances in her life?"

Peter returned to his chair. He spoke hesitantly. "I assume this is confidential, Dr. Larkin?"

The doctor nodded and laced his fingers across his stomach.

"Bronwyn has been very involved with her godmother, a Mrs. Norma Dinnick." Peter shook his head sadly. "She seems to have become obsessed with the old woman's estate, which I understand is very substantial. As Mrs. Dinnick has no children, Bronwyn thinks it's natural for it all to be left to her." Peter paused. "I should mention that although our marriage isn't perfect, Bronwyn wants for absolutely nothing."

"You mean financially?" The doctor rocked gently in his chair.

"Yes. Anyway, the problem is that Norma apparently has left part of her estate to someone else." Peter hastened to add, "Of course, she's entitled to leave it to whomever she pleases, but that's not what my wife thinks. Bronwyn was put up for adoption, but Norma, who was a friend of her biological mother, has always been a sort of distant benefactor."

The doctor began taking notes. "Yes, please continue."

"In any event, Bronwyn has been joking about eliminating the competition."

Doctor Larkin looked up. "Joking?"

Peter smiled. "I know it sounds strange, but you have to understand Bronwyn's sense of humor."

The doctor set down his pen. "Tell me more."

"It all spilled over this past Monday, when the competition was, in fact, eliminated. You must have seen it in the papers—Archibald Brinks was shot in court."

"He was a beneficiary of the Dinnick estate?"

"Yes."

Doctor Larkin sat back and massaged his brow. Peter pressed onward.

"I think my wife has taken it into her head that she is somehow responsible for his death."

"But she's not?"

"Good heavens, no! I can't imagine how she would be." Peter stood up before the desk, his hands dangling helplessly at his sides. "What can you do for her, doctor?"

The telephone rang.

When the doctor answered, the voice of the resident filled the room. "I think you should see Mrs. Saunderson immediately, sir. She seems entirely lucid right now, and she says she wants to see the police to make a confession and get it over with. Those are her words."

"All right, I'll be down shortly." After he hung up, he said. "It appears there's a lot to what you say, Mr. Saunderson."

"Now just a moment, doctor. I don't want my wife speaking with the police until I get her a good lawyer. I'll protect her in every way I can."

"Certainly not. I'll examine her myself, then give you a call. In the meantime, could you check and confirm what medications she's taking?"

"Certainly. I'll let you know." Peter shrugged himself into his overcoat and said good-bye.

Flanked by his two uniformed officers, Detective McGee returned to Paramour Antiques at precisely five PM. He waved the arrest warrant under Roger's nose.

"You are charged, Mr. Roger Blenheim, with conspiracy to murder one Archibald Brinks on Monday the twenty-fourth of November, 2003."

"But I don't even know him." Roger protested weakly.

He stood quietly as his rights were read to him.

"I want to call my lawyer."

"You can make the call at the station."

Roger went quietly. The officer in the back of the cruiser jammed up against him, grinned, and popped a piece of gum in his mouth. Roger wondered dully whether conspiracy to murder was as serious as murder.

The cruiser drew through a gate in the back of the old City Hall and into a courtyard. They opened the car door and dragged Roger from the backseat. Straightening himself with dignity, Roger said softly, "I am not resisting arrest, officer. You can let go of my arm, and I shall walk."

He stood unsteadily in the cobblestone yard and gazed up at the turrets, black against the sky. Each officer took him by the arm. Engulfed in fear and illness, his legs buckled and he almost sank to the ground. Taking a deep breath, he drew himself up straight and tall.

"Gentlemen?" Roger smiled weakly, "This is the second piece of bad news I have received today. My doctor told me I have HIV.

All three policemen swiftly stepped back.

"Jesus God!" The two officers glanced at each other. McGee chewed his cigar.

Sick as he was, Roger began to derive some pleasure from the situation. "Yes," he continued mildly. "Dr. Radlicov wants to put me on AZT immediately."

Turning beet red, McGee shouted, "Shut up! Just shut your fucking face! Get the hell into the station." None of the three men touched Roger again.

The booking went smoothly. First, they took his photograph and his finger prints. Then he was shown to a pay phone down the hall.

Peter had gone for the day. Roger left a voice message.

After taking his watch, they put him in a cell and left him alone. Roger judged it to be about six thirty when they brought him dinner, setting the tray on a small stool. The lights glared down on the glutinous brown mass of food. About to vomit, he pushed it away.

His sanity hinged on having his watch to keep track of time. In his bright box of a cell, the camera glared down on him from the ceiling. He could hear no sound. First, he paced the perimeter of his cell ten times. Then he sat on the edge of the cot, only to get up and flush the toilet. He paced around five more times. *Where was Peter?* Then he kicked hard at the painted concrete wall and finally slumped on the bed where he lay shivering under the blanket. The mattress stank, and the pillow was a dirty gray bag of lumps.

The heavy, metal door banged open.

"Blenheim!" the red face bellowed. Roger struggled to his feet. "Get your sorry ass moving!"

"Where?"

"Taking you to the interrogation room. Move it!" The guard shoved Roger to the door.

Roger began stammering. "But…but my lawyer's not here. You can't question me without my lawyer."

When he looked up at the guard, he saw the cruel twist to the mouth and the hard, dark eyes. He clung to the cell door. "You can't question me without my lawyer."

Roger did not notice the other guard in the shadows outside the door. Too late, he saw the swift movement of a dark figure stepping into the cell. He heard a strange whistling sound as the club sliced through the air above his head. The metal billy smashed across his right hand.

Writhing on the floor, Roger screamed hysterically. Crushed into a fetal position, he cradled his hand. Hot flames engulfed his entire right side. Whimpering and rocking, he heard the guard growl above him.

"Listen, you dumb fuck! That's where were taking you. Your lawyer's here and waiting for you. Get on your feet." No one reached out to touch Roger as he struggled up on one elbow and finally to his feet.

He was certain his hand was smashed. The guards made way for him. The walk from the cells was at least five minutes long. Stumbling in the dim light, he gingerly tried to move one finger and then another. The hand was black and badly swollen, but maybe all the fingers weren't broken. Unfortunately, sensation was swiftly returning. After walking for what seemed like miles, they rounded a turn in the passage and stopped before a broad wooden door. A guard reached in front of him and swung the door open.

Under a dim ceiling light, Peter sat at a small wooden table. He did not stand to greet his friend, but only motioned him to take the other chair. The guards withdrew and locked the door.

Roger sank into the seat. "Peter, get me out of here," he hissed.

Peter remained silent as he polished his glasses and peered at Roger.

Roger held up his hand, supporting it with the other. "Look what they've done."

"What?"

"They've smashed my hand."

"Who?"

"The guards!"

Peter slowly moved around the table to see. "Can you move the fingers?" Roger was able to wiggle all but the baby one.

Peter looked unimpressed. "Okay. I'll get the doctor at the infirmary to look at it. We'll file a report."

"Jesus, Peter! Is that all you can say?"

"What?" Peter sounded irritated. "What else am I supposed to say?"

"You could be a bit more sympathetic."

Peter took his time. He rose and leaned across toward Roger. Their faces were within inches of each other "Do you have any idea what serious trouble you're in?"

Roger lurched back. "I don't even know who Archibald Brinks is."

"He's the stockbroker who was shot in Osgoode Hall on Monday."

"You mean the guy who...right...it was all on TV. Somebody named Prince shot him."

"Exactly."

"So what have I to do with it?"

"They say they found the murder weapon at your place this morning." Peter could see every line and furrow etched on Roger's face. For just a moment, he was touched by the true innocence of his expression.

But then Roger's eyes flickered and narrowed. The lines of his mouth tightened.

"You mean the Gautier?"

"Whatever one they took this morning," Peter answered.

"But I gave you both of them last week."

Peter smiled pityingly. "Yes, but I gave them back to you on the Friday when you tried to blackmail me."

"Only after your check bounced." Roger sat limply on the straight-backed chair. His head was throbbing, and his hand felt like it was about to explode. When he looked up at Peter, it occurred to him that the bastard was enjoying his little drama. Something was masked behind the self important smirk. He was certain the pistols had not been returned until Monday night.

As if from a great distance, he heard Peter speaking. "Jesus, Roger! Wake up and listen. You look a thousand miles away."

Roger felt more ill than he had all day, but his mind was clearer than ever. He looked into Peter's eyes and saw that smirking mask again. "You're trying to frame me," he whispered.

Peter backed away. "Me? For Christ sake, you must be crazy. I'm trying to save your sorry ass!"

It was a strange experience for Roger. He remembered looking up into Peter's face so closely that he became aware of a strange odor, like venom. His stomach churned.

Silently, he mouthed the word 'motherfucker'. Then he was outside himself, feeling his whole being rising up within. Never had he experienced such power. He watched his own body springing upward at Peter with murderous energy.

Peter jumped back too late. Roger's good hand was around his neck, and he was being transported across the room. He was slammed to the concrete floor. Screaming, Peter clawed at the hand digging into his throat, but it was no use. Roger had mounted him and was crushing him into blackness.

The face above him was a contorted mask of rage mouthing again and again *motherfucker!*

Peter's legs flailed under the crushing weight. The room was closing in. Fighting for air, Peter saw only the twisted grin of the Devourer of Souls.

Then Roger released his grip. Tears flowed down his face. "Goddamn you for what you have done. I really loved you. And you betrayed me, you fucker!"

Neither man was aware of the guards racing in. Roger was pulled from on top and thrown across the room. One guard kicked him hard in the ribs and the other assisted Peter to his feet. As Roger lay curled up and screaming, he was handcuffed. Peter, sank to a chair and, choking for air, began to brush himself off.

"Blenheim, you've just added attempted murder to your list of charges," Peter hissed. "Find yourself another lawyer."

CHAPTER 24

▼

At ten next morning, Harry knocked on his father's door. Stanley answered after a few moments.

"I can shop myself, Harry. You don't have to bother," his father said, holding open the door.

"I know, Dad, but I need to pick up a few things myself." Harry knew his father was pleased.. He determined to make the outing a success.

"All right. I'll get my coat."

His father limped across the living room, sagging just slightly to one side.

"What's happening Dad? You're listing to one side," Harry said.

"Now don't start. I'm just fine." Stanley struggled with his jacket, but Harry hesitated to help. In the sunlight, his father's face looked worn and sleepy, with the corner of his mouth sagging down.

Entering the grocery store, Harry suddenly said, "Dad? Remember Saturday mornings, you used to pull me in the red wagon to go shopping? We'd make a game of how many bags you could get in the cart with me."

Stanley laughed. "Your mother used to get cross and say 'you're going to squish that poor little boy!'"

Inside, they slowly worked their way up and down the aisles. "I can't see so well this morning." Stanley squinted at his list. "I need some coffee and hot cereal. They should be in the next aisle over."

Harry hurried around the corner and found the items. When he returned, his father was leaning to the left over the shopping cart. "Dad? What's wrong?" He tossed the groceries into the cart and supported his father.

Stanley tried to push him back, but was too feeble. Alarmed, Harry righted him and slowly pushed the cart to the checkout, with his father clinging awkwardly to it.

In the car, Harry asked, "What's going on? You look like you're having a stroke."

"Nonsense! I'm fine. I didn't sleep too well on that sofa last night."

"On the sofa? You said you were going to get into bed."

"I turned the TV back on and drifted off, I guess."

Harry gave his father several sidelong glances.

"Damn it! Stop looking at me as if I'm going to keel over," Stanley said as he got out of the car.

"You almost did!" Harry rushed to collect the groceries and open the front door. "I'm worried about you. I think I should take you to the hospital."

"Stop it! I'm not going back there. You're going to drive me crazy if you keep this up."

In the kitchen, Harry put on the coffee, then sat across the table from his father. It was the house he had grown up in. He'd had his breakfast at this table every morning for almost eighteen years. The sun slanted in the window, making patterns through the blinds. Remembering the corn flakes and the orange he'd had every morning, suddenly he could see his mother washing dishes and Dad making little jokes as he helped him with his coat and schoolbooks.

How pale and worn this seventy-five-year-old man looked now. "Dad?" His father looked up from his paper. "I really think you should see a doctor." With new medications available, it was important for a stroke victim to get to the hospital as soon as possible.

Anger flared in the old man's eyes. Harry held his breath.

"What did I say? If you start ordering me around, this just isn't going to work. I'll get the house up for sale and be gone."

"I'm not trying to…"

Waving Harry off, he said, "I'm just short of sleep. I'll catch forty winks before lunch, and I'll be fine."

"Dad?" Harry touched his father's arm. "Why don't you lie down for a bit *now?*"

His father waved angrily. "Goddamn it, I'm fine. Can't I sit at my own kitchen table for a few minutes?"

Harry got up and poured the coffee. "What are your plans for the day?" Suddenly, he had the urge to be outside, to smell the garden, feel the grass underfoot and hear the birds, any birds, just as long as they sang. But it was winter.

"I don't know. Maybe watch TV, sit and read the paper. Go visit Bill across the street."

"Okay. Do you want me to hang around for a bit?"

"No, you get going, but maybe you could come back around supper. Have a bite to eat."

"Actually, I'm supposed to see Natasha tonight. But I could call it off."

"Not on your life, sonny boy!" His father winked and patted Harry's arm. "You don't go standing up a gorgeous woman like her."

My God, despite the arguments, we've talked more this last day or so than we ever have! he thought, heading for the door. "If you need anything, be sure to call me. I put my cell phone number by the phone." Harry felt uneasy leaving, but there was no other way. "Maybe I can come back tomorrow and have a game of cards?"

"Now you don't have to worry…"

Harry turned back and kissed his father, then left.

CHAPTER 25

▼

Peter, now the lawyer for Archie's estate, reported directly to the executor—George Pappas. He was duty-bound to make a preliminary inventory of its assets as soon as possible. Since the share certificate had not showed up in the Parrish estate, it had to be in Archie's stuff. If not, then Norma had it. Dear Bronwyn's godmother, the crafty bitch.

The day of the burial, Peter was in Archie's office. Offering up a silent prayer, he spun the vault's combination lock. Perspiration rolled down his cheeks, and his stomach lurched with fear and anticipation.

The door of the vault swung open easily. Peter grabbed the first bundle of papers and set them on the desk. When he had settled into the deep leather chair, he realized he was panting. Archie had plenty of assets, all recorded in reasonably current lists. He had made a few killings in the market and been wiped out at least twice. But the real money was safely tucked away somewhere else. His hands shook as he slit open the envelopes.

Pappas' booming commands echoed in his head. *You find that share certificate, Saunderson, or find somewhere to hide fast. Don't come back with excuses.*

He unfolded the first document. For God's sake! Norma's will. He tucked it in his briefcase. Peter stacked the remaining envelopes in a pile, trying to maintain a semblance of order. More shares, bonds, and debentures, but nothing relating to Elixicorp.

Find that certificate, Saunderson, or we'll be paying you a visit. Victor's pleasantly smiling face hovered before Peter as he continued his chore. At last all the envelopes were open and their contents spread on the desk.

Jesus! Money everywhere. Stacks of bearer bonds he could cash at any bank, but no Elixicorp share certificate. He picked up the phone, then hesitated. Call the airlines to book a flight? Too obvious. Pappas would be on him in a second. The train? Couldn't get far enough, fast enough. What about the bus? That was it. He could walk right now to the bus station and buy a ticket with cash. Totally anonymous. But a ticket to where?

Peter stuffed a dozen of the highest denomination bearer bonds into his briefcase. Within minutes, he was outside. With the bag clutched to his chest, he leaned into the icy wind slicing down Bay Street and headed for the bus station. Like an insubstantial moth, he was blown into a doorway where he took cover from the blast. Grit swirled up into his eyes, and he shivered in the alcove, wondering if he really cared anymore. Thinking he might get a bus to Florida or Vancouver, he stepped off the curb and into freezing slush, which slopped into his shoe. Shuddering, he was too cold to curse. Five minutes later, he reached the bus station.

In shock, he thought at first the ticket agent was Mr. Prince. Ridiculous! Prince was dead, his body exploded underneath the expressway. The man's chins sagged over his collar, but there was no bow tie. His belly bulged just above his belt, where the buttons were strained.

"When does the next bus leave?" Peter asked.

The ticket agent squirmed around on his stool and said in a falsetto voice, "Whitby at 11:30."

Whitby? Jesus! Peter's shoulders sagged. That was less than an hour away. Pappas would pick him up in time for lunch. "When's the next bus to Vancouver?"

The man laughed unpleasantly. "That's in the other direction, you know."

"What time?" Peter's voice was getting hoarse.

"Not till 12:30, my friend."

Peter set the satchel down between his frozen shoes. From his wallet, he extracted cash. No credit cards on this trip.

The man gave him his ticket and said, "Now you got time for a cup of coffee, friend."

Immediately, Peter recognized the tone. He looked up to see the ticket agent give him a lurid wink. He shuddered. Indeed, Roger had spoiled him for others. No one could ever compare to him in drag. By now, he should be used to propositions, but strangely, they always surprised him. He nearly stumbled over his satchel in his haste to get away.

In the washroom, he ran hot water over his hands and then soaked paper towels to wipe his face. In the mirror, he saw a pale and frightened man on the run. *Better than a dead man*, he thought. He caught a glimpse of the ticket agent waddling down the green-lit hallway. Quickly, Peter turned away.

The white stretch limo circled the block at a leisurely pace. George Pappas looked out at a glass office tower, reflecting a distorted image of the dingy bus station.

"You know what building used to be there, Victor?" asked the old man, pointing at the office tower.

In the front seat, Victor shook his head. "No, sir. What was there?"

The old man smiled in recollection. "The old Ford Hotel, where I used to meet Frank Vinelli for breakfast and talk over old times." Pappas paused to light his cigar. "Back then, Victor, you could trust people to do the job right the first time. Not like today."

"Yes, sir," said Victor quietly.

Peter entered the bus station restaurant and sat at the circular counter far from the window. Suddenly hungry, he ordered two poached eggs on toast, with bacon, orange juice, and coffee. He stared past the rows of chocolate cakes and blueberry and apple pies in the cabinet, and visualized the unending stretches of prairies he would cross until he came to the Rockies. He touched his ticket to Vancouver inside his breast pocket.

To his surprise, a sense of well-being and freedom flooded through him. Leave Bronwyn, the grasping, grabbing shrew, behind. He would not miss his law partners either. But the image of Roger, dressed up as Roxanna, made him wistful. But, no doubt, there would be others.

Outside, Pappas ordered his driver to park the limo across the street from the bays for loading the buses. He lowered the window and tossed out his cigar.

Inside, Peter skewered the bright yellow egg yolk and watched it run across his toast. Imagining life without Bronwyn, Roger, or the law, he reveled in the prospect of freedom. "Just walk away," he whispered. When he took his first bite, energy flooded through him. Then he grinned. "An opportunity to be seized."

Savoring each morsel of his breakfast, he thought that food had never tasted so good. As his eyes roved over the old-fashioned miniature jukebox on the counter, he calculated the value of the bearer bonds in the satchel at almost a million and a half. Nice start. Why stop in Vancouver? He could go on to Hong Kong. The prospects were unlimited. Glancing at his watch, he debated whether to have a second cup of coffee, since the bus wouldn't load for another half hour. He decided to browse the magazine rack.

The white stretch limo had moved onto Bay Street just beyond Peter's view. The engine idled gently and made little puffs of white in the frigid air. Pappas smiled wanly and ordered Victor to enter the restaurant.

Peter glanced out the window and shivered, knowing that he would not miss the godforsaken city and his shitty life. He leafed through magazines on cars and men's health. Time to start taking better care of himself, he thought. He could stay in Vancouver for a few days, then catch a flight to Hong Kong, maybe even a freighter. The romance of the notion appealed to him greatly. Stretching expansively, he reached for the latest Time magazine. Better have lots to read on the bus.

"Hello Peter!" The voice came from behind him, and a hand clamped his shoulder. Peter's gut knew before his head. He turned to look up into Victor's bland face. Shaking his head in disbelief, he backed away only to step into another man. Both of them had neatly combed hair and clean-shaven jaws. Their navy wool topcoats were identical. In a spasm, Peter jerked sideways. Each man took an arm, nearly lifting him off the ground.

"Mr. Pappas would like a word with you, Peter." Victor said in a friendly fashion. The other man picked up the satchel and swung it over his shoulder.

Outside, when Peter saw the white stretch limo, the image of distant mountains faded in his mind. Politely, Victor held the door open for him. He could try to run, but he would be lying dead on the ice and cement within seconds. There was no point in struggling, and he wondered once again whether he really cared. The car was warm and dark inside. Pappas watched him, red-eyed and rat-like.

"You didn't find the shares, did you Peter?" Pappas voice was smooth with false patience.

Terrified, Peter shook his head.

"You were trying to run away, weren't you?"

Unable to speak, Peter shook his head violently.

Victor turned around and took the bus ticket from Peter's breast pocket. Smiling sadly, he examined the ticket. "He has a bus ticket for Vancouver, sir."

"Nowhere is far enough, Peter. You know that." Pappas concluded quietly.

Slowly, the limo pulled away from the curb. The driver nodded, acknowledging some unspoken command from Pappas. They drove down Bay Street toward the expressway. Peter could not speak.

The white limo turned left and headed up the ramp to the expressway, which ended in mid-air.

"Please, Mr. Pappas…"

Pappas offered Peter a cigar, which he silently declined. "Where do you think that certificate might be? You tell me the Parrish estate doesn't have it. Running away tells me you didn't find it in Archie's. Now you wouldn't be hiding it from me, would you Peter?"

Aghast, Peter shook his head. "Mr. Pappas, I've been completely loyal to you for twenty years. Please…" Now the limo raced along the roadway high above the city and lake.

Pappas waved his hand to silence him. Then he nodded in the direction of the satchel. "What's in there?"

"Just some of Archie's assets. I was taking them to record them properly."

"In Vancouver?"

Peter was silent. Tears sprang to his eyes. "Please, sir. I panicked. I wasn't thinking straight."

Pappas smiled grandly. Peter could only focus on his cracked and yellow teeth.. "Please forgive me, sir. Please don't…"

The old man turned his face to the window. The limo pulled to a stop at the barricades. "You've seen how we deal with incompetence, Peter."

Peter was overcome with the memory of Mr. Prince's cowering bulk, stooping to undo his shoelaces at the edge of the precipice. "Mr. Pappas. You must believe me. Please forgive me!"

"I don't like begging, Peter." Pappas puffed on his cigar. "Tell me why I should forgive you."

Peter saw the body of Mr. Prince arc out over the edge. He saw Prince's sock fly skyward. "Because…" Peter was shaking violently. "I was frightened. I made a foolish error. Please, sir. I have done my best. I know it's nowhere good enough…"

Pappas smiled almost gently. "You do not deserve it, but I am going to give you one more chance."

Peter nearly collapsed in relief. "Thank you, sir…I am very grateful," he whimpered.

Pappas cut him short. "There is one last task for you."

Stumbling over his words, Peter cried out, "Thank you. Whatever it is, I'll do it!"

Pappas bent close to him. "Norma Dinnick has that certificate. Get it from her, and kill her." He turned away in disgust. "That shriveled old cunt!"

Peter stared dumbly at Pappas. "Of course, sir. I'll do it right away."

Pappas patted his hand. "This is your last chance." He nodded to Victor, and the limo turned abruptly and raced back to the ramp. At King and Bay, Peter jumped from the car and hurried inside his office. Shivering, he huddled into his desk chair and telephoned Ross Brackley.

CHAPTER 26

▼

When Harry was getting ready to see Natasha, he decided to check on Stanley before he shaved.

"I'm fine, son! Couldn't be better. Why aren't you off to see your lady friend?"

"I'm going soon, Dad. I just wanted to be sure you're okay. How was your afternoon?"

"Good! Bill came over, and we had a beer together. Mother's in the kitchen fixing the supper."

Harry stared at the receiver. Not more about Mother! "Dad? Are you sure you're okay?"

Stanley growled, "Yes! Now will ya stop bothering me?" He hung up.

Was his father hallucinating, like Norma with her upstairs tenants? He decided to call again from Natasha's place. Beset with images of his father slumped at the bottom of the cellar steps, he headed out.

Turning down Bathurst Street, he passed under the railway viaduct and into a desolate row of darkened garages and boarded-up storefronts. Large chunks of black sludge flew up against his windshield. Turning his wipers on high, he saw a long, white limousine slowly pass him and then pull into his lane. The windows were tinted, so he could not see any of the passengers.

Harry froze. Surely not Pappas's men! He dropped back and pulled onto a side street. The limo braked, turned, and followed him. Stopping, he locked his doors and searched for his cell phone. The limousine glided past. Closing his eyes, he exhaled deeply. After a few minutes, he backed up and continued down Bathurst Street, glancing every so often in the rearview mirror. To push Pappas' men out of his mind, he tried to concentrate on the evening ahead.

He was, he had to admit, worried about his performance the other night. As soon as thoughts of Dad overtook him, passion went into a tailspin. On top of that, *he* had shut her out by running off. Ironic, how silence had always frightened him! It had grown like a plague in his marriage to Laura. His love affair with Katrina had ground silently to a halt. And so, with Natasha, he felt it important to talk. And who was the one to walk out? *The fool*, of course!

It made perfect sense to live together, to try it out. More than anything, he wanted to be sure of her. He decided to discuss it over dinner. He thought of her question. *What do you think love is, Harry?* He saw no difference in their answers.

Natasha welcomed him at the door. Immediately, he felt the surge of desire. He stepped inside and drew her close. Her kiss was warm and full of promise. Smiling, he hung up his coat, and she returned to the kitchen.

Over her shoulder she called out, "Harry, please pour us some wine and come talk to me."

Her tone was lovely and seductive. He hurried to find the wine glasses and join her in the kitchen. Back turned to him, she washed carrots and beans in the sink. Drawn by her lovely, natural grace, he reached behind her and, touching her breast, kissed the nape of her neck. She smiled and leaned slightly into him as she continued her work. For moments, they stood close together without speaking. He watched her deftly peeling carrots and then cutting them into delicate strips.

"Harry, would you set the table, please?"

Happily, he rooted about for silverware and plates, reveling in thoughts of domesticity. Surely she belonged with him. Then he poured her the wine. She stopped her work to take a sip. They sat at the counter in companionable silence.

She touched his knee. "Can you stay the night?"

"Of course," he whispered close in her ear. Suffused with happiness, he wondered how to experience their love as an everyday event. He covered her hand with his. Smiling, she withdrew it to put on an oven mitt.

"The beef bourguignon needs a stir," she said, sliding off the stool. Within moments, she had lifted the pot from the oven and removed the lid. Harry was overwhelmed by the rich, delicious aroma of her cooking.

Just before she served the dinner, he called Stanley.

"How's everything, Dad?"

"What the hell are you doing?"

"Pardon?"

"Why aren't you romancing your girlfriend? Something wrong with you?"

"Just checking to see you're okay."

"Well, stop. I told you I was fine." He hung up.

Harry frowned. It seemed like he was slurring his words.

They sat at the kitchen counter to eat.

"How *is* your father, Harry?" she asked.

Harry grinned. "The good part is that we're talking. When I *really* forgave him, that just seemed to get us started."

"Wonderful!" Natasha was pleased to hear his excitement.

He told her about his father running back home from the hospital and threatening to leave for Halifax. "All I said was *let's start talking now.*

"He must have seen that you really meant it. That's great."

"But I'm really worried, Natasha. I think he may be going to have a stroke, if he hasn't already. There's a bit of sagging on his left side, and I think his speech is a bit slurred."

"Is he okay alone?'

Harry threw up his hands. "Maybe not, but I really have to let him live his own life. Otherwise, there'll be no connection at all."

She smiled in sympathy and touched his hand. "Very wise, but it's hard to give the ones you love the space they need. Perhaps he'll ask for help if he trusts you not to take over."

"I guess that's the best I can hope for."

When they were done, she cleared the plates. Harry helped put everything in the dishwasher as she served the fruit and cheese for dessert. In the living room, they drank their coffee.

Feeling a twinge of nervousness, he began, "Natasha, we were going to talk about the future…"

She came to sit beside him, gently touching her finger to his lips. "This isn't the time for talk, Harry. Just show me how you love me." She ran her hand along his thigh.

They rose and went down the hall to her bedroom. Standing by the bed, they undressed each other, letting the pleasure build slowly. Then she motioned him to lie down. Harry was amazed, as ever, at the way she could transform his fantasies into reality. Smiling, she slid on top of him. Soon, Harry was overwhelmed by her loveliness. There was no time for thought or hesitation. Immediately, he was ready for her. Afterwards, they fell asleep, bodies entwined. Sometime around two, they awoke to make love, slowly and sleepily, before drifting off again.

At eight o'clock, Harry awoke rested from the most peaceful sleep he'd had in weeks. She rose to make coffee. Together, they spent an hour in bed leafing through the Sunday papers.

He sat up and put his cup aside. "Natasha? Let's talk now."

"All right, Harry." She folded up the paper.

"We've been seeing each other for almost a year."

She smiled slightly at his formal tone.

He cleared his throat. "I'd love it if we could try living together. You know how much I love you."

She kissed his cheek. "Harry? Tell me again what you think love is."

He was taken aback. "You mean a definition?"

She nodded. "Yes. I mean *your* definition. Have you thought about it since we last talked?"

He playfully snuggled down beside her and began kissing her shoulder and neck.

She laughed and pushed him away. "No. I mean it. You wanted to talk, so let's talk."

He sat up straight. "All right. I think it's about loving and caring about someone so much that you want the person with you all the time."

"So it's about how a person makes *you* feel?"

Wary of a trap, he said, "Well, yes. But, not just that."

"What else then?"

He lay back against the pillow and stared at the ceiling. "It's wanting the person because you think she makes you a better person. Which you do."

"And?"

He sat up and fidgeted with the papers. "I don't know. What do you think?"

She took his question seriously. "Love gets you outside yourself and into another person's life, another world. At first, you almost lose yourself in exploring that person. You measure yourself and your life to see if there's a need and a fit. Once you're in that person's world, you want to stay there. You don't lose your own self, but something bigger is created."

"Is that different from what I've said?"

"Yes. Very." She turned to him, "You think of love from your own perspective. I think it's about knowing and understanding another person enough to let him be himself. Like you're doing with your Dad. You love him enough to let him try being on his own without controlling him. Even at the risk of losing him."

"But aren't we saying the same thing? You're in my world to make it better, and I'm in yours for the same reason."

She shook her head. "Suppose you love someone deeply, or at least you think you do, but they're not ready. Can you ever love someone enough to let them go, if that is what they want?"

Frowning, Harry asked, "Is that what *you* want?"

"No. But I want more time to know you better. Let it happen. Besides, unless you really know someone, how can you say you love them?" She kissed his lips softly.

He knew he sounded foolish, but could not resist. "How much time?"

She drew away from him and put on her robe. "It's like with your father. If you love the man, as a son, you have to let him be himself. If you don't, how can you ever know you really love the person and not just some idea of him?"

Harry began to dress. "So what are you saying, Natasha?" He spoke stiffly.

She came to him at the window. "I'm saying that we just might have something wonderful here, which could last a lifetime. We need to give it time. Time to really know each other. Sometimes, Harry, I think you are in love with a fantasy, not with me."

Harry sighed. Only an idiot could miss her message. He wasn't being shown the door. He promised himself to relax and let it happen.

CHAPTER 27

▼

Ross Brackley watched Norma's darkened apartment building from underneath the willow tree in the back yard. Orders from Saunderson were orders from the top. No screw-ups.

He had said "I want those goddamned shares now. Do whatever's necessary to find them—and when you've got them, kill her."

Stamping his feet in the cold, Brackley took a last pull on his flask, then wiped his mouth on his sleeve. He knew he was on the bottom rung; his feral instincts made him wary.

The back porch light cast shadows across the lawn. Brackley tried to stay in the dark as he trudged to the front of the building. He could see her, asleep in her chair, through the bay window. He opened the outer door to the foyer.

It was so dark and cramped inside, that he stumbled. Something soft and feathery whisked his ankle. Jumping back, he kicked out. A soft, snarling body of fur lay at his feet. He felt along the wall in search of a light switch. When he switched it on, the foyer was illuminated in a ghastly, pale yellow light.

"Jesus Christ," he swore under his breath. A rat-like ball of fur lay curled about his feet. Recoiling in horror, he smashed his skull against a coat hook. Cursing again, he poked at the creature with his foot. At first, the stunned animal stirred only slightly. Then, shakily, it brought itself to all fours and hissed. *A goddamned cat!* With a bark of laughter, Brackley pounced on the animal, opened the door, and flung it out onto the lawn.

Norma was snoozing in her armchair, still waiting for the taxi driver to take her to Madrid Towers. She was so tired that she wished to slip away forever into the soft, seductive twilight, but there was still too much work to be done. She had to secure the shares, just as Arthur had said.

Her eyes flew open at the sound of frenzied banging. *They can't be back upstairs so soon. Why won't they leave me alone? I'll be joining them soon enough.* She cocked her head to one side until she realized that the banging was from the front door.

"Just a minute!" She shuffled across the living room, stopping to smooth a bed sheet covering the chesterfield. "I'm coming! Don't bang so." Reaching the door, she stopped and listened intently.

"Who is it?" she demanded.

Another crash rattled the door.

"Please!" she shrieked. "Who is it?"

"I'm from Mr. Jenkins office," boomed the voice on the other side of the door.

Thank heavens! The taxi driver, she thought.

Norma twisted the wires from the latch and reached up to remove the chain. Outside, Brackley, his patience wearing thin, whistled tunelessly through his teeth. After several minutes, the door creaked open. Suspicious eyes peered out.

"Are you here to take me to the home?" Norma asked.

"Sure, lady, but Mr. Jenkins sent me for the shares. I gotta take them back with me."

"What shares?" Norma asked.

"The Elixicorp shares, lady." Ross Brackley tossed his coat on the chesterfield and cracked his knuckles.

She backed away from the immense man. Harry knew she didn't have the shares, and he would never have sent the beast now standing before her.

Norma gathered up her strength. "Young man! What is your name?"

Ross was actually a bit intimidated by the fiery little woman. "Brackley, ma'am," he said. *Doesn't matter if she knows my name*, he thought. *She'll be dead soon enough.*

"Sit down at once," she commanded in her most imperious tone. "I'll get the shares, but you must be patient and wait here. I'm an old lady, and if you come barging into my home, you'll have to wait until I hunt them up."

Brackley sat down and picked up a magazine.

Norma tottered off toward the bedrooms. At the kitchen door, she turned back to scold him again. Then, slipping into the kitchen, she reached under the counter and took out the cast-iron frying pan. Slowly, she crept down the back hall to the bedroom, frying pan in hand.

Brackley sprang from his chair and began to pace the living room. What in hell was the old broad doing? At last he heard her call.

"Young man, please come. I need some help."

Instantly, Brackley was down the hallway and into her room. He saw her half-buried in the closet.

She craned her neck to see him. "Well, don't just stand there gawking! I'll never find those shares if you don't help me get this box out."

He pushed her aside and then, dropping to all fours, he crawled into the closet. Norma smiled to see his huge rear end bobbing as he struggled with the box. Lifting the frying pan from the bureau, she took aim and brought it down swiftly on the back of his skull.

Brackley lay sprawled in the closet, but only for a moment. Grasping the back of his neck, he leapt to his feet, bellowing incoherently. With blood flowing down the side of his head, he lunged at her. Norma hurried from the room and tried to lock the door. But she was too late. He staggered after her.

Norma ran to the bathroom, locked herself in, and collapsed, quivering, on the toilet seat. For a moment, all was silent. She clutched the frying pan as if clinging for to life itself.

In the hallway outside, Brackley leaned against the wall and positioned his foot just above the lock on the door. A few hard kicks would smash it in. The first crashing blow nearly splintered the door from its hinges. "Open the door, you fucking old hag!" he roared.

Leaning against the wall, he raised his leg and positioned his foot just above the lock on the door. A few hard kicks would smash it in.

Shaking in terror, Norma heard the crashes. One, two, three! The wood splintered around the lock. Four, five six! The door bounced and swayed on its hinges.

"Oh, Arthur, help me!" she screamed, sliding to her knees and knocking her head on the porcelain sink.

Finally, the door caved in. Brackley towered above her.

"You goddamned bitch! You tried to kill me!" Reaching down, he grabbed the back of her neck. With one arm, he snatched her from the floor and flung her into the bathtub. "Where are the shares?" he shouted.

There was no reply. The tiny body was slumped awkwardly in the tub, entirely still. Brackley stood above her, his huge hands dangling uselessly at his sides. *Shit! Now I have to tear the place apart.*

Suddenly, he was swept with deep dread. He knew what happened to those who failed. He knelt by the side of the tub and stared at her. Grasping her jaw, he turned her head sharply and felt for a pulse. He could find none.

Instinct told him to run, but his fingerprints would be all over the place. With a wet cloth, he tried to rub her face and arms. Shit! Even worse. Now his blood was on her neck. Heart pounding in his chest, he stuffed the cloth in his jacket and ran from the apartment. Outside, he squeezed behind the wheel and sped from the driveway. He was a dead man. No one could hide from Pappas.

The bathtub was hard and cold. Every fiber of Norma's body screamed in pain, but that meant she was still alive. With her body immobilized, her mind was released to trip through years of confused recollections of George. Soon she did not know if he were dead or alive.

At the King Edward Hotel, that cold December night in 1963, the prospectus for the Elixicorp shares was launched. George had spun his seductive tale of riches for the elite of Toronto. How they fell for it! Only he could have pulled it off. Lying helpless in the tub, Norma's rage and humiliation rekindled.

George had towered over everyone at the party later that night in the suite. His bark of laughter, his gravely and seductive voice, and his brilliant patina of sophistication and wealth made him irresistible. Like a moth to the candle, she was helplessly drawn to him. Around George, she understood lust.

"Norma, come here!" he commanded.

Arthur was nowhere in sight. Probably hanging back in some corner, she thought. She went to George.

"Where's your husband, Norma? He shouldn't leave you alone with me like this." Pappas winked and encircled her waist with his arm. "Tell Artie he's lost this one!" When he tossed back his head in laughter, a gold tooth glinted in the light. Surrounded by his retinue, Pappas had everything.

Another glass of champagne mysteriously appeared in her hand. She giggled as he tipped it upward for her. Then George was gone, and another man stood next to her. Touching her arm, he gently guided her to another room.

"Mr. Pappas will join you soon, Mrs. Dinnick."

When he snapped on a lamp, Norma saw that she was in a beautiful bedroom. In silence, the man withdrew. Mouth agape, she explored the immense marble bathroom fitted with gold, then returned to the bedroom and smoothed the burgundy silk bedspread.

Scarcely glancing at her, George entered the room. "Take that dress off, Norma. Get under the covers."

The ultimate moment of her fantasies had arrived. Aching for him, she said, "There are people out there. Arthur's around somewhere."

Pappas waved dismissively. "There's a man at the door. No one will come in. And Artie's a bit under the weather right now."

Sitting on the bed, he pulled her down beside him. "I said, get undressed."

Norma quivered with excitement and hastened to obey. In silence, she lay down for him.

Now, as she lay in the bathtub, Norma remembered every detail. George had only removed his jacket and unzipped his fly. Then he was above her, grunting and wheezing. So vivid was her recollection that she twisted away in the tub, crying out, "Please, George, I want you so much, but slow down." She clung to him in the darkness.

Like a dumb and blind beast, Pappas thrust himself inward without a thought for any pleasure but his own. Desperately, she tried to catch his rhythm, but it was no use. Pain seared inward and upward. She saw his eyes roll upward at his lone climax and then, grunting and heaving, he collapsed onto the bed. It was over in less than a minute. He rolled sideways and lay panting beside her. Norma was stunned and heartbroken.

In search of a washroom, Arthur opened the door and felt for the light switch. For years to come, he would wish he had never found it. The ceiling bulb lit the room in a harsh and ugly light.

Norma's shrieks hung in the air. Pappas stared hard at him as he stopped to adjust his clothing. Arthur slunk from the room. Outside, he leaned against the wall and covered his face. Why didn't he seize the rapacious fornicator? Because the beast was George Pappas.

Shivering in the bathtub, Norma sought an ending to her nightmare. She hated George for dashing her dreams. He was no lover at all, just a blind, brutish animal, who thought only of gratifying his own pleasure.

In her mind, she created a different ending. In fury, she saw her own strong hand rising above his shoulder. She saw the flashing blade plunging deep into Pappas' neck.

He would be nothing without me. Everything he has was obtained by me.

In her vision, blood spurted everywhere. Eyes bulging, Pappas shied off like a panicked beast. Frenzied, he tried to pull out the knife but could not. The wound was too deep, and it was too late. Pappas faded quickly and Norma watched his body collapse in spasms. Funny little gurgles came from his mouth and his eyes grew flat and dead.

Norma, in her version, heard the wind whistling down from the high meadow behind Mama's house. She saw the dark shadows on the ceiling of her bedroom in Mama's house, and she shuddered. All alone then, and all alone now. Stranded in the bathtub, she was convinced that George was dead.

Mr. Grieves, the lone tenant, heard Norma's cries. He banged on the door and then tried the handle. The door swung open. He found her, fully clothed, in the bathtub. He dared not touch her, but called for the ambulance.

When the paramedics arrived, they hoisted her onto a stretcher. "You related, sir?" they asked Mr. Grieves.

He shook his head and backed out of the apartment. "I'm just a tenant. Her name is Norma Dinnick. That's all I know."

Once strapped onto the stretcher, Norma began to cry, "Harry? Where are you? I need you now." She clutched the paramedic's sleeve.

"Who's Harry, ma'am? Your husband or your son?"

Norma struggled to sit up, but the straps held her tightly. "Please, Harry! They've captured me again."

The paramedics smiled at each other. "Not another one!"

"I want Harry, my lawyer," Norma demanded.

"Ma'am, we're taking you to hospital, not jail."

She told the emergency room nurse that a Mr. Brackley had attacked her in her very own home. But, failing to provide the name of the Prime Minister or the day of the week, Norma was admitted to hospital for psychiatric examination.

The next morning, Norma blinked her eyes open. She was surrounded by orange fuzz, which she concluded was a blanket. Her hands and nose were cold. She heard noises off in the distance but could not turn to see. She was captured, bound in place.

"Help, please! Somebody help me." She strained to listen for a reply, but heard none. Ten minutes later, the curtain around the bed was torn back, making the metal rings screech on the track.

Norma saw shadowy figures surrounding her. She supposed that the ones from upstairs had come for her. Arthur, George, David and Archie were all beckoning her. She either joined them or stayed behind to be put in jail.

Dr. Waisberg, head of the geriatric department, stood at her bedside. In tow were residents, wearied from hours of speculation upon the madness of a slew of patients. All were used to discussing the patients' maladies as if they were also deaf, dumb, and blind. Someone in the back row stifled a yawn.

"Preliminary diagnosis?" barked Waisberg.

"Paranoid schizophrenia," one intern piped up.

Dr. Waisberg was a tall, gaunt man whose spectacles persisted in slipping down his nose. Before him, he saw an exceedingly frail woman of greatly advanced age, peering up at him with keen interest.

"Arthur! Thank heavens you've come for me." Norma, face wreathed in smiles, struggled to sit up.

The doctor proceeded to undo the first clasp of straps. "Nurse? Why is this patient confined?"

"She's been demanding to be let out of jail. Earlier, she slid off the bed and tried to escape, doctor."

One resident unwisely snickered. Dr Waisberg swiveled about in the cramped quarters, almost twisting himself up in the curtain. "Dr. Friedlander, since you find this case so amusing, would you care to come forward and share your insights?"

Silently, the mass of residents parted to make way for the hapless Dr. Friedlander, then regrouped around the bed. Waisberg continued to unbuckle the straps. Once freed, Norma grasped the doctor's hand so firmly he winced.

"Arthur! Take me out of here." She blinked up at him happily.

"Madam, I am Dr. Waisberg. Who is Arthur?"

Norma saw only her Arthur, mouthing words, which made no sense. He looked so stern—what could he be saying? *Norma, you have betrayed me!* she heard in her tired mind.

Norma burst into tears. Her shoulders shook so piteously that Dr. Waisberg was moved to slip his arm about her. Awkwardly, he patted her back.

Through gasps and sniffles, she demanded, "Arthur, how can you accuse me of betrayal? Everything I've done has been for you."

The residents were riveted by the pleading in her eyes.

"All these years, I've kept the shares from David, George and Archie!" Norma cried out, twisting from the bed so violently that the doctor lurched back, almost tearing the curtain from its rings.

Balancing herself on the very edge of the bed, she raged, "You infuriate me, Arthur Dinnick! I know I wasn't one hundred percent faithful, but George raped me at the King Edward. Even though you walked in and *saw* he'd raped me, you didn't rescue me."

Norma drew herself up and said with great dignity, "I killed George because you weren't man enough to protect me. I stabbed him to death."

With his mouth agape, Dr Waisberg made notes at a furious pace. The residents tried to hide their grins.

"I hated that rapacious…beast! And I *so* wanted you to help me." Norma tugged on the doctor's sleeve. Waisberg tried, without success, to free himself.

"David wanted the shares, too." Guile softened her tone. "So I had to stop him." Her jaw jutted out defiantly. "Only I could have persuaded him to climb the Statue of Liberty with his weak heart."

Dr. Waisberg was attempting to peel her fingers from the buttons of his white coat. Stunned into silence, all the residents gathered at the head of the bed in a tight knot.

"So what if David and I were lovers? You were gone, remember? But he was nothing to me." Norma sat back on the bed, releasing the doctor.

She began inspecting her fingernails. "But I made absolutely certain he didn't get the shares." Sighing deeply, Norma continued, "I had to stop Archie, too. I knew what would happen if I sued him and George, but he deserved it. Archie was absolutely the worst, trying to drive me mad so I couldn't change my will. Pestering me for the shares. He drugged me! He tried to starve me. He only bought Coke and doughnuts for me to live on." She giggled. "So George finished him off. I thought it was very clever *and* such fun, setting the cat among the pigeons."

Dr. Waisberg shook his head and clicked his ballpoint pen nervously. Consulting his clipboard, he asked cautiously, "But didn't you tell us that you stabbed George?"

Norma stared at the doctor as if he were an obtuse child. "That's exactly right, Arthur. I did say that."

Doctor Friedlander spoke tentatively. "But sir, she didn't say exactly *when* she stabbed George."

Waisberg gave the junior his best withering glance. Collectively, the retinue shuffled outside to the hallway. Waisberg cleared his throat. "Friedlander! Given the diagnosis of paranoid schizophrenia, what should we prescribe for the patient at her age?"

"Sir?" Friedlander shouldered his way to the front. "But what if the diagnosis is wrong?"

"Wrong?" Waisberg glared at the young resident over the tops of his glasses.

"Yes, sir. What if everything she's said is true?"

"That's ridiculous!" spluttered the doctor. "She's an old woman who is clearly hallucinating and completely disoriented. Do you really think she is capable of such acts?" As if offended, he concluded, "She thought I was her deceased husband, Arthur." Waisberg snapped his book shut. "You, Harcourt! What do we prescribe?"

From the back, Harcourt spoke. "For emergency treatment, Haldol, sir."

"Fine! At least someone is paying attention here," Waisberg grumbled. "Next patient!"

Norma's behavior became increasingly bizarre as the night wore on. She veered from cowering in her bed to skittering out into the corridors to beg passersby for forgiveness and release. She demanded the presence of her solicitor, Harold Jenkins, to free her from her unjust incarceration. Occasionally, her face was wreathed with smiles as she looked heavenward, saying. "I'm coming as soon as I can, Arthur. Don't rush me."

At last the night resident, Dr. Holloway, entered her room. Without a word, he held up a needle and took her arm. Norma screamed and wrestled away from him. Two nurses held her legs and arms. Blackness swept over her, and soon she was asleep.

The night resident noted her chart. Lost in his study of it, he returned to the nursing station and read more about her confessions of murder. He reached for the phone and called Harold Jenkins, who was listed as her solicitor.

The doctor got Harry's voice mail. "This is Dr. Holloway calling from the Toronto General Hospital about a client of yours, Norma Dinnick. She's made some very unusual statements, which I would like to discuss with you as soon as possible." Holloway left his pager number and hung up.

CHAPTER 28

▼

Harry drove home from Natasha's around noon on Sunday. His cell phone rang.

"Mr. Jenkins? It's Doctor Gervais calling from the Toronto General Hospital calling. Your father is in emergency. I'm afraid he's had a stroke."

Nearly dropping the phone, Harry wheeled the car around. Pangs of guilt assaulted him as he asked, "When did it happen? Is he conscious?"

"Yes, his speech is affected, but we're sure he's asking for you."

"I'll be there in five minutes."

In Emergency, he was shown into a tiny cubicle with green curtains drawn around it. His father lay under a flimsy blanket with a cone over his nose for oxygen.

Harry touched his father's hand, then sank to a chair. Stanley looked shriveled up like a dry husk. "Dad?"

Stanley's eyes flickered in recognition.

"Dad, I'm *so* sorry! I shouldn't have left you alone."

Stanley tried to mouth a word or two. Harry bent closer and strained to hear, but there was nothing.

The doctor appeared from behind the curtain. "You're his son?"

Without taking his eyes from his father, Harry nodded. "Yes. I'm Harry, his son."

"Your Dad's suffered a mild stroke, but we think we've got him on the right meds in time. We'll have to admit him for observation."

"Can he move?"

"Yes, but he's weak on the left side. His speech is impaired, and we suspect he doesn't understand what's being said. "We're going to do a CAT scan to assess the damage."

"What can I do?" Harry felt helpless and guilty.

"Stay with him, if you can. Talk to him. If he seems tired, let him drift off."

When the doctor left, Harry pulled a chair up and rested his head against the bed rail. His father blinked but did not speak. Then he drifted off to sleep.

Harry went to find a cup of coffee. In the empty waiting room, he sat down and leafed through magazines. CNN blared out the latest news on Iraq. Looking about, Harry saw a deck of cards on a far table.

His eyes stung with tears. Dad used to entertain him with cards on long summer afternoons on the porch, when it was too hot to move. Anna sat nearby, always alone with her books. Had she lived, he might not be in this waiting room, with his heart breaking for all the lost years between them.

He tried hard to remember his father before Anna's death. He had been an easy, friendly man, open to life and to people. Not like himself, who analyzed and scrutinized each particle of experience until the life in it was extinguished. Once Dad had loved and accepted life just as it was. And then Anna died and the light went out.

He pocketed the cards and returned to his father's cubicle. His father, and the bed, were gone. A nurse came in to say he had been taken for the CAT scan. Harry sat alone in the empty cubicle on a red plastic chair.

Absently, he began to shuffle the well-worn pack. He saw his father taking him by the hand along the street to the bakery, the shoe repair, and the fruit store. He must have been only five years old, but the memories had such intense clarity that Harry caught his breath. Dad stopped and chatted with everyone. That was his father before Anna died. Afterwards, he only went out to work, and Mother took over the shopping. Silence engulfed the house.

Harry was twelve when he stopped trying. No longer did he try to interest Dad in anything. What the hell for? Why bother? And then he was old enough to leave for University. Thank Christ he was out of that godforsaken house and back into life.

Even when he won his scholarships, Dad only grunted. Once in a while mother would call, trying to sound cheery, pretending Dad was just a little out of sorts. Nothing serious, of course. Goddamn it! Nothing was right, and Dad kept getting farther away from the world. Then he stopped caring. Once out of law school, he rarely saw his parents. After mother died, he left for good.

I want to go back and change it all, he suddenly thought. *But I can't. It's too late.*

Would he be different if he had not hardened his heart? But he only did so to protect himself from pain. Maybe he and Laura would have stayed together. Maybe Katrina would not have gone away without a word. *Who knows?* he sighed.

He knew, in his heart, that the yawning void within drove him to secure love. Natasha was talking about exactly that. Trying to fix people in place so they would not leave him. Never trusting enough to really love. He sank his head into his hands and closed his eyes. Somehow, he had to make things right between them. He smiled grimly at the irony of it all. Just as they were learning to talk, a stroke had rendered his father nearly incoherent.

The orderly wheeled his father's stretcher into the cubicle.

"Dad? You're awake."

His father smiled weakly. Harry found a Kleenex and dabbed at the drool trickling down his chin.

"How about a game of cards?" Holding out the deck, he shuffled and dealt the cards. "Pick them up, Dad."

His father's hands did not move. Picking the cards up for him, Harry organized the suits. Helplessness was reflected in his father's eyes.

"Dad?" Harry knew his father could not play, so he would play for him. His father had shown him all the suits when he was a little kid, sick in bed. "Point to all the Spades."

At first there was no response, and Harry thought it was hopeless. "Dad? Point to all the Jacks, and I'll give them to you. You've got a great hand here."

Still no response. Harry waited for what seemed like ages. With his hope almost gone, he saw his father's frail fingers creep across the covers to touch both Jacks.

"Come on, Dad. You can do it. Point out the Spades you want to play." His father's hand slowly reached out for the ten and eight of Spades. Tears welled in Harry's eyes when the old man's face creased into a crooked, lop-sided smile.

"You're doing it Dad! That's fantastic." Harry leaned over and hugged him for only the second time in many years.

The doctor appeared in the doorway. "Mr. Jenkins? Could you come to the nursing station so we can talk for a moment?"

Harry followed. At the desk, the resident consulted the results of the scan. "I'm afraid there's been some pretty extensive damage. We'll admit him so we can watch him for another forty eight hours."

"What's the prognosis?"

The resident shook his head. "Too early to tell, but I think you should be looking into nursing homes, if you haven't already."

"I was playing cards with him just now," Harry said. "And he could identify the suits." Then he realized how like an eager child he sounded.

"Terrific, Mr. Jenkins. Don't worry, we'll keep a close eye on your Dad."

Harry returned to the cubicle. His father was asleep with the playing cards spread on the blanket. Gently, he stroked his forehead and kissed him. Then he hurried from the room.

CHAPTER 29

▼

When the hospital called Harry to tell him about Norma, he burned with righteous indignation. Peter had promised to protect her. Instead, the bastard had set the beast on her.

"Peter! I want to meet with you immediately."

"I thought you might," said Peter softly. "I'll see you at the bridge at seven tonight." He hung up.

Thinking his anger was under control, Harry took the path downward to the Cecil Street footbridge. Covered in a blizzard of snow, Peter stood midpoint on the bridge, staring up at the night sky. He did not seem to see or hear him approaching. The wind picked up and howled down the valley road. Harry glanced over the edge of the railing to see the river, the rocks, and the roadway. Finally, he stood directly in front of Peter.

Peter's eyes were closed. His face was marble white in the stinging cold. Not until it happened did Harry know what he was about to do. Swiftly, his fist swung up and cracked Peter under the jaw on the left side. Peter's eyes flew open, and he staggered backwards. Jarring pain ripped up Harry's arm. He had never struck anyone before. He stepped back, anticipating retaliation, but Peter only rubbed his jaw thoughtfully.

"Thanks for sending Brackley to Norma, you bastard! You promised to protect her if I called the cops on your lover."

Peter nodded and said quietly, "I have a lot to tell you."

"A lot of explaining, too!" shouted Harry over the wind.

"I'm sure you want to know about the shares."

Stuffing his hands in his pockets, Harry nodded.

"I've spent most of my professional life trying to find the Elixicorp shares," Peter began, taking a cigar from his breast pocket. "And, Harry, I'm going to die because of them."

Harry chuckled, "Always a flair for the dramatic, Saunderson!" Dizzied by the height, he watched Peter lean against the railing. "What about them?" he asked.

Peter continued conversationally, "My major client was George Pappas. I don't have many others." Carefully, he slit the cellophane from the cigar, then proceeded to light it. "Within my first few months of practice, I was retained by Pappas to find the shares—by any means necessary. And Pappas never gives up."

Tapping Harry on the shoulder, Peter said, "Let's walk a bit. It's cold." The two men began the trek to the far side of the bridge, now slippery in the snow.

They stood under the white light of the subway entrance and Peter continued, "The money came from a massive fraud, conceived of and orchestrated by George and others. He bilked hundreds of investors. who put their life savings into a scheme to develop a drug to ward off memory loss."

Harry waited in silence.

Peter smiled wryly. "Of course, there was no such drug and no such research. But he sold the city's elite on the beautiful story, and so they clamored to throw money at him. Even after it was obvious that the whole thing was a fraud. Pappas was never charged. I suppose they were too embarrassed to admit their folly. You know, they still invited him to their dinner parties. But that's human nature, isn't it? People want to hang onto their dreams."

Harry was impatient with such philosophic musings. "Maybe so, but it wasn't just money, ripping off the wealthy. People have died because of those shares."

Peter chuckled softly. "No one knows that better than I, Harry."

They had reached the center of the bridge again. Peter stared over the railing. Tires hissed on the wet pavement far below.

Peter continued, "Pappas was the charmer and salesman, but Arthur Dinnick, our esteemed law professor, Archie Brinks, and David Parrish all had their roles. And, of course, Norma was a central figure."

"Norma?"

"Yes, Harry, *your* client."

"I don't believe it!"

Peter shrugged and smiled. "Some say she was the real mastermind. Anyway, Arthur outfoxed them all. He pulled off a fraud upon a fraud, by stashing the original certificate and the money somewhere. The bank branch and the account numbers were written on the back of the original certificate."

"How much was involved?"

"Initially about five million, but with compounding it's probably about fifty million by now."

"Holy God!" Dumbfounded, Harry tried to take in the news. No wonder Norma wanted the shares.

Peter continued, "So, for most of my career, I've tried to track the shares down—unsuccessfully, mind you."

Snow was falling heavily. Peter raised his foot and rested it upon the ledge at the railing. Harry gazed out into the hazy glow coming from the banks of office towers at the far side of the ravine. The rush of water and creaking of ice could be heard from the river below.

"You never found *anything*?" Harry asked.

"No, not really," Peter said wearily. "I've been all over Europe hunting for them. Pappas is convinced that Arthur stashed the money in a bank somewhere in Italy before he committed suicide."

"Suicide? Norma said he died of a heart attack."

Peter smiled slowly. "She also said David died of a heart attack. Makes you wonder, doesn't it?" He patted Harry's shoulder. "And what about poor Archie Brinks? I wonder who set up his execution?"

Harry was shocked. "You're suggesting Norma did?"

"Think about it, Harry. That nice little old lady certainly got the ball rolling when she sued both Brinks and Pappas."

"She wanted to get the matter dealt with in open court. Brinks was drugging her and she was frightened out of her mind by Pappas."

Peter smirked. "Of course, Harry. She's as sweet and innocent as a black widow spider." Peter waved his cigar dismissively then tossed it over the rail. As he watched the smoldering tip disappear, he whispered hoarsely. "But none of it matters now. If you have Pappas on your tail, suicide is the more attractive route."

The wind was howling so much that the light standards on the footbridge vibrated, creating an eerie, melodic hum. Although freezing rain lashed their faces, Peter calmly settled down to another cigar and slumped onto the ledge at the railing.

Harry stamped his feet for warmth. "Peter, let's get off this bridge. Go out for coffee or a drink."

Peter's laugh was a bark. "Just like old times, eh, Harry? Wouldn't think you'd want to be seen out with me."

"What the hell are you talking about?" Harry shouted over the howl.

"Don't tell me you've forgotten that you used to cross the street rather than be seen with me."

"For Christ sake! Do you blame me? You ruined everything between me and Katrina."

"Ah, yes, Katrina. Lovely girl, Harry. Ever see her again?"

"No." Harry huddled deeper into his collar.

"Ever wonder why?"

Harry did not answer.

Peter leaned back against the railing. "She used to confide in me sometimes. She thought you were a sanctimonious little twerp, who mistreated me terribly. Which you did."

"That's ridiculous!" Harry felt the old fury rising within and swung around. "So, I was right about you! You did break us up."

Peter waved his cigar. Harry was ready to it smash down his throat.

"It all fits together, Jenkins. All your life, you've been superior to us lowly folk. Were you really born that way?" Peter gave him a pitying smile. "Here's a perfect example. You think your client, Norma, is a sweet old woman in need of your gallant protection. You can't see she's a dangerous, conniving bitch who'd castrate a man just for fun. And *why* don't you see that? Because you're blinded by your own superiority. You think *she's* good, and everyone else is evil, because you're always on the side of truth and justice."

Rooted to the spot, Harry growled, "Shut up, Saunderson! You're no one to make judgments."

Still smiling, Peter continued, "You lord your superiority over one and all. Your self righteousness is one of your least appealing qualities."

For Harry, the words painted an ugly picture. It was like seeing a photograph of himself, his features drunken and leering.

By now, Peter's face was a frozen mask. Snow coated his hair and eyebrows. Mimicking Harry, he intoned, "I'm not like you, Peter." Standing on the ledge, he continued, "What you really mean is 'I'm not a sicko pervert like you!'"

"Christ! I never said that!"

"But you thought it, didn't you?" Peter said calmly. "So you needed a lesson. It was the little matter of the bath house receipts," he grinned. "I put them in your dresser drawer for Katrina to find. She thought you were there fucking any guy you could find at Romero's. From that moment on, she wouldn't come near you. You too were a sicko pervert. I tried to defend you, of course, but she simply wouldn't listen.

Harry did not move. He remembered it clearly. One day, Katrina had been studying alone in his room. Meeting her in the hall, he had tried to kiss her, but she backed away. And then, without explanation, she grew cool and distant. Soon, she avoided him whenever possible. It was over.

Grabbing Peter's collar, he yanked him close and shouted, "You framed me! You son of a bitch!"

Peter chuckled. "Of course! Why else would she leave such a sterling chap as yourself?" He threw back his head and laughed. "You see, people like you need people like me to shake you up a little."

Harry did not speak. Suddenly, a part of his life made sense. In a flash, he saw Madame Odella's nicotine stained fingers reaching for her Tarot deck. *The Moon card represents someone hiding like a cowardly puppeteer. You are paired. He is an instrument of your destiny.* Harry could not comprehend a mind, which so grossly manipulated others. He certainly had been *The Fool.*

Finally he said, "You really hated me that much? I never harmed you."

"You despised me. It was written all over you. *So* afraid people would know we roomed together."

"But I didn't think that!"

Peter laughed. "For Christ's sake, admit it. Or do you think you're above such base feelings? Come down from your throne and get your hands dirty once in a while. Live like the rest of us have to."

Suddenly, Peter began undoing his topcoat, letting it fly open in the wind. "Just so you know, I planted those bath house receipts so you'd know what it's like to be shunned and treated as less than human."

Instinctively, Harry stepped closer to him.

Peter turned away swiftly into the gale to look over the edge and up the valley road. When he turned back, he smiled oddly and said, "Funny. You're the third person to accuse me of framing them in the last week or so."

"What? Who else?" Harry shouted into the wind.

"Roger Blenheim. You were a tremendous help there, Harry. Roger's in jail. They charged him with criminal conspiracy in Archie Brinks' murder. He had the weapon in his cabinet, and the police found it—thanks to you." Peter stared down at his shoes, crusted with ice, then carefully stepped up on the ledge.

"Jesus! You planted that too? And had me set him up?"

Peter nodded. "Of course, Harry. I knew I could rely on your helpful nature." He sat on the railing.

"Peter! Get down from there. You're going to…" Taking a step forward, Harry reached out.

Peter sat forward. "Don't worry, Harry." He continued wistfully, "Maybe I shouldn't have done it to Roger. Not a bad chap at all. And, Harry, he is *absolutely fabulous* in drag! But then, you're far too straight laced to go for that."

Rubbing his hands together, Roger pulled up his collar. "He also loves to play with masks. Did you know that when you put on a mask, Harry, something fantastic happens. You get this amazing feeling inside, like you're someone else." He shrugged and smiled. "But then again, you wouldn't appreciate that sort of thing."

He hopped down from the railing and began to pace. "You see, when I put on the Gagiid or the Nisgaa mask, I felt this tremendous surge of power. Roger used to call it the power of the true self."

Harry spoke. "Peter, this weather is crazy. Let's get out of here. We can go for a drink…"

Peter turned on him. "Do you have any idea what I've been saying, Jenkins? Do you have any notion at all of *your* true self?"

Taken aback, Harry said, "No, Peter, I've never played such games or been interested in drag queens."

Peter roared with laughter. "Just as staid as I suspected. You poor bastard!"

Harry pulled on Peter's sleeve. "Look, let's go…"

Peter resumed his perch on the railing. "I shall confess, Harry. I did frame Roger. He was bleeding me dry, and also my wife, Bronwyn." Then Peter crossed his legs, causing his body to tilt dangerously backward. "I set Roger up for the conspiracy to murder Archie, and then I drove poor Bronwyn mad by making her think she's responsible for his murder."

"Peter! Be careful. You're going to fall." Harry stepped forward, his hand outstretched.

"The ever gallant Mr. Jenkins!" He laughed. Then all civility fell away, and he snarled, "Look at yourself, always on your goddamned white charger. Forever lording your *goodness* over the rest of us. Looking down on the lawyers who have to scrape the crud off the floor." He waved his hands so expansively that he threatened to tip over backwards. The sounds of traffic on the valley road were suddenly silent.

"Peter, don't!" Harry shouted. "Get down for God's sake!" There were only four feet between them. Harry dared not move.

"You know why I married Bronwyn? She was my entrée into the straight, respectable world. But she was a damned expensive one." He shrugged and grinned. "She deserves a little madness."

Harry could scarcely feel his own hands and feet. "Listen, Peter, please come down. Let's talk about this somewhere else."

Peter began to rock gently back, almost tipping over the edge and into the ravine. Then, standing up, he turned and faced the valley road.

Harry saw his chance. He took two huge steps forward, but before he could reach out, Peter turned back and resumed his seat on the rail.

"I'm flattered you want to save me, Harry, but if you try, I'll take you with me." Hearing the menace in his voice, Harry froze to the spot.

"I'm a dead man anyway. Pappas will execute me in an *excruciatingly* gruesome fashion. Probably castrate me first. So you see, this is really the easiest."

"Peter! Don't"

Swiftly, Peter rose and lifted one leg over the railing, teetering on its edge. "Funny thing about Roger. I think he actually *loved* me. I have no idea why." Turning back to him, he shook his head. "The whole idea escapes me. I don't know much about that sort of thing. Do *you*, Harry?" Smiling sadly, Peter turned and faced the edge again.

Harry lunged but caught only the corner of his shirt. "Peter! Talk to me, please!"

Peter swung his legs over the railing. Giving a curt nod and a formal salute, he said, "Good-bye, Harry."

Harry heard the shirt rip and felt it tear from his hands. Teetering for only a moment in the icy blast, Peter dropped into the darkness below. His white mask of a face was rapidly engulfed in the torrent of snow.

Peering into the ravine, Harry could hear or see nothing. He tore his fingers from the icy rail and ran to the white light at the subway pay phone. Pain stabbed his chest as he gasped into the receiver. "Hurry! My friend just jumped from a bridge!"

He gave the details, and the ambulance arrived within five minutes. He tried his best to answer all the officer's questions as the police fished Peter's body out of the river below.

CHAPTER 30

▼

Shivering when he finally got back home, Harry knew Peter's dead white face would haunt him forever. He set the alarm clock for seven AM in order to get to his appointment with Dr. Holloway at nine.

To warm himself, he poured a large snifter of cognac and lay on his bed. Not only Peter's face rose up to plague him. Saunderson had held up a mirror to reveal an ugly picture of himself, which he had not considered. If Peter were right, he would have to revise his ideas of Norma *and* himself. He finished his drink and exhaustion swept him into a deep sleep, with dark shadowy figures.

The next morning, Harry was at the hospital in good time. The weather had warmed up, and the snow had turned into brown and gray slush. Norma wasn't in one of the better wings of the hospital, Harry reflected. The psychiatric ward had its own separate entrance from a side street, with no public access from the main wing. The hospital's nineteenth-century architects had taken all possible precautions to prevent the lunatics from mingling with the sick and dying. But at least the narrow bars had been removed from the windows.

Inside, all traces of wing's original jail-like appearance had been removed. Corridors of light green linoleum spun out from the rotunda. The soft yellow walls were adorned with simple floral patterns in orange, blue and red. At last, he reached Doctor Holloway's office. Still in shock, he could not forget Peter's words last night, nor his twisted features as he jumped over that railing and dropped out of sight. Was Norma *really* the mastermind of the fraud—and perhaps a murderer?

He asked the secretary, "What's Dr. Holloway's specialty?"

"Geriatric psychiatry—the whole range of mental disorders associated with aging." When she smiled up at him brightly, Harry was suddenly aware of her glow. *The promise of youth in the midst of decay,* he thought rather sadly.

From the office, he could see a waiting room filled with the pale light of winter sun. The patients' wheelchairs had been arranged in a semi-circle, as if a sewing bee were in progress. Seemingly lifeless bodies were slumped to one side or the other in each of the wheelchairs. A dozen pairs of eyes were fixed on him. Some glimmered with curiosity, and some were dark and distant.

Soon, Harry was ushered into the doctor's cramped office. Holloway could not be thirty yet. His face was fresh and unlined, and his brilliant blue eyes sparkled as they shook hands.

"You're Norma Dinnick's lawyer?" he asked.

Harry nodded.

"This is a very strange case. I've not seen anything quite like it before." The doctor consulted his file.

Harry decided to say as little as possible. "Oh? And why is that?"

"The original diagnosis was paranoia and schizophrenia. But the only basis for that is a few incidents of rather bizarre behavior." The doctor looked up from his file. "You've known her for some time?"

"Yes, almost twenty years." Harry cleared his throat. "She's quite elderly and frail. A very intelligent woman. I understand she's been attacked, which might account for any disorientation."

"What attack?"

"You mean it hasn't been noted? Emergency told me she said she'd been attacked by a man named Brackley."

A look of confusion settled over the doctor's face. "No. It doesn't seem to be here. I'll get it from Emergency."

"Why is she in a psychiatric ward. Has she been violent?"

The doctor tipped his chair back and regarded Harry evenly. "I'll come straight to the point. Your client insists she has committed three murders. First Archibald Brinks, then David Parrish, and finally George Pappas."

Harry was speechless. Maybe Peter had been right. He asked mildly, "What do you mean 'insists'? Has anyone questioned her on these statements or tried to understand what she's talking about?"

"For obvious reasons, I didn't want to do that until we spoke."

Harry knew that psychiatric hospitals were dangerous quagmires. Even if Norma were a fraud artist *and* a murderer, he, as her lawyer, was required to protect her. Time to throw Norma a lifeline.

"It's absolutely ridiculous," he began. "First, a frail, old woman arrives in an ambulance. Although somewhat disoriented, she clearly states that she's been assaulted. She even gives the name of the assailant. Next, she's put in a psychiatric ward and no one thinks to call the police to report the assault. Under those circumstances, I'd be talking about murder too."

"Please, Mr. Jenkins."

"I can tell you, Dr. Holloway, that David Parrish has been dead for many years. With a history of angina, it was no great surprise that he died of a heart attack climbing the Statue of Liberty. Archie Brinks was shot by a Mr. Prince in open court at Osgoode Hall. I saw him pull the trigger. He would have been charged, but he was bumped off a few days later. As for George Pappas, to my knowledge, he is very much alive and exceedingly well."

Dr. Holloway's youthful face was strained. "That's why I wanted to discuss this with you."

"Fine, but is anyone going to report the attack by this Brackley?"

"Yes, of course."

Harry rose. Opening the door, he said, "I'd appreciate that—and as soon as possible. Now, may I see Norma?"

The nurse led him to the gathering of wheelchairs. It was hard to pick her out, in that sea of pea green smocks, but there she was in the back row, sitting up straighter than the rest of them. "Norma," he said softly.

She tilted her face upward in the pale sunlight. On her cheek, there was a nasty red and deep purple bruise, but otherwise she seemed unscathed.

"Oh, Harry! Is that you?" Her voice cracked and her eyes filled with tears. She took his hand and pulled him closer. "You've come."

"Nurse? I'd like to see my client alone, please."

"Certainly, sir. You can wheel her back to her own room. It's number 347."

Harry backed her out of her spot and headed down the corridor.

As soon as the nurse had disappeared, Norma began to chatter brightly. "Harry, you must get me out of here." Her tiny head, fringed with white hair, bobbed as they glided past more rows of wheelchairs with silent patients in them. "I have to get home and look after my apartment building. Rents to be collected and bills paid." Her hands fluttered as she spoke. "Besides, Harry, you would not believe the strange people in this place." She reached up for his hand. "Last night I feared for my life."

Harry wheeled her into her room and put her by the window. He sat down heavily in the armchair.

"How quickly can you arrange it?" she asked.

Harry was silent. At this moment she appeared perfectly lucid. It was certainly normal to want to go home. But here sat the woman whom Peter claimed was instrumental in a massive fraud. And now she had insisted she had murdered three people, backing up Peter's accusations. *As sweet and innocent as a black widow spider*, he had said. Expertly slipping from lucidity to madness at a whim, she had at the very least seriously misled her lawyer.

She leaned forward and took his hand. "Harry, you're not cross with me, are you? What's wrong? You look so stern."

He stared hard at her. "Norma, you're in a lot of trouble."

"Me? But what have I done?" Tears welled in her eyes.

"Do you realize what you've told the doctors?"

She frowned in recollection. "I told them a man named Brackley attacked me right in my own home."

"What else?"

She shook her head.

"You said that you've murdered Archie Brinks, George Pappas, and David."

"No!"

"You've been so convincing that they're wondering whether they ought to call the police."

"Oh, dear!"

"Norma, you've misled me about the shares. You insisted they belonged only to Arthur and you. Now, according to Peter Saunderson—Bronwyn's husband—you and Arthur were instrumental in a massive conspiracy to defraud the public."

Norma bowed her head. "Those shares! Such a curse. They've been poisoning our lives for years."

"I'll say. At least one person has already committed suicide because of them, and Archie's been shot. So where's it all going to end?"

Norma's face darkened. "It's very cruel of you to remind me of Arthur." She sniffled a little into her Kleenex.

"What do you mean?" asked Harry, on guard for further revelations. "I wasn't talking about your husband."

"Arthur committed suicide," she began quietly, but then anger flared in her. "George drove him to it."

"You always said Arthur died in his sleep of a heart attack."

"It's partly true. He died in his sleep of an overdose." She waved her hand dismissively. "I'm sure that it caused a heart attack. After all, George was going to kill him."

"Why?"

"Because he thought he'd hidden the money."

"Had he?"

"Arthur wouldn't cheat anyone! But George followed us to Monaco and would *not* believe everything was safe and soundly invested back home. Arthur even showed him some accounts he kept in a notebook. But Pappas wouldn't believe him. They took him to a cliff—it was at least a hundred feet down to the water." Norma began to sniffle. "Then they held him over the edge by his legs. They said that if he didn't come up with the money when he got home, he would suffer a very slow and painful death."

"So the fact that he committed suicide in Florence suggests that either he couldn't come up with the money, or he didn't want to." Harry watched her closely.

Norma hung her head.

At first blush, the story made some sense. He asked, "Where are the shares now?" He saw the hesitation and calculation in her eyes.

"Somewhere in Venice. Arthur went there from Florence by himself, so I'm not sure which bank." She studied her fingers, then looked up at him. "Thank God George is dead," she sighed.

"No. George is *not* dead."

Norma's features stiffened. Rage percolated just under the surface. "George raped me! That's why I stabbed him. He's vicious, a mad dog." Tears flowed down her cheeks, then suddenly stopped. Seemingly exhausted by her revelations, she slumped back in the chair.

"Raped you? When?"

"It was years ago," she said solemnly. "And then I killed him. Not because of the shares, but because he raped me."

"But Norma, Pappas was alive a week ago," Harry insisted. "You instructed me to sue him."

Her eyes grew flat and distant. "He was such a disappointment. So seductive, no one could resist him. But he was an uncouth barbarian," she said angrily.

Harry could sometimes catch glimpses of the beauty she must have been all those years ago. But now, her features distorted by her pain, he saw a bitter and disappointed lover. Still, no matter how much she wished Pappas dead, she could not continue to confess to his murder.

Norma?" He shook her shoulder gently. "George Pappas is *alive*. You must have dreamed it."

Her lips tightened. "If he is, he won't be for long." Her head began to droop and she made little snuffling noises and whistles with every breath. "I'm so tired, Harry."

Harry strolled down the hallway. Sunlight filtered through the dirty windows, making blurry patterns on the floors. Obviously, Norma was delusional one moment and lucid the next. But which story was true? He could not afford to be blinded by clever half-truths. Despite her trips from lucidity to madness, he, as her lawyer, had to get a straight story. And then protect her. If he could not convince the doctors that her murderous imaginings were figments of a distraught mind, then he'd better take down his shingle. After extensive testing, the medical profession would conclude she was incompetent and beset with paranoid delusions. At least partly.

When he returned to her room, he saw that her catnap had done her good. Sitting up straight in her wheelchair, she smiled brightly at him. Good, he thought. the mask of lucidity had returned.

"Harry, I've come to a decision." Her features took on a softness he had not seen before. Not a trace of madness. "I rather like it here. It's quite peaceful, in a way."

"This is a hospital. You can't stay here." Harry sat down beside her and took her hand.

"Something like it then." Her tone was resigned. "Will you see they take good care of me? I don't really want to go home after all." She looked into his eyes. Harry was always fearful when he saw such unmitigated trust. But then, it could be just part of her act. "Norma, you don't have to do this. You did not kill George Pappas. They can't put you in jail for that."

"Harry, I'm *so* tired. I need to be in a safe place, where you can look after me."

"Safe from Pappas?"

She waved her hand in the air and said uncertainly, "I don't know. From all of them."

Harry knew she feared all her visitors from upstairs. "The doctors will have to declare you incompetent. Shall I get them?" he asked.

For a moment, her eyes glimmered with bright intelligence, decisiveness and clarity. "Yes. It's definitely for the best."

Harry would always remember the vivid transformation in Norma when the doctors arrived. Her eyes became flat and vacant as she stared into the middle distance.

"Mrs. Dinnick? I'm Dr. Holloway. Do you remember me? This is Dr. Robertson and Dr. McCarthy."

No response. Norma's features grew stiff and frozen. Her head hung down at an odd angle.

"Can you hear me, Mrs. Dinnick?" asked Holloway as he bent closer.

Slowly, Norma raised her head and began to whimper. "They're upstairs now. All night long, making such a commotion." She threatened to burst into a wail. "Stealing my mother's Irish linens and lace." She grabbed Holloway's coat. "Make them stop, please!" Her cry was piteous.

The doctors administered every test they knew. Occasionally a glimmer of sanity surfaced before another plunge into her dark world. The doctors withdrew and held a conference in the hallway. Harry did not dare look at Norma, for fear of a secret wink. When they returned, they asked Harry to draw up the committal papers to sign. The outplacement department would be notified.

In the corridor, Harry leaned against the wall. Forms! Always forms with little boxes into which whole lives had to be crowded. But so often, *real* people with *real* lives could not be made to fit. Soon, he would be charged with overseeing both her well-being and her assets. In the sunny hallway, he shuddered.

After the doctors left, he asked Norma, "Do you want to stay in your room, or go for walk? I could wheel you around for a bit."

Craning her neck around, she grinned up at him. "Thank you, Harry. A walk would be nice. I'd like to see the other inmates. Find a very safe place for me, please."

Nodding, he unlocked her brake. Gently, he pushed her along the corridor, past the other patients. Some regarded them with great curiosity. Others were lost in their own worlds.

They came to a rotunda where the light streamed in through potted plants. Suddenly, she waved to him to stop. A man, wearing a green smock, sat on a bench.

Norma screeched, "No! Not you, George Pappas! How did you get in here?"

The elderly man did not look up. He continued to rock intently back and forth, whistling a tuneless tune.

"My God! Look at you!"

The elderly man jiggled a cane between his knees and took no notice of them.

"You've gone entirely to pot, George Pappas, sitting there sunning yourself like a fat, lazy cat."

Bending forward, Harry said, "Norma! That's not Pappas."

Her furious face bobbed in front of him. "I'd know that animal anywhere. Don't tell me he's not George." Twisting around in her chair, she grabbed the cane from the old man's hand.

"What did I tell you about those shares?" She smacked the old man's knee sharply. Harry struggled with her for the cane. "What a disappointment you turned out to be! You made a botch of everything, you greedy, stupid animal!"

Norma snatched the cane back from Harry. He tried to wheel her away, but she held fast to the bench.

"Besides, George Pappas, you're a fake!" She smacked him on the shoulder with the cane. "Making women think you were God's gift. Some lover, you were! Thirty seconds and its over!" In disgust, she sent the cane clattering to the floor.

The orderlies rushed down the hall to put the restraints on Norma. Swiftly, they wheeled her away. The old man sat alone and unperturbed.

Harry walked back to the nursing station and left his phone numbers. "Tell Dr. Holloway I'll be back with the papers later today."

Heading back for his car, he sighed. Lawyers were trained to seek the truth by drawing lines and making logical distinctions. That's exactly what he would try to do filling out Norma's committal form. But that form would never represent the truth of her life. In Norma's world, where all boundaries had been erased, how could *any* truth exist? In his world, Peter had painted him as a self-righteous prick, blinded to the realities of the world. Was that true? Poor Peter had drawn every imaginable boundary to find his own truth, but succeeded only in hiding his true self. So, did truth exist anywhere? Perhaps, he concluded, we all ended up with our own version of a truth. Harry tossed his case in the car and got in. No matter what, it was best that Norma live out her days in the safety of an institution.

CHAPTER 31

▼

A wave of weariness swept over Miss Giveny as she typed yet another will. Through years of skimping and self-denial, she had amassed a little money. Perhaps it was enough for her and her sister, Merle, to live on. Harry had said absolutely nothing about her notice.

When the telephone rang, she broke off from her typing. "Yes?"

"It's Bronwyn Saunderson calling. Is Jeremy or Harold Jenkins in, please?"

Miss Giveny could not understand why Norma Dinnick's goddaughter was calling. She wasn't a client.

"No, they're not. Shall I leave a message?"

Miss Giveny frowned as she scribbled it on a pad. Why was she at the Brentview Clinic? She rose stiffly and crossed the hall to Harry's office. Ever since moving into the new premises, everything had changed. Mr. Crawford would have put a stop to all the nonsense. He would never have hired such a slippery character as Jeremy.

She entered Harry's office and stared at the clutter on his desk. The envelope containing her resignation sat there, unopened. Stunned by wildly contradictory emotions, she hesitated several moments, then folded the envelope and slipped it into the bosom of her blouse. She returned to her office and closed the door.

Jeremy entered the office whistling. Pretty soon, he'd talk to Harry about getting his name on the door. Also, they'd have to get rid of that old bag Gladys Giveny. He tossed himself into his desk chair and gazed down into the atrium. It was a comfortable sort of practice, but it had no *really* wealthy clients. He wondered how old Harry was. Jeremy could buy him out in a few years, with any luck. But how to lure the old man into retirement?

"Mr. Freemantle! Where have you been?"

Jeremy jumped. Christ! The old battle-axe was on the war path again. "What?"

"You should read your messages. Your Aunt Bronwyn wants you to call."

Jeremy exploded. "Listen, Gladys, I know you've been here since the dawn of time, but I happen to be the lawyer, and you are the secretary. I don't have to explain where I've been. Why in God's name Harry puts up with your constant complaining and shoddy work…"

Miss Giveny stood motionless for several moments Her breathing was harsh and her look one of pure hatred. She would not allow this snake to force her out. Mr. Crawford's firm was at risk.

Jeremy slammed the door. He read the first of four messages from his Aunt. He assumed she was at the Brentview Clinic to dry out. When he called, he was immediately put through to her private room.

"Thank God you've called. I desperately need your help," she said.

"Why are you at the Brentview?" Jeremy quickly assessed the situation. Obviously the worst of the hysteria was over, leaving only a certain dramatic flair.

"Peter is trying to drive me mad by framing me!" Although her voice was low and intense, not one syllable was slurred. "You must help me. It's all about Norma's will and Archie."

"What the hell are you talking about?"

"Come up here now, and bring Harold Jenkins. I need both of you."

Later, Jeremy stood in Harry's office. "I've no idea what she's talking about, Harry. Something about Peter framing her."

Harry stared down onto the Bay and Richmond Streets intersection. "I do." He turned to face his junior. "I'm afraid Peter is dead."

Jeremy sat down heavily. "What? When?"

"He committed suicide late last night. He…jumped off a bridge."

"Oh, my God!" Jeremy looked away, then buried his head in his hands. When he looked up, Harry was shocked to see his face, a grotesque mask of fury.

"Jesus! The goddamned coward!"

"Why do you say that?" Harry asked carefully.

"Isn't it obvious? Nobody should do that, no matter what!"

"I think he was afraid of what might happen." Harry appraised his junior. "He said a George Pappas was going to kill him."

"Who's that? I never heard of him."

"Nor had I—until you mentioned him a few weeks ago."

"I did?"

"Yes. You spoke to me about Peter's being blackmailed and having some underworld connections."

The boy shrugged. "I guess I heard it from Bronwyn."

Unease settled over Harry. He could never be sure about his junior. "We better go. Someone has to tell Bronwyn about Peter."

Bronwyn's condition had improved so much that she had been moved to the low-security wing. She was delighted with her airy, chintz-filled sitting room, which overlooked the wooded area at the back. After she had reached Jeremy, she sat down to examine her nails, which had gotten into a frightful state. Carefully, she arranged the tiny bottles of polish brought to her by the nurses, who were delighted at her interest in a manicure. Her nails were brittle, with lots of snags. No matter. She would simply cover them up with glossy red—blood red. Hard as nails. She held them up to the light at the window and nodded her approval.

When she turned back into the darkening shadows of the room, she caught a glimpse of Archie's face. She sighed, thinking he might always be with her.

"How well do you know Bronwyn?" Harry asked Jeremy as he pulled into the clinic parking lot.

Jeremy was startled from his reverie. "Oh, I don't know. She's been married to Peter for ages. When I was at boarding school, sometimes they invited me over for dinner." He flashed a brilliant smile at Harry. "Why?" he asked.

Harry knew only a little about Bronwyn through Norma and her will. But sometimes, like now, a name in a client's will suddenly jumped off the page and acquired a startling life of its own.

"She does have one problem." Jeremy let his words hang in the air. "The bottle. I thought she was here to dry out," he concluded solemnly.

"How do you think she'll take Peter's death."

The boy answered promptly. "Devastated. Just like me." They got out of the car and climbed the front steps. "Do you think Peter really framed Bronwyn? With what?"

"I think we'll find out, Jeremy."

A nurse showed them to Bronwyn's room. She was sitting cross-legged on the bed, wearing a beautiful Japanese dressing gown. Lost in a study of her nails, she did not look up.

Standing before her, he said, "Bronwyn, I'm Harry Jenkins. You asked me to come." His junior hung back at the door.

"Did you bring Jeremy?" she asked not looking up.

Harry frowned. "Yes. Don't you see him? He's right at the door."

Jeremy stepped forward. "Auntie?" He took her hands. "Here I am."

Bronwyn merely nodded. They sat down.

Harry hated breaking terrible news to people. "Bronwyn, I'm very sorry, but I have some very sad news to deliver."

"Archie's come back?"

Harry took a deep breath. Was there any reality in the world? "No, but I'm afraid Peter is dead too."

At first, Bronwyn did not reply. Instead, she picked up a nail file from the bed and began furiously filing one nail. "Does that mean I am free?"

Harry was speechless. He watched her finish her work. "Yes, I suppose so. Was he keeping you here?"

"Yes. He framed me."

"With what?"

"Archibald Brinks' murder. You must have seen it on the news."

"Yes, actually, I was in the court that day. And last night, just before he died, Peter admitted he framed you."

Bronwyn looked up sharply, focusing on him for the first time. "You saw it? How did he die?"

Harry took her hand. "He committed suicide by jumping off a bridge." He was amazed at her reaction. Tossing her head back, she laughed, "So Pappas got him?"

"How do you know about Pappas?"

Bronwyn examined her hand and began her nail-filing once more. "I found out he was Peter's client." She began rocking gently on the bed. "Peter was trying to set me up as Archie's murderer."

"Why would he do that?" Harry asked her.

Her smile was bitter. "Because he hates me. He wants to be rid of me, so he can run off with Roger. And he doesn't want to have to pay me." She leapt from the bed and stood before Jeremy. "Give me a cigarette, darling."

Jeremy fumbled in his pockets. "Sorry…looks like I'm out."

"Shit." Bronwyn flounced back onto the bed. "Archie wanted to keep Norma from changing her will, but she went ahead anyway. She was going to leave it all to me. I had the motive, and so Peter tried to frame me as Archie's killer."

Harry looked at her sharply. "How did you know about changes to her will?"

Bronwyn was oblivious to the steely edge in Harry's voice, but Jeremy was not.

"Harry?" he began tentatively, "It's true she knew about the changes."

Harry turned on his junior. "How?"

In contrition, Jeremy stared at his shoes. "I took a copy to her."

Struggling to maintain an even tone, Harry said, "That is completely and utterly in violation of every code of ethics, every canon of professional conduct!" As he spoke, he felt the sharp edge of righteous anger rising out of control. Then he saw the white mask of Peter's face, dropping into darkness and out of sight. He tried to moderate his tone. He struggled to understand the boy who stood before him.

Finding a package of cigarettes in a drawer, Bronwyn proceeded to light one. "So, Mr. Jenkins, am I free to leave this place?"

Harry had almost forgotten her presence. Looking keenly at her, he said, "I can't advise you, Mrs. Saunderson. Norma Dinnick is my client."

Bronwyn shrugged and blew a smoke ring.

"Did Peter ever see Norma's will changes?" he asked as calmly as he could.

"Sure," she said, as if the question were of no importance. Absently, she began chipping away at the glossy red polish on her nails. Little red flecks of paint flew onto the white towel beside her. Soon, she was scraping her hands and wrists with her nails.

Harry stood and collected his brief case. "Good day, Mrs. Saunderson," he said at the door. Jeremy followed at his heels.

In the car, Jeremy sat beside him gnawing a thumbnail.

Harry said, "I'm getting you back to the office as fast as I can. Then, *you*, Mr. Freemantle, will clear out your desk."

"Harry, please. I apologized. I'm sorry. Nothing like that will ever happen again. I promise."

"Do you really think you can make everything right with an apology? Do you have any idea what you've done?" Staring at Jeremy, Harry tried to see behind the smooth and youthful countenance. He wracked his brain for honest understanding of what motivated such a dissembler, but all he could see was Jeremy's blank face, unmarred by any trace of conscience. For once, Jeremy sat in silence.

Harry's anger came in waves. "You simply have no concept of a solicitor's role. You think law is just a ticket to wealth, with no responsibility to the client. First, you breach the fundamental trust between solicitor and client by showing a draft will to a contemplated beneficiary. Then you leave a copy so that it can be seen by whomever."

Harry glanced across at his stony faced junior. No response. Red taillights flashed off his right front fender. Slamming on the brakes, he just missed rear-ending the car which had cut in front of them. "Moron!" he muttered. Stuck in traffic on the ramp, Harry breathed deeply until his chest stopped heaving. "And don't think of asking me for a reference, because you know what it'll say."

Jeremy sat in silence for the remainder of the drive, thinking of the future. Time to get out. Lawyers like Jenkins lived in the Stone Age—they were going nowhere.

At last they turned off the ramp and headed west into the downtown. Harry squinted into the slanting orange rays of brilliant light.

Thinking of Jeremy's youth, he tried to reason with him. "You don't understand what giving the will to Bronwyn has done. It unleashed a whole sequence of events which ended in your uncle's suicide."

"How so, Harry?" Jeremy sounded bored.

"If you hadn't handed over the draft will, no one would know what Norma intended, and Archie would probably be alive."

"That's ridiculous! I'm not responsible for that."

Harry pulled into the office parking lot. Staring straight ahead, he gripped the steering wheel. "Maybe your actions didn't *cause* all the events, but they sure helped touch them off."

Jeremy smiled scornfully at Harry. "Thanks for all the advice, old man. You must be getting senile to make all those crazy connections"

"Get out," Harry said quietly. "Your pay check will be ready for you in the morning."

"I'm not coming back here. I want my check now." Jeremy, jumping from the car, slammed the door, and marched toward the building.

Harry followed as closely behind him as he could. A disgruntled ex-employee could cause no end of trouble to the office and his practice. But it was all over within fifteen minutes. With a bag slung over his shoulder, Jeremy stood at Miss Giveny's desk.

"I want my check now, Harry," he said.

"Miss Giveny," Harry said mildly, "please prepare Mr. Freemantle's check for any outstanding pay and I'll sign it." He turned back on Jeremy and spoke coldly. "Mr. Freemantle has been fired by me for serious professional misconduct. He receives nothing more than the basic amount."

Nodding curtly, Harry retrieved all keys from the boy. "Good-bye, Jeremy." They did not shake hands. When he was gone, Harry called the locksmith for emergency service in changing the locks.

Suddenly weary, he checked his watch and decided to go home. Within twenty minutes, he was walking into his house. Mail was scattered in the front hall, but he did not bother with it. Upstairs, he took a hot shower to relax, but his mind still raced. Rules of conduct in law practice served a necessary purpose. Case in point! All hell had broken out when Jeremy had shown Bronwyn the will.

Norma floated before his line of vision as he let the hot jet course down his back. Last week had been such a jumble of contradictions, he could scarcely sort them out. But one matter had to be resolved. Roger Blenheim remained in jail on charges of conspiracy to murder. Peter had flatly stated that he had planted the gun in his bedroom.

Obviously, Peter's admission would be central to Blenheim's defense. Harry tried to recall the rules of evidence and remembered something about 'dying declarations.' Because a deceased person could not be cross-examined, his statements could not be used in evidence for court. But there were exceptions. *Statements made by a person who knows he is about to die are admissible into evidence.* Theoretically at least, someone about to die is not going to lie. Surely to God, someone standing on the railing of a bridge, in a blizzard, not only *knew* he was about to die, but *intended* to die. Harry snoozed for half an hour, then set out for the police station.

The desk sergeant took down all the information. The judge would deal with the matter in the morning.

Harry stood at the door about to leave. "Where is Mr. Blenheim now?" he asked.

"Downstairs in the lock up."

"May I see him?"

The sergeant shrugged. "Suppose so. If he wants to see you."

Harry waited for ten minutes, until he was led to an elevator at the back of the Old City Hall. In silence, he and the guard marched through gray concrete hallways and finally reached a small room lit by a single overhead lamp. Harry sat down, and a tall, haggard looking man was escorted in.

"And who might you be?" Blenheim asked politely. "Excuse the state of the room, but I don't have many visitors."

"It's a long story, but I'm a lawyer who knows your friend, Peter Saunderson."

"And how *is* Peter—the prick?" Roger smiled faintly.

Hearing the pain in the man's voice, Harry hesitated. "I'm afraid I have *very* bad news, Mr. Blenheim. Peter died last night."

Roger was perfectly still for a long moment. Finally his eyes darted to his hand, which Harry saw was inexpertly bandaged. "Jesus!" Roger's voice broke. "What happened?"

"He committed suicide by jumping off a bridge. I was there."

"But why?"

"He thought someone was going to kill him."

Roger nodded imperceptibly. Harry saw that his eyes were damp. He looked away. "Poor, stupid little bugger," he whispered.

"I *am* sorry…"

Blenheim looked up at him. "We're you a friend of his?"

"Not really, but I've known Peter since we were in law school."

"He never figured out how to live his life, you know." Roger seemed to be talking to himself as he continued. "He thought he always had to hide who he was. He used to love playing with the masks. Said that's when he became his true self."

"Peter did talk about the masks," Harry said quietly.

Roger continued as if he had not heard Harry. "He tied himself down to a wife and the damned corporate ladder." A tear rolled down his cheek. "That wasn't him. He should have just been himself."

Harry could find nothing to say. Of course, Roger was right. But staying true to oneself was not so easy for someone like Peter.

Roger seemed to collect himself. "So, I wonder where that leaves me? He tried to frame me, you know."

"I know. That's why I'm here. Before he jumped," Harry cleared his throat, "he said he'd planted the gun at your place."

"Ah, yes. The Gautier," Roger said softly, as if lost in thought. Then he appeared to come to life. "A beautiful little pistol., silver and elegantly scrolled. It has a mate. They're dueling pistols. I made Peter a gift of them. Funny how he used them to betray me."

Harry smiled sadly, thinking of his father's blunt, ugly gun. Funny how it had started them talking.

Roger spoke again. "So he's dead. How does that affect me?"

"I think his statement is admissible evidence, but you need to ask your lawyer. I'm ready to help any way I can."

Roger bowed his head and then smiled up at Harry. "You know, I actually loved the little son of a bitch." He began to chuckle.

"Peter knew that," Harry said quietly. "That's just about the last thing he said."

Roger pushed his chair back. "So this information can get me out of here?"

"I think so. Get your lawyer to call me." Harry gave him his card, and the two men shook hands. Then Harry hurried from the jail and returned home.

CHAPTER 32

▼

As Harry opened his front door, the telephone rang. Pushing aside newspapers and the remains of dinner, he snatched up the receiver. It was Natasha. He sank into the arm chair.

"When can I see you?" he asked. His eyes roved around the room. Beside the television sat a basket of laundry. At least it was clean.

"How about tomorrow?" she said.

The brilliant, winter sun revealed a coating of dust on the coffee and side tables. One of his slippers was stuck under the couch. The home of a fusty old bachelor, he thought.

"Why don't you come over here for dinner?" he asked. Although he had not made an actual meal for weeks, he wasn't bad in the kitchen.

"You cook, Harry?"

"You bet. I was a short-order cook, as a summer student." He could get the place tidied up for tomorrow.

After she agreed, he hung up and stretched out on the couch. The events of the last few days spun in his head. He saw Norma's wizened face twisted in hatred as she raised the cane against the man she mistook for Pappas. And then Peter's salute, before he dropped over the railing. In his exhaustion, too many questions swirled in his mind. Roger and Bronwyn were victims of Peter's malicious manipulations. Just as he and Katrina were. Where *was* Katrina now? For a moment, he toyed with the notion of finding her. He snapped on the evening news and, in minutes, was asleep.

At ten thirty, the telephone rang. He rose swiftly to the surface of his dream of Katrina and answered.

"Your father is in surgery, Mr. Jenkins."

Harry swung his feet to the floor and sat up. "What happened?"

"There was evidence of a brain aneurysm. The surgeon is trying to prevent damage."

Harry was at the hospital within half an hour. He paced the hallway outside the surgery until a nurse insisted he wait down the hall. For a moment he sat upright on a creaking plastic chair molded for a body entirely different from his own.

Jumping up, he returned to the desk and asked, "Is it a very long operation?" They did not know.

He paced the gray tiled hallway under the florescent lights until he came to an empty waiting room. Magazines were scattered about, along with coffee cups and chocolate bar wrappings. Waiting for news, he thought. Hundreds of people had sat in this desolate room trapped in an eerie, fearful suspension between despair and joy. Some won a reprieve; others did not. The ice in the drink machine began clunking and spluttering. The spout of the coffee machine drizzled.

At the far end of the hall, he saw a red-lit sign. *Quiet Room,* it read. Harry approached, and, after only a moment's hesitation, opened the door. The room resembled a chapel except that only a podium stood at the front. No vestige of any religion was in evidence. He sank onto the red, padded bench. A huge metal box, which Harry assumed was an air-conditioning unit, was built into the wall behind the podium. Mysteriously, it began to gurgle and sigh as if coming to life in the dead of winter.

For years, he had simmered with resentment at his father. Sometimes he had been all but consumed by the restless, angry energy swirling within him. Only now was their relationship beginning to mend. His father's words, so plainly spoken, had been filled with the hope of his forgiveness. *Because I'm still alive, so maybe it's not too late.*

Why had he, a middle aged man, been unable to escape his childhood? Dumbly, he stared at the gray steel air conditioner as if it could provide an answer. Suddenly, he wished he knew how to pray.

Dad's reaction to Anna's death might have been a mental illness. People talked these days of post-traumatic shock, but there had been no such words back then. He tried to remember whether mother had sought help. Harry, to his shame, certainly had not. But he had been quick enough to cast blame and wallow in his hurt. Although he was the child, he did eventually become an adult—or so he thought.

Without children of his own, he had trouble comprehending his father's reaction, which he thought extreme. The enormity of such loss escaped him. His wife, Laura, had always been too busy for children. He heard her voice: *Sure you'd help with a baby, Harry, but that means the responsibility would fall mostly on my shoulders.* If there were no love, why bother with children?

It was simple. He equated his father's silence with a lack of love. There could have been a hundred other reasons. Perhaps if someone had reached out, it might have been different.

Harry caught his breath. An unearthly wailing came from the hallway. The door to the Quiet Room flew open. A tall, bony woman, wearing a mauve dress and yellow shawl, clung desperately to the arms of two men. One was old and hunched and the other, muscular and attentive.

The florescent lighting illuminated the woman's face raw with agony.

"No! No!" As if possessed, she shook violently and her voice slid up octaves. "By the blood of Christ, no!" Clasping her hands to her ears, she began to moan, her eyes ricocheting about the room.

She screamed at the ceiling. "Why have you cursed me? He *cannot* be taken so soon."

She flung herself to her knees before the podium. "He is too young! Why?" Hugging herself, she rocked back and forth. The young man, his face stained with tears, encircled her shoulders and tried to raise her up, but she refused all comfort.

The old man sank to the red padded seat behind them and buried his face in his hands. He groaned, "My son, my only son!"

Throwing her arms heavenward, the woman shrieked, "Take me! He is too young!"

Babbling, she beat upon her breast and tore at the buttons of her dress. She screamed. "Why have you cursed me, Jesus?" Spent, she fell prostrate before the podium, her entire body heaving.

The old man was silent. Then his shoulders convulsed, and he muttered, "My son. Dear Jesus. Not my only son." He leaned on the young man, and, through gentle sobbing, he whispered, "It is too great a price. I cannot bear it. Why did they beat him, so...savagely?"

A priest, black robes flowing, came in clutching a Bible and a Rosary. He spoke to the old man. "What has happened, my son?"

The man struggled to control himself. Through broken sobbing he managed to say, "They took him by car to a side road, north of the city. And there they beat him with a tire iron and a shovel." The old man's shoulders convulsed. "God forgive them. They *do* know what they've done."

The priest touched the man's shoulder. "But why, my son?"

"Because he was different from others. God have mercy, but he loved a man." Weeping, he asked the priest, "Why is *any* love a sin, Father?

Harry saw the priest's lips tighten for an instant as he turned away. Then shoring himself up, he intoned, "The Bible says it is so, my son."

Harry was sickened. *Where can love, forgiveness, and compassion be? If it is not found in this rabid priest does it exist anywhere?*

Sinking to his knees, the priest reached out to the woman. She twisted away in agony. Shrieking, she rose to her knees. Blindly, she scuttered across the floor to huddle in a corner. A doctor, her white coat flapping, grasped the woman's arm. With a nurse's help, she stilled her and expertly injected a drug. A swift and deep slumber engulfed her. Orderlies gently lifted her onto a stretcher, and the doctor stopped to smooth down the stiff fabric of her dress. The priest had gone.

Harry pressed his hands against his face. With all his heart, he wanted to pray. He had just witnessed the unholy wrenching of the spirit at the loss of a child, caused by blind hatred. As he touched the tears on his face, he thought of Peter, years back.

Then he began to understand. "God forgive me," he whispered. "I have known nothing! My father died along with Anna. I did nothing to help. And the world twisted and destroyed Peter."

At last, he rose and slowly made his way down the now silent hallway to the desk.

"Mr. Jenkins, we've been looking for you. The surgeon would like to speak with you."

A tall man, a mask covering his mouth and nose, approached Harry and gestured him into a waiting room. Harry sank, in body and spirit. The doctor closed the door and removed his mask. Harry sat down.

"Your father has come through the operation better than we expected."

"He's alive?" Harry said in wonder.

"Yes, of course. Although we can't be sure it won't happen again, there are medications…"

Harry was on his feet, grinning. "Thank you, doctor." He pumped his hand. "Thank you *so* much. That's wonderful. May I see him?"

The doctor shook his head. "He'll be in intensive care for a few days so we can keep an eye on him. You can come in the morning."

Harry shook the doctor's hand once more, then hurried from the room.

So stunned was he that he marched past his car twice in the darkened parking lot. As he stared out at the damp fog rising from the pavement, his mind raced with possibilities. At the very moment of his asking, he had received the answer. The agony written on the woman's face blinded him with flashes of understanding of his father's silence and his own emptiness. The priest's turning away told him everything about Peter's life, and much about his own.

His rational mind told him that those who found special significance in synchronous events were desperately seeking solace. But how *had* it happened? For once, his mind grew still.

Finally, he spotted his car. Sitting behind the wheel, he caught his grinning face in the mirror. Never before had he experienced the sensation of warmth and stillness now flooding his entire being. His brain no longer tormented him with questions. His heart understood. The world took on unknown dimensions. And his father was alive.

At home, Harry took a hot shower and climbed into bed. He realized he was still grinning. In the morning, he awoke exhausted. His sleep had been a continuous riot of dark shadow and bright light. But no remembrance of his dreams remained.

He drank a cup of coffee at his kitchen table. His brain labored to put the woman's face into a safe and rational context. By the time he had shaved and dressed, she had begun to fade from his consciousness. No doubt, it was a singular event. He could not dissect it, categorize it, or explain it. Nor could he dismiss it.

At 7:00 AM, Harry gowned to enter the ICU. Heart monitors bleeped in feeble and unconvincing rhythms. Occasionally soft weeping came from behind the curtains of cubicles. Harry sat for two hours at his father's bedside.

Suddenly, long-forgotten bits and pieces of his father's stories floated up to him and set him to reminiscing aloud. Softly he sang tag ends of rhymes and songs learned from his father. When he forgot parts, he simply hummed. Sometimes he thought his eyelids fluttered, but he could not be sure.

At last, Stanley's eyes blinked open, then filled with recognition. "Son," he whispered.

Harry grasped his hand. "Dad, I'm *so* sorry!"

Stanley tried to shake his head. "No…no," he mouthed.

"I shouldn't have left you alone," Harry whispered.

There was no response for several moments. Stanley's hand tapped his. "I love you, son."

Harry's eyes stung with tears. Almost choking, he said, "Dad, I love you too. I'm so sorry we've missed so much together."

Stanley struggled to take a breath. The words came slowly, one by one. "I wanted you to go and see your lady friend…."

The doctor appeared from behind the curtain. "You're his son?"

Without taking his eyes from his father, Harry nodded. "Yes. I'm Harry, his son."

"Your Dad's come through the operation better than we hoped. He was talking during the night, but his speech is impaired. Lots of word salad."

"Pardon?"

The doctor smiled. "His speech is garbled. The words sound all right, but usually they don't mean much together."

In silence, Harry stared at the doctor. His father had just said the most important, meaningful words he had ever heard from him.

When Harry left the hospital, the clang of streetcars, the hiss of tires in traffic, and the swift movement of early morning shoppers—all the noise and motion that was downtown Toronto—blurred his vision of the night before. The woman's face had grown hazy, and her wrenching screams no longer echoed in his mind. Even the memory of the priest had faded. But he sought to keep the feeling close to him.

Turning up a road, which ran past a park, he thought of Natasha. Today he would bring her to his house. They would talk. His thoughts stalled.

The sun's rays flashed across his windshield, nearly blinding him to the snow-covered hills on either side. From his left, a dark object shot down the hill and into the road. Slamming on his brakes, he swerved sharply to the right. He just missed it.

He jumped from the car. A small child, encased in a pink snowsuit, screamed as she struggled up from underneath a sled. Her foot caught in the pull-rope, yanking off her boot. She toppled to the ground once more. Harry rushed to pick her up, as tears streamed down her cheeks. Her face was covered with mucous from the crying. He grabbed a bunch of Kleenex from his pocket and gently dabbed her nose. She began to quiet. He marveled at how tiny and perfect she was. Thank God, she seemed unharmed. He found her boot and put it on her foot.

"Amy! Are you all right?" a voice cried from the hill.

Harry turned to see a black figure in the snow running and waving frantically.

Slowly, he set the little girl down. "She's okay!" He called out.

The woman, somewhere in her late forties, approached him. Strangely, he thought of Peter and the bridge. The little child ran to her and buried her face in her coat.

Harry's heart constricted. He knew her at twenty yards. "Katrina?"

Cautiously, she drew near, holding the child by the hand. "How do you know my name?"

He stood before her. "It's me, Harry." He held out his hand.

Confusion flashed over her face.

"Harry Jenkins." he said glancing down at Amy. "From years ago," he added quietly.

Katrina's hand flew to her mouth. Then she smiled. "I don't believe it! Harry, what a way to meet after so long."

He managed a laugh. "Is she yours?" he asked nodding at the little girl who peered up at him.

"Yes. She's my granddaughter." She began dusting the snow off the child's mittens.

He wanted to say *how lovely you look.* Instead, without thinking further, he told her, "How happy you look. Life has been good?"

When she smiled, he saw the young woman who met him at the bridge almost every night for the better part of a year.

"Yes, I've been fortunate."

"You have children?" He laughed. "Stupid question."

"Two. A son and a daughter, one husband and two grandchildren." Briefly she touched his hand. "It's amazing to meet like this after so many years!"

"How is your mother?"

"Not bad," she shrugged. She's amuses everyone in the nursing home with her fortune-telling."

He was driven to ignite her memory. "Do you remember Peter Saunderson, who lived upstairs with me?"

She frowned and then shook her head. "Mom had so many tenants over the years. I could never keep them straight."

There was no point in telling her about Peter. He stepped back. "Well, I'm glad Amy's all right. No harm done?" The child shook her head and stared down at her boots clasping her grandmother's hand.

A man shouted from a car just parking on the road. "Hi Amy! Hi Mom!"

"Daddy!" The little girl broke free and ran to the man getting out of the car.

Katrina introduced them. "This is my son. His name is Harry, too." She gazed at Harry, then gave him a brief smile and got into the car.

Harry stood, transfixed, at the side of his car. Then he slid behind the wheel and headed for home. He could not deny his sense of connection to forces of which he had no understanding. A chapter of his life had opened for just a moment, then closed.

He sighed when he opened the front door. In two hours, he would pick up Natasha. Facing a monumental clean-up job, he tossed his coat aside and marched into the kitchen. The morning light cast a pallor over the room.

First he unloaded the dishwasher, and then put in all the dirty dishes he could find. A full load. The refrigerator was nearly empty. Lots of jars of pickles, mustard, and mayonnaise, but no food to eat. They would shop together for dinner.

As he worked, his mind floated over the last week. Images flew up to him in no particular order. He paused to squeeze out a worn dishcloth, which he decided to toss in the garbage. Lately, existence had seemed a meaningless jumble where nothing fit in any pattern. Now, he dimly perceived something—he did not know what—linking everything together. Outside, he stuffed plastic bags into the tins. He cursed under his breath at the mess the raccoons had made. Plastic spoons, Styrofoam plates, and coffee grounds were spread out on the snow bank. He rushed in the cold sunlight to collect them.

As he stood in the den, he laughed and was suddenly suffused with an energy he had never known. A fusty old bachelor, he thought! Time for something new. Get rid of the old. He vacuumed the carpets and dusted the furniture. For a moment, he sank to the chesterfield. Time to get a maid, he thought.

Taking the stairs two at a time, he headed for the bathroom. In fifteen minutes, he had scrubbed the tub, the shower, sink and toilet. Slowing down, he sat in the spare bedroom at the front of the house. His mind spun from one image to the next, with Norma dominating. He saw her creeping up the stairs to the empty apartment. He contemplated her life—or what he knew of it.

A few times, she had spoken of her early years up north; the absent mother, the cold and creaking house, and the fear. She had come to the city determined to escape the emptiness of the north. Hungry for security, safety, and love, she had risked everything to protect the shares. That huge pot of money had governed her life, and still, no one seemed to know just where it was.

He thought of Katrina. Incredible to have found her at that moment in time! He knew something was at work in his life. He finished dusting the tiny room and stacked some books in the corner.

Harry got fresh linens from the closet. Stripping the bed, he tossed the old sheets into the hamper. He smoothed the bottom sheet across the queen-size bed. Then he sat down and gazed at his bed. He loved Natasha beyond any understanding. She was his spirit guide, the one who had come like a warm breeze when he needed her most.

He saw himself in Madame Odella's front parlor. From behind the kitchen curtain, Katrina smiled and pointed upstairs. Katrina said she had been fortunate. Still, he thought, with a small smile, she had named her only son Harry.

Fitting the corners of the sheet, he imagined Natasha lying there with him. He wanted her with him always, but perhaps it would not happen. He saw her deep brown eyes looking up at him. Were his imaginings and fantasies too *real* for them? He spread the comforter on the bed and changed the pillowcases.

At one o'clock, he picked Natasha up. She reached to put her arms around his neck to kiss him. His hand lingered on her breast. He felt as nervous and alive as the first time he had come to her.

"What have you planned for me?" she laughed.

Relaxing, he said, "Let's shop at the St Lawrence Market, and I'll make dinner at my place."

"Sounds wonderful." After looking out the window, she turned back to him saying, "Harry? What is it? You seem different."

"A lot's been going on," he said slowly.

"Tell me." She gazed at him intently.

He was delighted to talk. "Where to start?" he sighed. He stretched his arms and placed his hands on the steering wheel. Looking straight ahead, he said, "Last night, they operated on my Dad for a brain aneurysm." He looked across to see her intense concentration. "It went well, and I guess he'll be okay."

"Thank God, Harry."

He nodded. "But there's so much more. Something very strange happened. While I was waiting for news, I sat in the Quiet Room, you know, like a chapel."

Suddenly, his words tumbled out. "And at the very moment I was trying to understand my father shutting us out, the most amazing thing happened. It was like a..." He faltered for words. "Like a play acted out right before my eyes."

He told her about the elderly parents whose only son had just been murdered because he loved a man. And the reaction of the priest. "I witnessed...no...I felt and shared their horrific, helpless grief. I experienced it myself, first hand." He sat back, exhausted with his telling. "It was *my* grief," he whispered.

She covered his hand. "You know, Harry, sometimes we get exactly what we need at just the right time."

Harry sighed and contemplated the connection he felt. "You're right, Natasha." He laughed at the sense creeping over him. "Scary, isn't it?"

"Yes, but it's wonderful too."

"More things like that have been happening." He took her hand. "When I was in law school, I was in love with a girl who lived downstairs. Her mother," he laughed, "was a fortune-teller named Madame Odella."

Natasha's gaze was steady as he described Peter's machinations. "A piece of my life has fallen into place, too." In a rush, he told her about Katrina and her sudden coolness and the reason why. As he spoke, she became very still when he told her about the bathhouse receipts. "And then, to top it all off, I saw her today."

"Who?"

"Katrina. So unbelievable!" Harry felt breathless. "Her granddaughter shot out in front of my car on her toboggan. Thank God I stopped in time."

Harry caught his breath. "Katrina was right behind her. We talked. She's lived a wonderfully normal life—husband, children, grandchildren."

Natasha touched his shoulder. Suddenly, he felt he could talk all day and night. "And in the past two weeks, everything's gone crazy." He told her about Norma and the paradox of her madness and lucidity.

She said, "Isn't her madness and lucidity all a part of her? She's not one or the other, but both. The whole thing. Two sides of the coin. Same with Peter."

When she had finished, he said, "So, just as I've been thinking nothing fits together, a few things fall into place."

"Those are amazing stories, Harry. No wonder you've seemed all bottled up," she said. "But why are you so surprised? Life can be like that, if you just accept it."

They gazed at each other. Maybe now was the time, he thought. "Natasha, can we talk some more about us today?"

"Yes. I think we should."

His heart sank at the faintness of her smile and the coolness in her tone. "Let's get the shopping done first."

They found a parking spot on a side street near the market, which was an ancient barn-like structure covering several blocks near the waterfront. Sharp rays of sun came out and touched them as they hurried through the freezing blasts of wind. Inside, stamping their feet in the cold, they saw steam rising up from the floors. The smells of cheese and meat permeated the great, noisy hall. Crowds rushed by as they hesitated, not knowing where to start. He took her arm, and they headed for the butcher shop. Behind the counter, white-coated butchers moved in secret rhythms, as if some mysterious force had choreographed their work.

Harry took a number and joined the line. "My special chicken stew," he said close to her ear. Smiling, she leaned into him.

He was frustrated. One moment she was aloof, and the next, her lovely intimacy surfaced. In confusion, he wondered which was real. He ached for her.

Carrying packages bound in brown paper, they hunted for fruits and vegetables. Searching through the carrots, potatoes, and red and green peppers, he looked up to catch her unaware. He longed to fathom the mysteries that drew him so helplessly to her. Finished with the shopping, they drove to his place in silence.

She was delighted with his house. With ease and grace, she wandered from one room to another as if she belonged there. She sat at his desk in the den.

"Now I understand you better." She rose to examine his bookcases, smiling from time to time as she recognized a book. "Your reading material, Harry, says a lot about you."

"Really? And what do you find so telling?"

"You're a Renaissance man. Look at the variety. History, literature, art...a little science."

"Well," he shrugged, slightly embarrassed.

"But where are the law books?"

"At the office."

She smiled and curled up on the chesterfield. He poured the wine and brought a glass to her.

"That says a lot, too."

"I like to keep the business at the office."

"So you're not 'in love' with the law?"

At first, he thought the notion absurd. But if he did not love the law, why had he devoted his career to it?

"I think the law is simply a tool, a dull one at best, to help people with real problems. To me, a lawyer's a little bit like a carpenter trying to build something new out of the rubble."

She cradled her wine glass against her breast and looked out the window into the darkening garden. "You know, Harry, your stories tell me you're open to a lot more than you realize."

He moved closer. "Meaning?"

"Those kinds of answers, like the woman in the Quiet Room and meeting Katrina, only come to people who are attuned."

"I suppose…" He could think of nothing else to say.

"I want to get to know you better, Harry," she began quietly. "That's important before we consider living together. But the stories you've told me today bring me much closer to you."

How like her, he thought. She was refusing now, but hope was always implicit. "All right," he said carefully, wondering what she meant about the stories.

She shifted closer to him on the couch. "Also, I'm going to be away for a bit."

"What?" He sat up straighter.

"Not for long. Just a vacation."

"By yourself?"

"No."

Harry felt his gut contract. He set down his glass down and rose to get the wine.

From the table, he said, "May I ask with whom?"

"Yes. A girlfriend, Sheila. We've had the trip planned for a long time. We're going to Europe."

"You never said anything…"

"I know. But it's only for a month."

"A month?" Harry said dully. He poured her wine.

Natasha laughed. "It's not that long, Harry. You should see yourself. You look lost already."

He looked closely at her. He had to believe her. "I love you, Natasha," he said quietly.

She came to him and touched his cheek. "And I love you. But I don't want us to rush. Just let it happen."

He smiled sadly, "Okay." He stood up. "I 'm going to get the dinner ready."

In the kitchen, he sliced the chicken breasts. He cursed when he nicked his finger with the knife. Suddenly she was behind him, lightly kissing his neck. He smiled and held her in his arms.

She moved away. "Shall I cut up the vegetables?"

"No, Madame," he said with mock severity. "The chef is in *his* kitchen."

The white, silky flour slid through his fingers as he coated the chicken. He felt the old rhythm and remembered how he had cooked with Laura. For a moment, he stared out the window. The sharp odors wafted upward as he sautéed the onions, mushrooms, and garlic in the golden butter. When he set the chicken in the pan, he stood motionless, watching the bubbles slowly exploding. This time, he would make it work. But how? By letting go, by releasing, she would come to him when she was ready.

In the den, they drank more wine and listened to old tunes from the 1940's. While the stew simmered in the kitchen, they fell into a companionable silence.

As he served the dinner, she said, "You're very good in the kitchen, Harry."

He pulled out a chair for her at the dining room table.

"And elsewhere, I hope?"

After they had eaten, he took her upstairs to his bedroom. As they lay in bed, he drew her close in wonder at her being. Looking into her eyes, so deep and reflective, he knew he was at the very beginning of something he could only dimly perceive.

When they made love, they were slow at first, soft and gentle. But soon passion swept over them like a thunderstorm breaking. Finally, they fell asleep in the warmth of deep satisfaction. Much later, he awoke to the silence of the house and her gentle breathing beside him. He got up.

Light from the bathroom fell softly across the bed. Harry saw the contour of her shoulder and arm underneath the white sheet, which rose and fell with her breathing. Not daring to disturb her, he knelt in silence before her.

Transported outside his own body, he was overcome with the desire to know the dreams, fantasies, and mysteries she held within. He would enter her world with love and understanding, and he would never leave. The awe he felt at her closeness made his breathing slow and deepen in rhythm with hers. He watched his hand reach out from the shadows to smooth the sheet. She was in his bed at last, and, fearing a mirage, he dared not wake her.

In the past two weeks, his world had been shaken. His mind had become a jumble of colliding, conflicting events and consequences. Now he felt her power to draw his life together. A still peace gently settled over him like a silken web of meaning. Released from his frightened self, he knew he could let her go.

Without rational analysis, he understood in his heart that Norma was both mad and lucid. Behind Peter's cunning and guile lay the bruised and bloody face of the young law student who had no notion of love, yet was loved. Perhaps just in time, he understood his father's pain, so that now the healing could begin. And then, once more, he gave thanks for the gifts he had received: the unholy agony of the woman in the Quiet Room, the priest's denial of compassion, and the sudden appearance of Katrina to close a chapter in his life.

Harry, who had sought to cramp life close to his heart for fear of loss, now grasped the final paradox. Without seeking control, he could relax and let life happen. Ironically, the final paradox was that, despite appearances, there was no paradox at all.

A unity lay beneath the world. Through the clash of opposing forces within him, he could see the totality. He prayed that this glimpse of understanding would never leave him.

They did not waken until the next morning at ten o'clock. Harry went downstairs to make coffee and start breakfast. He hurried to get the newspaper from the front porch. The cold morning air cut at his ankles. Back in the kitchen, he set the paper on the counter and took the eggs from the refrigerator. He could hear Natasha running the shower upstairs. Filling his coffee cup, he carried it and the paper to the sunlit den.

The headline read:

MOB BOSS PAPPAS SHOT… body found at foot of bridge.

"My God!" Harry whispered. He read on. Moments later, he set down the article and stared out the window. Norma had said Pappas was the only person alive who knew about the shares. But where in hell were they? When he heard Natasha on the stairs, he went into the kitchen and cracked the eggs into the frying pan.

978-0-595-40760-6
0-595-40760-9

Printed in the United States
78201LV00005B/3